GUARDING INNOCENCE

JAMES ROSENBERG

PART 1

CHAPTER ONE

PITTSBURGH'S GOLDEN TRIANGLE EXTENDS from the junction of the city's three rivers. Skyscrapers dot the horizon, creating an unforgettable welcome to those fortunate to receive their first glimpse after leaving the semi-darkness of the Fort Pitt Tunnels.

Up a winding road to the east sits the Oakland section of town. A bustling, urban, multi-cultural hub which houses the city's namesake university and its nationally ranked hospitals. Throughout the day, its sidewalks fill with students from all parts of the world and others seeking first-rate care and treatment. At night, energy teems as young people search for a new dining establishment or a place to order a cocktail with friends.

The law school, built in the heart of Oakland over four decades ago retains a modern look given its sleek five-story design. The curved plaza in front welcomes visitors, but once inside the atmosphere is more austere, with large auditoriums lining a gaping atrium where light streams through floor-to-ceiling windows. Most of the time, it's quiet, with just the faint sound of a professor teaching behind closed doors. When a lecture is over, however, hordes of students stream out to head to their next class or to the lounge on the bottom floor to hang out before mammoth study sessions.

Never one to have a long-term plan, Cam Crewell had applied to law school in part because his dad wasn't about to let him "waste months" playing video games in his basement. He also couldn't think of anything better to do. Unlike most of the go-getters who were in his first-year class, he had sleepwalked through orientation without charting a definite path for his future. He didn't have a spreadsheet with alternative career options like others in his first-year section, who seemed to know exactly what they wanted from law school and where they would be ten years after graduation.

Law school so far hadn't lived up to his expectations, which, given his general unwillingness to push himself too hard, had not been set high in the first place. In no small part because of the constant pressure of keeping pace with a bunch of overachievers, since he started at Pitt Law two months earlier, dread coursed through his veins every minute he was awake, and often kept him staring at his ceiling at night. The dripping exhaustion of never getting a solid night's sleep only exacerbated his constant feeling of being over-whelmed.

Reading opinion after opinion for five different classes, memorizing the facts while understanding the court's reasoning and how the case fit in with the dozens they had already read, made his head spin. Others in his class seemed to absorb this information and spout their breakdown of the day's cases without effort. He struggled just to keep up with the work, let alone provide cogent analysis when called on. As his confidence waned, he felt like he teetered on the edge of falling into a chasm. His dad always told him how helpful a law school education would be, even if he didn't end up being a lawyer. At this point, he wondered what law firm would ever want to hire a nervous, insecure wannabe.

Cam jogged into the immense auditorium for his Con Law class and took his seat in the second row. For once, he felt prepared. He had briefed the one case assigned and reviewed all the others cited in the body and the footnotes, as well as subsequent Supreme Court cases relying on this decision. With his computer booted, he opened his notes and aligned his pens and markers in front of him. He drummed his fingers on the keyboard, waiting for the lecture to begin so he could, for the first time, speak his mind.

Two minutes later, Professor Jorge Bolle appeared and faced the seventy students who occupied less than half of the available seats. Face hidden behind a dark, scruffy beard, he spoke in a New York lilt with a voice that sounded like his throat was filled with gravel. "Good morning. Today, we start our examination of the Second Amendment and the right to bear arms. Who wants to tell me the holding of District of Columbia v. Heller?"

Each time one of the law professors sought out volunteers, tension overtook the room. Everyone understood that accepting the challenge might endear them to the professor, but a mediocre analysis subjected them to ridicule from both the instructor and the entire class. No one accepted one of these offers without first considering the potential consequences.

Cam's hand shot in the air.

Bolle flashed a wry smile and pointed in his direction. "Ah, Mr. Crewell, glad you decided to join the discussion today. Please proceed."

Cam ignored the veiled insult and cleared his throat. "In the lower court, six residents of D.C. sought to enjoin enforcement of three provisions of the District's Firearms Control Act that banned the registration of handguns, prohibited the

5

carrying of unlicensed handguns or any other 'deadly or dangerous' weapon capable of being concealed. The U.S. Supreme Court took up the case in its first review of the scope of the right to bear arms in decades."

"Excellent," Bolle interjected. "What did the Supremes do?"

Cam threw his shoulders back, and continued, "The Court affirmed the Circuit Court's decision and struck those portions of the Act which interfered with an individual's right to carry guns. In recognizing the 'Individual's Rights' theory of the Second Amendment, Justice Scalia found that the operative clause of the Amendment compelled that, 'the right of the people to keep and bear arms, shall not be infringed.'"

Bolle nodded approval, while Cam bit his lower lip suppressing a smile. He didn't have much time to enjoy his success.

"That's crap," a female voice yelled from the other side of the room. Bolle swung his head to find a young Asian woman with straight black hair and emerald eyes standing with one hand on her hip and her other in the air.

"You don't agree, do you Ms. Long?"

She let out an extended, dramatic sigh. "How could I?" Many of her classmates laughed. "The Court ignored most of the language of the Amendment to achieve a result that violates the fundamental rights of citizens."

"Explain how your analysis is better grounded than Justice Scalia's," the Professor directed.

"Do you think they even spent any time reading the text of the Amendment? Doesn't seem like it." She glanced around. "The Amendment states, 'A well-regulated Militia, being necessary to the security of a free State, the right of the people to keep and bear Arms, shall not be infringed.'" She paused for effect. "It's clear that any right to bear arms is in the context of being in a militia, not for personal use. This has been

6

bastardized for centuries and shouldn't prevent states from regulating individuals' use of weapons."

A slow, muffled clapping came from a couple of people surrounding her. A woman with red hair slapped her on her back. Long sat down with a smug expression on her face.

Cam shot to his feet. "That's not the way the Court views it. The Second Amendment gives individuals the option to carry a gun if they choose. The court's opinion is well-reasoned and supported by past precedent in a line of cases dating back centuries upholding the individual's right to bear arms."

Before he could finish his sentence, Long jumped back up, her eyes narrowed and her finger pointing across the room at Cam. "It's logic like yours which leads to people carrying semi-automatic weapons down public streets claiming they are making our neighborhoods safer. Do you realize how stupid you sound knowing how many people have died in the service of so-called Second Amendment rights?"

"You just want to tell people how they should run their lives." Cam shot back.

Long leaned forward in Cam's direction. Everyone in the classroom waited for her comeback. "That's moronic. You're the type who wants to tell a woman what to do with her body. Men like you think you know what's best for all people and can't imagine that women might have a smarter way of doing things." Her shoulders shook as she spoke.

All eyes swung to Cam, who waited a moment and then threw a smirk toward his opponent. "That's the problem. You don't even recognize how consistent my positions are. More than anyone, I am for individual rights. Do whatever you want in the privacy of your home. You won't hear me squawking about what you do alone, and if that includes carrying a gun, so be it. My position is well-grounded, rational, and consistent, which you refuse to recognize."

"What I don't understand is your indignation in supporting a cause where the person's claimed right hurts other people. When you carry a gun and it kills someone, it violates all our rights. Your 'individual rights' argument is pathetic and moronic."

Cam wanted the last word, but Bolle interrupted, walking forward with his hands extended in front of him. "Excellent discussion. Let's try to avoid the personal name calling, but you have set forth both sides of this argument. Let's get some others involved in the conversation." He pointed to a student in the first row and directed him to discuss how much regulation a state could impose on an individual's ability to carry an assault weapon. He didn't allow either combatant to reengage for the remainder of the hour.

Once class ended, Cam spied Ms. Long outside and made a beeline towards her, gritting his teeth while forcing out a short animalistic grunt. She crossed her arms as he approached. "Libs like you always distort the facts to support your side," he shouted.

"And you conservatives want to be able to show off your guns, and don't worry how many people die in the process."

He threw his head back laughing. "Sophia, haven't I told you? I'm a Libertarian, which means I don't care about guns so much. It's too much fun arguing with you. You can be so uptight."

Long smacked Cam on the shoulder. "And you think all the women are checking you out when you preen in front of the whole class. If only someone had informed me what a pompous ass you were, I would've made sure we found a different set of roommates."

"People will judge us by the company we keep." He smirked. "By the way, we still live by your rules. No guns in the house. We're proving all types can cohabitate without violence."

Cam tapped her on the shoulder. "See you at the house later."

"Of course. I'll remind you how much smarter I am when I get back home."

CHAPTER TWO

THROUGHOUT HIS LIFE, CAM forced himself to repeat phrases of positivity he read online or made up to fit a particular situation. "Life is a vessel for prosperity," was his go-to confidence builder beginning in eleventh grade. In college, at least the second time, he relied on, "Winners don't compromise," to visualize a future filled with success and all the material rewards attached to it. No chant or mantra, however, could help him overcome the lingering doubts about his competence which had nagged him since starting law school.

During his tenure in college, he managed to put his life back on track and assumed he would remain on an upward trajectory. He couldn't define what success meant, but he needed to avoid being trapped in a common life or becoming a minion to someone else's accomplishments. The goal was always to be top dog or perched up high, staring down at everyone else struggling with the climb.

Cam sat with two other young adults adjacent to a rickety, wooden table in the living room of their shared house where they grabbed breakfast before dashing off to class, held impromptu beer-infused discussions of life or, like now, gathered in spirited study sessions exploring nuanced distinctions of arcane legal topics. A placid smirk stretched across his face as his head bobbed side-to-side so he could address his two best friends.

Cam's long, wavy hair pointed in every direction, out of place after a series of head rubs had tussled it out of its usual well-maintained style. He leaned forward in his chair, papers strewn on the table. He rotated his head to his left. "Keep them coming. We're on fire." They studied together often, but most times let their sessions devolve into quibbling about whose local sports team would beat the other or whose college exploits were most interesting. Today, for one of few times, they maintained their focus on their studies.

The young man in long shorts and an olive-green t-shirt caught his stare while rummaging through a sheaf of documents. "We're still on Con Law. Explain the concept of penumbra of rights found under the First Amendment."

Cam squinted at his friend. "Marco, you may try to challenge me with the harder essay questions, but you don't intimidate me." He raised his eyebrows, his eyes opening wide before responding, "The penumbra of rights under the First Amendment to the U.S. Constitution was first identified in the Supreme Court opinion of Roe v. Wade. In that case, the Justices upheld a woman's constitutional right to an abortion, even though nothing in the Constitution or the Bill of Rights articulates anything close to providing such a right. Rather, according to the Court, such a right was found in the shadow of privacy rights contained in the First Amendment, which before this decision included the right to free speech and assembly, but not the right to abortion."

Cam raised a finger, "But there's more." His eyes darted back and forth between his two friends. "Last year, the

Supreme Court overruled Roe, which raises the question whether the Court will overturn other rights found under this concept like gay marriage and contraception."

Marco shrugged his shoulders, an expression of wonder stretched across his olive-toned face. "Damn, dude, off the top of your head, without looking at your notes. You kind of nailed it. Avoided the political trap so no one could tell where you might fall on the spectrum of support for abortion and got right to the heart of the matter. Well done." He held out his hand for a fist bump.

Cam tapped his friend's fist with his own and then directed his attention to the other man in the folded metal chair on his other side. "Hit me with another one," he said, smacking his other friend's knee.

"Fine, let's move onto race. Can a state propose a law that suppresses the ability of black people to vote?"

"Nice, D'. Perfect question, coming from our African American housemate," Cam said. "The short answer is no, but like most things we are learning in Con Law, there are no short answers. The better answer is that states cannot enact laws which purposefully discriminate. If a law is facially neutral, however, it may pass constitutional muster even if it affects a protected class of people more than others. We don't have unlimited time to respond to these questions, so I will say no more."

Marco stretched his arms high above his head letting his mouth open wide in a full-faced, unrelenting yawn. "Let's stop there. We've been going at this for three hours. I feel like we are almost ready for the exam, and we've reached the point of diminishing returns."

D'Andre threw his book on the ground, but feigned annoyance. "Shut up, you wimp, can't handle any more?" He leapt out of his chair, making some guttural noise, and then punched

Marco's arm, who winced, but who then tossed the book sitting on his lap at D'Andre's head. D' ducked out of the way, allowing it to hit the bookcase behind him. A loud crash echoed through the living room.

D'Andre stood to examine the cracked glass object now lying in pieces on the floor. "Billy," he moaned as he fell to his knees. He covered his eyes. "You were our best bong. You helped us through some tough times in this sewage pit." He raised his head and leered at Marco. He growled, "Now you broke it." He bit down hard on his lower lip.

The three housemates stared at the broken pieces. "Tragic," Cam said in a deadpan. He shoved Marco. "You killed Bill. All he's done is protect and nurture us. Retribution must be given to pay for your sins."

He grabbed a stained pillow from the couch and began pummeling Marco. D'Andre seized a bigger cushion and used it as a battering ram to knock Marco down. They climbed on top of him and resumed their assault.

Marco squirmed as the thrashing continued unabated, his giggles intermixed with pleas to escape. He tried to wriggle free, but his jeans lowered on his waist, exposing the black band of his underwear. D'Andre clutched the uncovered portion and tugged upward, causing a high-pitched yelp to escape from Marco's mouth.

Cam rushed to assist and both yanked harder as a small ripping sound escaped from Marco's pants. "We need to get it over his head," Cam said as they worked to stretch the fabric further.

With his butt arching higher due to the force being applied, Marco offered a pitiful squeak. "These are my best underwear."

"Not anymore," D'Andre said, laughing as he tugged harder.

As the undergarment stretched beyond its maximum elasticity, the front door opened, and Sophia entered the house. Her eyes widened examining the scrum on the area rug before her. "You're all idiots," she said, dropping her backpack underneath the coat hooks on the exposed brick wall. "Is this what you've been doing all afternoon? I guess this is why you'll lose the bet." Her face brightened. "Being our maids for a month. That will be rather entertaining watching you grovel."

The boys released their holds. They stood and tried to regain an appearance of propriety by running hands through hair and shoving shirts into pants. Marco reached behind and smushed the remnants of his underwear back into his shorts. Sloppy grins, like those of six-year-olds caught sneaking candy, covered their faces.

"C'mon, Sophia. We're taking a break from studying," D'Andre said. "Need to blow off some steam."

Sophia's long hair swayed in a circle as she scoffed and shook her head. "I don't care what you were doing. We were in the library for hours, killin' it. No way you dimwits will beat us."

The boys pouted in unison. Cam chirped, "We know the bet. Just because you all graduated from a top-ten undergraduate school and we all went to state schools, doesn't make you smarter. We're working as hard as we ever have. Haven't had a beer in days. I think we might be able to pull this off. We'll be ready once finals start. There's no way your collective grade point average for this term will beat ours." He pointed at her chin. "First week of next semester you'll be cleaning the house while we order you around. Lock it in."

Sophia smirked and tapped him on his arm. She whispered over her shoulder as she turned to walk away, "You're in way over your heads."

The boys remained speechless as she sauntered out of the room.

CHAPTER THREE

CAM CHILLED IN HIS second-floor bedroom, chuckling to himself. The image of Marco's underpants pulled up over his head was running on loop in his mind. He leaned against the wall, underneath a Brothers Osborne poster, while his legs angled towards the bottom of the unmade bed. A faint, rhythmic thumping emanated from his ear buds. His head bobbed, yet his eyes remained closed. The thoughts of case reviews, in-class interrogations, and the supposedly friendly competition dissipated, and he drifted into semi-consciousness. Random fantasies of the women from school mixed in his imagination with those of one of his housemates. His lips curled into a smile.

An unexpected depression at the far edge of his mattress jarred him out of his stupor. His eyes blinked open to find a young woman with fiery red hair examining her phone. "Gabrielle, you scared the crap out of me," he said. "I thought we had a rule about respecting each other's privacy?"

She scoffed. "You boys never respect our need to be alone.

How often do you use our bathroom? I've had to do my hair so many times after one of you despoiled ours. It's nasty. But that's not why I'm here, of course." She rolled her eyes.

Cam swiped at his nose and lifted himself into a seated position. "Why are you here?" He ran his tongue around his teeth and tasted the beginnings of a filmy sleep residue. He turned his body a bit so he wouldn't breathe on her.

She placed a hand on his leg. "You need to think about the big picture and what actually matters."

He gazed at her hand and then raised his eyes to stare at hers. No expression showed on his face.

"You and I have to make peace," she continued. "We're so distracted. Not focusing on what's important."

Cam shook his head to release the cobwebs built up during his brief siesta. Despite her sometimes-goofy appearance and speaking like a teenager, Gabrielle was the most practical of the women who lived on the third floor. All three oozed intelligence and competitiveness, yet she had the ability to interpret the significance of small events and how they could affect their futures with greater clarity than anyone else in the house. The purpose of her sudden appearance still eluded him for the moment.

"I'm not following. What's the problem?"

"Your focus is out of whack. You don't perceive what is truly important." Cam's face displayed no comprehension of her concern, so she continued, "I understand the girls came into the house all cocky and we coerced you boys into betting us, but who cares whose grade point is higher at the end of the semester?" She shook her head and clicked her tongue. "Everyone's attention is on the bet, but no one is thinking about the mock trial competition." She stared hard at him as he raised an eyebrow without speaking.

She sighed and said, "Cam, does it matter who wins the

wager? So what if you're our slaves for a month? Where does that leave us?" She smacked his knee. "The trial competition has the life altering reward. Broadside, Taylor, and Sanders in New York has promised two paid internships to the winners. Getting a summer position with them would give any of us a leg up."

She stopped and glanced up at the ceiling. "We signed up to be on the same mock trial team. We're partners, but if we can't get our act together, we won't have a chance. I want one of those internships, so I'm telling you now, stop. Stop messing around. Don't worry about the bet. Start thinking about the competition." She offered him a small smile. "Focus on us, not them. Got it?

From his prone position, Cam saluted. He was about to respond, but his cell phone buzzed on the table next to the bed. He grabbed it and rolled his eyes. "Let me answer this," he said, raising his index finger. "It's my sister."

Gabrielle stood to leave. Cam lifted the phone to his ear. "Hey, Ilana, why are you calling me in the middle of the day?"

Gabrielle turned to wave goodbye and saw Cam's face turn an ashen shade of grey. He bolted upright. "Ilana, what are you saying? I can't understand you. What's the matter?"

Gabrielle remained silent and reached a hand towards Cam's shoulder as he leaped off the bed. He was shouting, "Don't worry. I'll meet you in twenty minutes. Are you okay?" He paused to listen for a moment. "Love you, too." He threw his phone in his pocket.

Cam jumped around the room grabbing his wallet and throwing on a pair of shoes. Gabrielle stood motionless, appearing helpless. "Are you okay?" she asked.

His voice cracked as he said, "My dad passed out walking down the stairs. They called 911. They're on the way to the hospital." He grabbed her shoulder. "Can I borrow your car?"

Gabrielle reached into her pocket. She tossed her keys to Cam. "Call us when you can. Do you want me to go with you?"

He shook his head. "Thanks. I got this."

Gabrielle didn't move as Cam leaped down the steps, taking two at a time.

CHAPTER FOUR

THE FADED GREEN, TWO-DOOR Honda with dents on all visible surfaces, hurled over the speed bumps in the parking lot of Presbyterian Hospital without apparent concern for potential damage to the undercarriage of the car. Built a century earlier, the towering brick building remained part of the expanding hospital network extending its tentacles beyond its original neighborhood in Oakland and into other areas of the city and region. It shared the area with the other major tenant, the University, making Cam's drive to find out what happened to his dad palatably short.

He ran into the emergency room, his head turning in all directions trying to regain his bearings. A grey-hair at the information desk directed him up an elevator and to a private waiting room where three people waited for him.

Upon entering, he saw his sister, clad in a lightweight purple T-shirt and jeans with parallel pre-fabbed tears extending down the legs, reclining in a cozy chair. She caught his eye and leaped up to engulf him in a hug. When she tried to talk, her body heaved, and she couldn't form any words, just pitiful gasping sounds which were muffled by Cam's bulky sweatshirt.

"Ilana, are you okay?" Cam asked, grabbing her shoulders with his face inches from hers.

As she rested her head on his shoulder, Cam waved to the skinny adolescent staring at the ground, his hands in his pockets and long hair hanging in front of his face. Cam waggled his finger to invite his brother to his side of the room. When he didn't respond, Cam said in almost a whisper, "Max, are you okay?"

Max shuffled over and Cam grabbed him so he would join their scrum. He allowed Cam and Ilana to put their arms around him, but his hands remained dangling at his sides.

The woman in the plastic chair at the edge of the room sat motionless. Her gaze focused just above the three kids. She didn't say a word.

Cam rubbed his brother's head as the siblings swayed together. Ilana's muffled crying was the only sound in the room save for an old black and white clock ticking in the background.

They released from each other, and Cam approached the woman who stood and extended her hands as if she was the queen greeting one of her subjects. "It's good to see you, Cameron," she said. She swiped at her skirt to eliminate any possible wrinkles.

Cam avoided any physical contact. "How are you, Miranda?" He didn't wait for an answer. "What happened to my dad?" He turned his back and took a seat in the round armchair on the other side of the room.

Miranda walked over to Cam, her makeup smooth, without any hint of imperfection, as if she had spent an hour putting it on for a night out on the town. The cream-colored blouse she wore looked like it had just been pressed. A whisper of fragrance, like an ocean breeze, arrived a moment before she sat next to him.

"He's in surgery now. We're not sure what happened, but he was walking down the stairs and collapsed. He tumbled to the bottom and was unconscious." She twisted her head away and placed the back of her hand over her mouth to muffle a sob. A small tear appeared in the corner of one of her eyes when she turned back.

Ilana took the seat on the other side of Cam and continued. "Max," she looked at her younger brother, "called 911 right away. He was very calm. You would have been proud of him."

Cam nodded at his brother and returned his attention to Ilana. "How is he?"

Her sandy blonde hair swayed around her shoulders as she shook her head "The ambulance brought him here. We really haven't talked to anyone yet. We're just sitting here. It hasn't been that long, but I'm so nervous."

Cam put his hand over Ilana's shoulder allowing her head to collapse on his arm. Max picked at his fingernails.

During the next few hours, they remained in the type of anguished purgatory known only to those who have waited for news about a loved one receiving emergency treatment. After a period of anxious anticipation, a doctor dressed in hospital issued scrubs poked his head in the room. "Can I enter?" he asked, as if they would deny him entry.

Tall, with a scruffy, angular face which exuded confidence, but not arrogance, he sought out Miranda. "You're Henry's wife?"

"Miranda," she said. "How is he?" She dabbed a tissue to her eyes.

"He's in recovery. He had a nasty fall and ended up with a subdural hematoma, with significant swelling on his brain. We needed to alleviate the pressure, which I think we accom-

21

plished--at least temporarily. The cardiac testing we performed confirmed he suffered a heart attack. I presume that's what led him to fall. He will require a more involved workup." He took a breath. "By the way, I'm Doctor Latavius Please call me Brian."

Miranda forced a smile. "How's he doing now?"

"Resting for now. It's a shock for him to find himself in the hospital. At this point, I don't believe he understands what's happened. He'll need to be in here for a while."

Cam inched forward. "When can we see him?"

Doctor Latavius held up a hand. "Not for a few hours at least. He's been through a lot. I'm hoping later this evening you can say hi."

Silence overtook the room allowing the doctor the chance to duck into the hallway. Ilana joined her two brothers by the television and pulled them in close to her. She couldn't stop herself from crying.

CHAPTER FIVE

THE SUN HAD SET LONG before Cam and his family had an opportunity to check on his dad. The tangled mass of tubes and IVs feeding his body medicine, fluids, and nutrition almost hid him from sight. They stood in a semi-circle at the foot of his bed, but only spent five minutes offering vague assurances of good health, support, and love before Henry fell back to sleep.

He was so groggy while awake, he could only open his eyes for a few moments. They couldn't tell how much pain he was in, but he didn't exhibit any outward indications of major discomfort. His inability to speak, combined with his complete lack of movement, save for a couple of finger twitches, provided Cam with no assurance that his dad remembered what had happened to him or if he even realized he was in a hospital.

They left the room expressing platitudes of relief to each other attempting to compensate for their feelings of dread. This did little to reduce the family's anxiety. After a few seconds, they became quiet, realizing they understood so little about Henry's condition and discussing it only increased how stressed they all were.

Cam and Ilana walked together down the hallway. "Are you okay?" he asked.

She took a deep breath before responding. "It's been so weird lately, and now this." She stopped and turned to her brother, her eyes wide and her pupils big like black opals. He stopped walking, waiting for her to continue. "Dad's been trying hard, but she makes it impossible. You've spent time with her. She's like plastic. Nothing's real."

"Has she been making any effort?" Cam asked, rolling his eyes.

"In her way, I guess. The problem is she doesn't have the ability. She never wanted kids. They've been married for three years, but we have no connection."

Cam nodded. "I've never had to live with her for very long. I try to avoid even coming over for dinner. You and Max have to put up with a lot that I never had to." He paused for a moment. "How's he doing?"

She turned her head away from him. "Can't say. He's pretty quiet. That's normal for boys like him, but he spends a lot of time in his room when he's home. He wants to spend time with his friends as much as possible. He's not looking to hang out with us." She sighed. "I wouldn't say he was very happy before this happened. What's he going to be like now?" She threw her hands up in the air. "Miranda's going to be in charge."

"Is he getting into trouble?"

She shook her head. "I don't think so. He's a good kid--just a little quiet."

Cam leaned into his sister. "I'm worried about him." He again grasped her shoulders. "I worry about you too."

Ilana smiled, but didn't respond.

Cam continued, "How's Miranda been? Are she and dad getting along?"

"I miss mom. I never understood why he married Miranda so quickly."

Cam bit his lower lip. "We've talked about this before. He was lonely. Miranda has a lot of good points." He chuckled and looked at the floor. "I think."

"Well, I hope her good points materialize soon because that woman is going to have to figure out how to take care of dad and learn how to be a mother—real quick." She smacked Cam's arm. "Can't imagine why that should be a problem for her."

CHAPTER SIX

CAM TILTED HIS HEAD to the side as he walked down the creaky wooden steps after a night of fitful sleep back at the house. He made an exaggerated sniffing sound and shrugged his shoulders. "Do I smell French toast? Here?" he said to himself in a hushed whisper. Dressed in a pair of baggy blue-cotton pajama bottoms and a wrinkled grey T-shirt, he turned into the kitchen to encounter a bevy of activity.

He held his hands in front of him, palms outward. "Whoa, what is happening? Everyone is up at eleven on a Saturday." He looked around the room. "People are cooking food, using pots and applying heat." He walked over to the long table in the living room. "The table is set--with real dishes." He leaned over to the petite woman carrying a ceramic gravy boat with steam rising from the top. "I didn't realize we had actual dishes." He touched her arm. "Kate, what are you carrying and why does it smell so good?"

She placed the container on the table. "It's syrup. Real maple syrup. Not that Mrs. Butterworth crap you boys like to pour on your frozen waffles." She pulled out a seat for Cam and tapped him on the butt. "Please sit. Brunch is served."

"This is rather unusual," he said, looking around as he sat. "We've lived in this house together for two months and we haven't cooked a group meal yet. Have we prepared any meals?" He shrugged and grinned. "What's happening?"

The other five residents of the house took their places filling the mismatched wooden chairs surrounding the table. "You had a pretty rough night. We're worried about you," Sophia said, pushing her hair out of her face.

A moment of silence overtook the room before they all started to speak at once.

"Are you okay?"

"How's your dad?"

"When's he getting out of the hospital?"

"How's your brother handling things?"

Cam shook his head and held up a hand. "This is too much to handle for me. I don't think I've eaten anything since I went to the hospital yesterday." He reached for the stack of French toast and stabbed at three pieces. The feeding frenzy was on and the rhythmic clatter of people loading their plates with the fruit, eggs, and bacon filled the room. A sweet aroma and a quiet hum hung over them as they devoured the food.

After a few moments of everyone focusing on getting food in their mouths, Cam waved his fork in the air attempting to grab the group's attention. "I didn't know any of you could cook," he said. "Maybe we should do this more often."

Marco smacked him on the shoulder and said while finishing up an oversized mouthful, "We have a lot of talent in this house. D'Andre is responsible for the French toast."

D'Andre stood with a half-bow. "The secret is lots of vanilla. And making sure the bread doesn't get soggy before putting it on the griddle." He nodded and sat down.

Marco continued, "Gabrielle made the fruit salad and Sophia, Kate, and I cleaned the downstairs and set the table. Kate was responsible for the fantastic napkin origami."

Kate blushed. "We all wanted to do something to show that we cared and are worried about you," she said. "We've only met you boys a couple of months ago and it might be rocky at times, but we're figuring out how to deal with your idiosyncrasies. We wanted to be here for you."

The girls put their arms around each other. Sophia retold the story of the girls meeting as freshman at Michigan and spending the next four years almost inseparable. She gushed as she talked about how they joined the same sorority, had the same classes, and spent too many weekends partying.

Marco wanted his chance to talk and raised his voice to be heard. "Yes, we've heard your story many times before and let me remind you that the bonds between the guys may not be as long lasting, but they are as strong as yours. Yes, we only met the week of law school orientation, but what a week we had. I don't think we slept. We met some interesting women and discovered some of the more unique spots in Pittsburgh which most people never experience. Maybe we'll be able to show you some of them after we're done studying for finals."

He nudged Cam, who added, "We found this house and given its proximity to school, agreed this was the best place to live. Plus, it was the cheapest, and the only one that fit within our budget." He turned to the women. "I'm glad you saw our posting and decided to live upstairs. Who knows who might have ended up renting the other rooms. Olivia?"

They chuckled at the image of the person with the reputation of being the most sexually active in their class living upstairs.

"These floors squeak a lot," D'Andre said, "I don't think we would ever have gotten any sleep." They laughed and continued stuffing food into their mouths, even with the pace slowing from the rampage at the beginning of the meal.

D'Andre leaned forward to be seen. "Not sure how we all ended up here, but I'm glad we're figuring it out. We have a bunch of unresolved tension in this house. I hope we can make it through the year without any blowups."

Gabrielle scoffed. "Not sure what tension you're talking about." She turned her head side-to-side peering into the eyes of everyone at the table. "Who has tension? Anybody?" Her eyes locked on Cam. "You got tension?"

Cam's face flushed. He waved his hand at Gabrielle. "Tension? Not me. I crush pressure. I have no worries about finals or cases or anything else. Nothing they do can interfere with my ability to focus."

Everyone laughed. "I come from a long history of too much parental involvement." Sophia said. "I come by worrying naturally." She leaned into Cam who was seated next to her. "The tension will consume you because you will never forget about the bet. We are here right now in a moment of great harmony, but once we leave the table, that ends. Let me remind you that the bet is on. Our grades on first semester finals will destroy yours." She pointed at the three boys. "We girls will channel all the tension fed to us at school and then ace all of our tests destroying you and allowing us to win our bet." She smiled, but her eyes didn't change.

Gabrielle caught Cam's attention and rolled her eyes.

Cam stood and grabbed a plate. "Breakfast was awesome. Thanks. I guess I'm going to have to study now." The rest cleared the dishes and the mood sobered up somewhat as they recognized they faced another afternoon with their heads buried in their books.

CHAPTER SEVEN

A SMATTERING OF PEOPLE REMAINED in the hospital cafeteria. Some sat alone, staring off in the distance killing time. Others huddled in small groups whispering, like they were in church. Cam, dressed in shorts and a grey T-shirt due to the hot weather that had lingered into the fall, leaned back in the faux leather booth across from his sister. He sipped a cup of coffee while she caressed a mug of hot chocolate.

Ilana didn't speak. Her eyes drooped from numbing weariness. They had sat for almost ten minutes without uttering a syllable, staring through the large window at the array of colors the sun created as it lowered in the sky. Both were having difficulty containing their boredom having arrived at the hospital earlier in the morning. The dark bags under both of their eyes and their inability to sit still betrayed the worry gnawing at their insides.

Earlier, they had spent hours sitting with their dad who still was having difficulty communicating because of the medications he was receiving and the lingering possibility of, as yet, undiagnosed cognitive issues. He had undergone so many tests already they had lost track. The doctors still hadn't finished the battery of examinations they wanted to complete so they could determine his level of impairment. After their dad fell asleep, they came downstairs to study and kill time until sneaking in a final goodbye before visiting hours were over.

"He's not getting better," Ilana whispered, covering her mouth.

"Sure he is," Cam said, "He's getting stronger."

Ilana blew out a huff of air. "He better. Life with step-witch isn't much fun."

Cam gave her a quizzical look.

"She's funny. Every morning she gets up and spends a half hour putting on her makeup. She looks great, but she's just coming here. It's pretty much all she has to do. It's not like she's working."

Cam laughed. "They've been married for a while now and we still don't know much about her. She never had kids. We don't know what happened in her first marriage. We don't know her family." He paused to glance up at the ceiling. "None of them came to their wedding. It was small, but it wasn't that small."

A smirk stretched across Ilana's face. "I never got why dad ended up with her. She's so much different than mom."

"Maybe that's the point. Dad and mom were together since seventh grade. He never was with anyone else. Miranda is different, for sure. She's everything mom wasn't. She likes to go out and party. Mom was all about the family. Miranda's all about. . . well. . . Miranda."

Ilana scrunched her face. "I miss mom."

Cam didn't respond for a moment, then added, "I do too."

The conversation halted with both staring over the other's head and ignoring the textbooks open on the table. Cam twirled a highlighter between his fingers, while Ilana bit her lower lip, her hair falling over her eyes. The squeak of the rubber wheels of a walker rolling on the tile floor remained one of few sounds in the cafeteria.

A few minutes later Cam tapped his sister on her arm and twitched his head to his left. Ilana turned and spotted Miranda walking the buffet line selecting a couple of items she placed on a tray. After a brief discussion with the cashier, she approached their table. "Kids," she said, "I'm so embarrassed. I left my purse in your dad's room. Could you lend me a few dollars for my coffee and crackers?"

Cam nodded and reached into his pocket. He handed her a five-dollar bill. "Of course."

She thanked him and added, "I would sit with you, but I want to get back upstairs for a few minutes before closing. You understand, don't you?" She walked away to pay for her food.

Cam snorted. "There's something ironic about that, isn't there?"

Ilana laughed. "There's something ironic about everything with that woman."

They shook their heads and stared down at their books, pretending to read.

CHAPTER EIGHT

NINE PEOPLE SQUEEZED AROUND the table in the living room area, passing bowls and plates engaging in boisterous shouting and indiscriminate conversations occurring in between the primary activity of shoving food into mouths. Thanksgiving break gave a brief respite from classes and despite occasional bursts of studying, the law students tried to squeeze in some serious relaxation time to allow space for reinvigoration.

Cam was the only one in his house who lived in Pittsburgh, but the rest wanted to avoid the nightmares associated with holiday travel, electing to stay in town and recharge, despite missing time with their families.

Cam's family had, while his mom was alive, held a traditional celebration complete with a too big turkey, mashed potatoes, gravy, cranberries, and an assortment of pies for dinner. After hearing stories of Cam's Thanksgivings from years past, the rest of the house decided to stay put and have a blowout Thanksgiving dinner of their own. They planned a menu and then invited Cam's sister, brother, and stepmom to celebrate at their house.

Before the meal started, tucked in a corner away from the lighter banter, Cam, Max, and Ilana reminisced about Thanksgivings growing up when their mom woke early in the morning to make the turkey and their dad spent most of the day setting the table and making sure the house was ready for the family and friends who would arrive to share in the celebration. They barely acknowledged the holiday since their mom's death, most times ordering in a turkey and eating it while watching football, just the four of them, with Miranda often in another room, sitting around feeling the emptiness of their mom's absence.

During his final years in college, after his mom's death, Cam would return home from his undergraduate studies for the holiday, but always cut the visit short finding any excuse to return to school before the weekend was over. Miranda, trying to keep family harmony, tried to instill some traditions back into the family, but tradition to Cam included his mom and whatever Miranda thought they should do clashed with Cam's recollection of how his mom did it. He never would agree to meet her halfway. The weekend would be, without fail, depressing; the five of them sitting around the table, with the memories of their mom hovering, suffocating their interactions.

They couldn't talk about the past and didn't have enough shared memories to talk much about the present. To him, it was stilted, awkward, and painful, forcing him into near silence. Ilana and Max followed Cam's lead, eating with their heads lowered, not adding to the conversation, only to bolt to their rooms at the earliest possible moment.

The meal his housemates planned retained many of the qualities of the Thanksgivings Cam remembered from his youth. Once everyone found a seat, conversations sprung up at every corner of the table, interrupted by an occasional burst of laughter. Dishes moved at a feverish pace as they slopped food onto their plates, mixing the mashed potatoes with the cranberries, and even allowing the applesauce to co-mingle with the turkey.

Miranda was not an integral part of the dynamic. She participated, attempting to talk with all the friends and learn a little bit about each of their backgrounds. Given she didn't arrive with a strong foundation of each person's history, she was having difficulty keeping names, faces, and personal tidbits straight. She forced a smile while conversations whipsawed around her.

As the eating frenzy slowed, the volume in the room diminished. Four empty wine bottles rested in the middle of the table while people sipped at the remnants in their glasses. Hushed, small conversations broke out. Food comas set in, mellowing out everyone, with interactions becoming more intimate.

At the far end of the table, Marco leaned into Max trying to find an area of commonality. His attempts to gather any information were rebuffed by one-word answers and sheer avoidance of providing any substance. After significant cajoling, Max confided in Marco that he wanted to try out for the freshman basketball team at school, but worried about the potential embarrassment of getting cut.

On the other side of the table, Ilana was much more willing to share, and whispered to Kate, hoping Miranda couldn't overhear, how much she wanted to become a better dancer, but how her dad didn't allow her to take more classes. Next to them, Cam and Gabrielle discussed potential team makeup for the mock trial and fantasized about winning the competition and what it might mean for their resumes.

The conversations continued to diminish in volume, while increasing in intensity. Around the table, bodies leaned in closer, interacting with rapid hand gestures. No one noticed when Miranda's cell phone vibrated in her pocket. She took it out to look at the display and excused herself, heading to the kitchen. A minute later, she returned, her face devoid of color. She stood motionless at the head of the table, her finger pointing at her phone. All eyes drew towards her, and the room became silent.

Her mouth moved emitting only guttural sounds until she said, her voice cracking, "It's the hospital." She caught Ilana's eye. "Your dad just passed away."

For a moment, no one moved or said a word, until Ilana screamed and ran away. Max looked side-to-side; his mouth wide open but nothing came out. Cam ran over to him, almost knocking plates off the table as he shoved his chair back and smothered him in a hug. His roommates surrounded them with hands placed on their backs and heads. The only sound in the room was the brothers' sobbing.

CHAPTER NINE

DARK, MENACING CLOUDS HOVERED over the house. Cam's family trudged inside, followed by his housemates, pain etched on their faces, too weary to say anything, and their emotions worn too raw to try. At any moment, another thunderstorm of tears could rain down, like it had for the past three hours. They threw their coats on the hooks in the entryway and wandered inside looking lost and purposeless.

Sophia had arranged for a few classmates to bring over snacks and some sandwiches so something to eat was available when they returned from the funeral. Miranda offered no opposition when Cam's female roommates asked her if people could come over to their shared house so she wouldn't have to worry about hosting at hers. She placed herself in a corner of the dining room, away from others, dressed in a simple black dress. A small band of pearls hung just below her neckline. She held her hand at her waist and examined her nails, manicured with a gleaming, coral red polish.

Cam walked in circles from the living room to the kitchen and back, not able to sit and unable to accept that he had just buried his father. His loosened tie swayed as he walked. Ilana and Max stood in a corner next to each other, their faces almost matching shades of a ghastly white, not willing to interact with the few people who nibbled on the food.

Kate sidled over to Cam and leaned her shoulder onto his arm. He glanced at her, an ironic smile on his face. She looked up at him. "Your dad sounded like a great guy," she said. "Your words were wonderful."

"Thanks," he mumbled, not attempting to add to the conversation. He had written out a eulogy the night before trying to find words which would adequately summarize his dad's life, but struggling because he wanted to tell the perfect anecdote and offer the proper tone. His primary focus was on his dad's life before he met Miranda, when Cam felt the family was at its best, but he also snuck a couple of tidbits about the family since their marriage. His stomach churned as he wondered whether he had managed to avoid offending Miranda.

"I didn't realize he started his own business before he became a professor. It sounded like you have your dad's sense of humor." Kate continued, still trying to get Cam to engage.

Cam nodded but didn't respond. Kate put her arm around him and squeezed.

D'Andre, on the other side of the room attempted to pull Max into a conversation, but with similar results. Not a word came from Max's mouth as he stared off into the distance. The button-down shirt he wore to the funeral hung untucked, while tufts of his hair pointed in different directions. He made no attempt to fix any of this.

Gabrielle grabbed Ilana and guided her towards the food. Ilana resisted any attempt at sustenance. The plastered-on smile Ilana wore in no way hid her pain. Gabrielle managed to get her to answer questions about her dad, but soon realized that she could only focus on the period when her mom was alive, and had no interest in discussing anything more recent.

A decent number of people had come to the funeral, but many less returned to the house. After a bit of time passed, the few who remained said their goodbyes and ducked out. Cam's friends, without any fuss, went through the living room, clearing the paper plates and putting the remaining food in the refrigerator. Cam watched from the couch, while Ilana sipped water and Max picked at some of the remaining veggies. Once the room returned to a semblance of normalcy, Cam's housemates excused themselves to go upstairs to put in some studying time. They mumbled quick goodbyes and offered hugs before exiting, leaving Cam alone with his family.

Their dad had been the leader of the family, even if he asserted authority sparingly. Miranda now was the oldest person in the family but had never exercised a parental role before. They stood spaced out around the room, waiting for someone to say something or offer some direction to the group. Max chomped on a celery stick to compensate for the awkward silence.

The sound of sliding chairs and quick bursts of conversation from upstairs leaked through the ceiling until receding into nothingness. Cam pictured everyone at their desks with law books open, typing notes on their computers. He longed to be in his room without the gnawing pain he felt in his stomach. After another bout of silence, Ilana walked over to Cam and looked him in his eyes. She said, "Can I stay here tonight? I don't want to go to the house."

Cam looked over to Miranda who shrugged, her face expressionless. "Sure," he said. He swept his hand around. "There's no room down here to sleep. Plus, everyone will be up early in the morning. You'll have to sleep on the floor in my room."

A small voice chimed in from the corner. "Can I stay here also?" Max said, his eyes still looking at the floor.

"Of course, Boo," Cam responded, invoking his brother's family nickname. "I'm sure there's enough space for everyone."

Miranda grabbed her purse from the table. "I guess that means I'll go home alone." She sighed. "I wish your father was coming with me."

Nobody could figure out a response, so they stood motionless, until Miranda turned and walked out the front door.

CHAPTER TEN

THE PINEY, PUNGENT SMELL of coffee wafted up to Cam as his eyes opened after a fitful night of sleep. Ilana and Max slept close to each other on the floor under sleeping bags. He listened to their breathing, thankful they weren't awake. The three of them had stayed up late reminiscing, knowing sleep would be elusive. He wanted them to stay asleep as long as possible.

He yanked his covers off and tiptoed over his siblings, then walked down the stairs tugging on the now wrinkled navy-blue sweatshirt he had fallen asleep in. He ran his fingers through his hair, but it returned to the unruly mess he found when he awoke. At the bottom of the steps, the girls sat at the big table in the living room, dressed in corresponding sweats of green, blue, and pink. They waved and smiled as he shuffled past heading to the dish-rack by the sink to grab a mug.

He returned, placed the mug now filled with steaming coffee in front of an empty chair between Sophia and Gabrielle, and headed to grab his backpack hanging by the front door. The floor groaned as his bare feet moved along its surface. He slunk into the chair and slid his computer out of the bag and onto the table. It hummed, once booted, in harmony with the three nearby machines, like puppies yelping in play.

The girls stopped their work and raised their heads, six eyeballs appearing just above their screens. Their eyes darted back and forth, first examining Cam's actions then returning to catch each other's gaze. Cam clicked on his keyboard, oblivious of any activity around him.

"What are you doing?" Gabrielle asked, emphasizing each word, and shaking her head.

Cam didn't respond, so she stood and walked over to him. She shook his shoulder "Are you studying?"

He nodded. "We have three cases for contracts we have to outline for tomorrow. More for Con Law and Torts. We got a lot of work to do." His eyes returned to his computer.

Kate smacked him on his other arm. "You buried your dad yesterday and haven't had any time to grieve. You look like hell, but that's not the point." She paused. "Let me repeat—you buried your dad yesterday." Sophia and Gabrielle bit their lips waiting for Cam to respond.

He closed the screen to his computer and rested his arms on top. "My dad wouldn't want to cause me any problems. He wouldn't want me to worry about my studies."

"What makes you say that?" Sophia asked.

"It's just the way he was. He worked hard. Didn't make waves. He always said he didn't want to be a burden to us when he died. He wasn't. He wouldn't want to interfere with my life."

Sophia shook her head. "That's crazy. He was a huge part of your life. You need some time off to get your head straight. School's tough enough when everything is normal."

Cam shrugged. "I'm fine. I miss my dad already, but if I'm not doing something, I'm going to go nuts."

"You'll go nuts if you don't take a break," Kate said. "Take a few days. Relax. Have you informed any of your professors about what happened?"

He shook his head. "I'm not getting behind. This is too important to me. If I take time off now, I'll never catch up. I might have to drop out." His voice trailed off.

"You've been pushing yourself hard since the first day of class," Sophia said. "And now this."

Cam reopened his computer. "I've made up my mind." He pointed at the screen and raised his eyebrows. "You want to talk Con Law?"

The women ignored his question and for the next thirty minutes they didn't speak, focusing on the assigned cases, outlining the facts and trying to understand the courts' holdings.

As Gabrielle stood to stretch, two more bodies shuffled into the room yawning.

"I thought you both might sleep until noon," Cam said to his siblings, raising his head to greet them. "You want some something to eat?"

They both nodded with a hint of a grunt. Max's hair stood almost straight up, mimicking his brother's appearance.

"Grab some of the leftovers from Thanksgiving or grab some waffles in the freezer. We don't have much to eat because," he paused, "we never have much to eat here."

The two kids shuffled into the kitchen. After a moment the small microwave kicked into action. It dinged like a bell a minute later, and they returned each carrying a steaming round waffle.

Cam rolled his eyes. "Grab a plate next time. Enjoy your breakfast. I'll take you back to your house once you're done."

Ilana and Max ate their breakfast while standing. Neither said a word.

CHAPTER ELEVEN

CAM HADN'T EATEN IN Poli's in years. Old-world charm combined with a garlicky aroma greeted patrons coming to dine. The tank of lobsters plunked in the middle of the front lobby made the restaurant look like it belonged in a gangster movie from the fifties.

His family had spent many evenings eating there when he was growing up. His dad always suggested it when his mom wanted the family to go out to eat. He hadn't consciously avoided it since his dad remarried, but they didn't take the family out to eat as much. Miranda didn't cook often, but she'd rather order in than sit in a restaurant.

He wasn't sure why she wanted to meet and was confused why she suggested meeting here when it had no connection to anything they had done since she joined the family. But maybe that was the point. The sight of waitstaff in starched white shirts and black vests triggered a flash of memory and he pictured younger versions of himself, Ilana, and Max sitting across from his mom and dad in a corner booth.

He stood inside the plate glass entrance doors and shook his head to bring his mind back to the present. He glanced left and right while pulling at the sleeves of the sports-coat he had thrown on twenty minutes earlier. A young woman, noticing he was looking for someone, took pity and pointed to Miranda tucked away in a booth in a secluded seating area.

The woman led Cam to the booth dodging workers who hustled to meet the demands of a busy Friday evening. Dishes clattered at nearby tables as he slid in opposite to Miranda.

"Hi," he said, starting to extend his hand, but pulling it back before completing the gesture. "You look great."

He wasn't kidding, either.

She wore a light blue dress that accentuated her petite figure, and her makeup highlighted her deep blue eyes. A hint of lilac scent lingered over the table. Her hair bounced just above her shoulders, recently cut and styled.

"Thanks," she said. "How are you?"

Cam's gaze didn't meet hers. "Fine, I guess. Classes are tough, but they keep me occupied. Less time thinking about other stuff."

"I'm worried about you. Are you really okay?"

"Sure. It's been three weeks since my dad died. I'm still numb, but I'm dealing with it." He paused. "How are Ilana and Max? They don't tell me much when I call. I should stop over at the house, but like I said, classes are busy."

A waiter stopped over to check on them. Miranda said she only wanted coffee and didn't want any food. Cam shrugged and copied her order. Menus remained unopened at the edge of the table.

The waiter returned with two cups and filled them from a silver pot. Miranda ripped open three packets of sugar and poured them into her cup.

"Your brother and sister seem to be doing fine. You're right, they don't talk much, at least not to me. They're going to school and so far, I think they're keeping up with their homework. Ilana works on her college applications, but I'm not sure where she is in the process. Your dad helped her with her essays. I'm no good at that stuff."

Cam squirmed in his seat and swiped his lips with his napkin. "I'll check on her and make sure she gets her applications done."

Miranda picked up some creamer and poured it in her cup. She twirled a spoon around the edge, watching it mix with the coffee. She raised her head. "I have something I have to tell you."

Cam stiffened, sensing he was about to figure out the purpose of their meeting. "Go ahead."

She didn't say anything right away, turning her head towards the windows at the edge of the restaurant. She spoke without looking at Cam. "When your dad and I got married, you and your brother and sister were older. I could never replace your mom and I never tried."

Cam nodded without responding.

"I had a nasty divorce before meeting your dad. 'Damaged goods,' he called me. He was right and he was good for me, but he was in charge of everything. He ran the house, paid the bills, worked, and took care of you kids. I thought my job was to make him happy, and I think I did that pretty well."

"Dad was so much happier than right after mom died."

Miranda chuckled. "Thanks. The point is your dad never expected me to be a mother to his children and I never looked at myself as one. You were his kids."

"So, what are you saying?"

"I had never been to Pittsburgh before I met Henry. This isn't my home. My family is on the west coast. So are most of my friends." She paused and met his gaze. "I'm moving back."

Cam bolted up in his seat and smacked the table causing

the cups to rattle and the silverware to shake. "What are you saying?" he repeated.

"I can't stay here. I'm leaving in a couple of weeks. I'm putting the house up for sale."

"What about Ilana and Max? Have you thought about them?"

"I have. Max is in high school. Ilana's going to college next year. I figure you and your family can look out for them until they're on their own."

"You've got to be kidding. I'm not their father. We don't have any extended family. You saw how much of the family came to my dad's funeral. None. Because we don't have any."

"Cam they're good kids. You'll do a fine job looking after them. I have confidence in you."

"I can't believe you're leaving. You're just going to wash your hands of us? Typical."

Miranda pouted. "I need to worry about me. Like I told you, my deal with your dad didn't involve raising kids. I'd do more harm than good if I stuck around." She forced a smile.

The veins on Cam's neck popped out. He balled his napkin in his hand and squeezed. "I'm not sure what I can do about this, but you can bet I'll think of something." He stood and pulled a ten-dollar bill from his wallet and threw it on the table. "This one's on me. I hope you have a great life."

He walked away from the table without turning back to her. When he got to the front door, he slammed his open hand against the glass. The thud echoed through the restaurant causing the patrons to turn their heads towards the door. By the time the door closed, he was halfway down the block and the customers had returned their attention to their meals.

CHAPTER TWELVE

BLINDS COVERED THE TWO windows in Cam's bedroom, blocking out any sunlight. A desk lamp provided the only illumination, leaving the room in a perpetual state of shadow. The door to the closet was closed, but the aroma from the stack of dirty laundry still managed to waft into the room.

Cam sat on his bed, his head resting against the wall. He clutched his two pillows to his chest. Max sat near the bottom of the bed and faced his brother. To their right, Ilana leaned back in the desk chair, staring up at the ceiling.

After leaving the restaurant Cam raced over to his dad's house, wanting to make sure he arrived before Miranda returned. He picked up his siblings to bring them to his house. He marched them upstairs to avoid any distractions from his housemates.

Ilana scrolled through her phone while Max made shadow puppets on the wall. Cam squeezed the pillows, not sure where to start.

He threw his hands over his head. "I just met with Miranda."

His siblings offered no response to indicate they were listening.

"Pay attention." Cam clapped his hands. "We have to talk."

Ilana spun the chair to face Cam. Max swung his legs around so he could sit up straighter.

"We have problems." Cam didn't say anything further until he made sure he had their attention. "Miranda says she's leaving town. We have to decide what to do."

Ilana picked at her hair. "What do you mean, she's leaving town?"

"Just what I said."

"So where are we going?" she said in a monotone, without any apparent concern.

"I don't know." His voice lifted with exasperation. "I don't think you understand. She's not coming back."

"She's leaving without us?" Max asked.

"Yes, without any of us."

Ilana and Max stared at each other and shrugged. The room went silent until Cam again said, "I don't understand what's happening, but we have to make some decisions."

"I'm not moving." Ilana said, "I want to keep my room."

"Me too. I can't deal with this." Max chimed in.

"Unfortunately, it looks like you'll be going somewhere. We have to figure out where. This is way above my pay-grade." Cam slapped the wall behind him.

Cam didn't have anything more to say. His head spun as he began to understand the gravity of their situation. Ilana and Max sat in silence.

———

AN HOUR LATER, Cam returned to his house after dropping Max and Ilana off at what, for the moment, was their home. He slammed the front door after entering and fired his keys in frustration at the wall leaving a small hole in the plaster.

"Nice," said Marco, one of four in the room with books opened for studying. "That comes out of your share of the security deposit."

Cam picked up his backpack and heaved it on the table. He muttered something inaudible and kicked the chair hard enough that it landed on its side with a thud.

"Hey, what's going on here?" Kate asked, her face scrunched in annoyance because Cam's entrance interrupted her studying.

"It's a little complicated," Cam responded, fast walking around the room without any apparent destination.

The four others looked back and forth at each other. Sophia threw a pen at Cam to slow him down and said, "Sit. Tell us what's going on."

Cam slumped into a chair and pouted. "Like I said, it's complicated." He struggled to put together words. "My stepmom has decided to leave town. She doesn't want to bother with my family anymore. Ilana and Max won't have anywhere to live."

Despite a tendency to hang in the background during high pressure situations, Marco walked over to Cam and put a hand on his shoulder. "That's rough, man." He paused for a moment before asking, "What the hell are you going to do?"

Cam sighed. "Don't know. I'm going to have to make sure they're okay. I'm not leaving them without a place to live. They both go to school here, so we're staying in the city. I was thinking that I might have to find a place where the three of us can live."

Marco shook his head. "That's not much of an option. You can barely afford this dump even with the six of us splitting everything. Do you have any idea what it would cost to rent a small place by yourself and then have to pay all the utilities?"

Cam's head spun. "Somehow I have to figure out how to pay for law school. Plus, next year Ilana's going to school. And then in a few years it will be Max's turn. We can't afford all of that. Let alone take on new expenses." His head drooped. "We're screwed."

"How are you going to pay for all of their college?" Sophia asked, lowering her voice.

"I have no idea. My dad put aside some money for our college, but he told me a long time ago that it wasn't enough to cover all of it. I've taken out a ton of loans already and I guess Ilana and Max will have to also. We're going to be paying off our loans until we start receiving Social Security."

"Damn, dude," she said, "this is rough."

Gabrielle walked around the table and leaned over Cam, her hands rubbing his shoulders, her red hair falling on his back. "I have a thought." She backed away from Cam so she could see everyone. "It might be a little crazy, but you're in a desperate situation."

Cam turned around in his chair, so he faced her. "Go ahead. Nothing you say can make my life any crazier."

Gabrielle laughed, covering her mouth with her hand. "Here's what I understand about your situation: You're in school here. Your brother and sister have nowhere to live, but also need to go to school around here. You can't afford a place to live by yourself." She stopped to look around, but nobody spoke. "There's only one solution. It's rather obvious."

She waited for someone to complete her thought, but no one did, so she finished it herself. "Your brother and sister move in with us."

The room fell into complete silence, and nobody even

twitched. The suggestion was so outrageous to everyone in its audacity they couldn't respond. How could two high school kids live in a house with a bunch of self-absorbed law students who already were crammed into too little space and who left the house in a constant state of disarray?

Cam jumped in to articulate more of the reasons why this idea was ludicrous. "They're kids. We're not really adults. None of us are in a position to act like a parent. We're first-year law students and our focus is on that. Not raising kids." He scoffed. "Look at this house. Is this a good place for kids?" He pointed to a stack of beer bottles on the windowsill and then to a pile of dishes in the sink. "We can't do this. I can't do this." He grabbed his face with his hands.

Marco spoke again, "Listen Cam, it's an outrageous idea, but I'm not sure you have any other options. You can't drop out now, because if you do, you'll never make it back. You'll end up a produce manager at the Eagle and have regrets for the rest of your life. You've told me about your plans. Crush first-year grades, get a high paying internship, and later make partner at some national law firm. Gab's plan might be the only way you're ever going to stay in school and the only chance you have of reaching your goals."

Sophia leaned forward to speak for the first time. "Nobody's asked me, but I'm not so sure that living with us would be the best idea. Look at us. We sleep late. We don't eat well. We swear a lot. Not sure this is the best environment for a couple of impressionable high schoolers."

"This is too much," Cam said. "We all need to think about this. You're being so generous, but I'm not sure this has any feasibility. How about we let this sit for a couple of days and then decide if it's doable? Tomorrow morning you'll wake up and realize this idea was silly. Either way, I'm touched by all of your generosity." He went around hugging everyone in the room.

They returned to the table and reopened their books. The demands of their professors would take precedence over Cam's struggles for at least the next few hours of studying.

CHAPTER THIRTEEN

THE STRESS OF HIS DAD dying and the responsibility of having to care for his brother and sister sapped Cam of most of his remaining energy reserves. It was a vivid, fall Saturday and Cam stayed in bed with the covers over his head in a deep, near-coma sleep. He forced his mind to turn off and his body responded with hours of uninterrupted sleep, the first time he managed to stay asleep without waking in a nervous sweat since his dad had gone into the hospital.

Around noon, he trudged downstairs to find all five roommates in the living area, wide-eyed and appearing to be waiting for him They were out of their sleep garments and the downstairs was devoid of the usual clutter with most items back in place for the first time in weeks.

Kate stood to pull out the only open seat at the table. She motioned for Cam to sit. He complied.

Marco ran to the kitchen, returning with a mug of coffee, steam twirling out the top, and a toasted bagel slathered with cream cheese. He set them in front of Cam. Sophia grabbed a napkin and placed it in his lap.

The group looked at Cam while D'Andre took a position at the front of the room near the faux fireplace. He cleared his throat and made sure he had Cam's attention. "We've been up for a while talking, trying to find a solution to our problem." He swept his hand around the room to include everyone. "We went through a bunch of options, but none were workable, because they involved a significant outlay of cash, which none of us seems to have."

Two of the women giggled, but D'Andre continued, "We've spent a lot of time trying to come up with workable solutions, but we realized the only viable way to deal with your situation is to have the Crewell clan move into our cluttered, unkempt, yet comfy house."

Cam threw his head forward to speak, but D'Andre cut him off. "We have thought through every objection you could raise. We decided that your family would need three rooms and some privacy, so you will be getting the three bedrooms on the third floor. The women will be moving down to the second floor with us."

Marco turned and held out his hand to fist bump someone, but no one returned it, leaving him with his hand clenched in mid-air. He shrugged and said, "D' and I will share a room. So will Sophia and Gabrielle. Kate gets her own room because of her over-expansive wardrobe. We've checked our schedules and we have enough variation in class times that we should be able to have someone home at most times so if Ilana or Max needs something, we can help. We have three almost-working cars between the six of us, so I think we will be able to drive everyone wherever they need to be."

Cam stood and interrupted. "Guys, it's not just a matter of moving a few rooms. They're high school kids. They'll need lots of help in areas none of us would ever think of before they happen."

Sophia extended her hand to take her turn to speak. "Cam, I thought this was a bad idea last night and I'm still not convinced. But we know a little bit about high school. It wasn't so long ago we all were there. We actually have a lot to offer them." She pointed to the refrigerator. "Look, we made a chore and dinner chart. Everyone must do their share to keep the house in good order and everyone has a day of the week where they have to make dinner. Ilana and Max have their own night and with the six of us, we got every day covered. I think we thought of every contingency."

Cam rolled his eyes. "You haven't, but I appreciate that you are considering some of the possibilities. This is an impossible situation. I need to do what's best for all of us and I need to make a decision in the next few days before Miranda leaves and they don't have a place to live."

Gabrielle approached Cam and placed a hand on his shoulder. "We're in this together. We'll do whatever you need."

Cam smiled as his eyes glistened.

CHAPTER FOURTEEN

THE CURTAINS HER MOM bought for her on her thirteenth birthday no longer covered the windows. The framed pictures of her at the ballet barre and playing soccer were off the wall, piled in a corner. Boxes filled with clothes and the mementos from her childhood were stacked throughout the room. In the midst of this chaos, Ilana sat on her mattress, now barren of sheets and comforters. She wouldn't look at the remnants of her past, just staring at her fingers clutched in her lap. One tear fell and splattered on her jeans.

With his hands in his pockets, Cam shrugged. His eyebrows arched high over his eyes. "I'm not sure if we have any other options. Where would we live? How would we pay for it? I checked with your school and you're still able to attend, so nothing changes in that regard."

Ilana shook her head and her body heaved. Cam sat next to her on the bed and put his arm around her. "This isn't what I expected either. I'm not saying it'll be easy, but it's the best I could come up with. Miranda didn't give us a lot of time to think this through."

"Screw her," Max said, marking his first words since they arrived fifteen minutes earlier. He sat on the floor, his eyes cast downward and his back against the wall. "This is all her fault."

Cam bit his lower lip. "Fault isn't important. Figuring out what to do, is. Do you think you two can have an open mind about living at my house?"

"I want to keep doing dance," Ilana said, swiping at her eyes. "I want to see my friends, and next year I'm going to college."

"All doable," Cam said. "What about you, Boo? Thoughts?"

"It sucks. She sucks. Living in another house would suck. Ninth grade sucks."

"Good. Anything else you want to add?"

"Yup. I need help with my science project that's due on Tuesday. Miranda walked away when I asked her."

"We have a lot of smart people in the house. Maybe someone can offer you some guidance."

Max threw a balled-up sock against the wall. "I'm sure they're going to drop everything to help. I also have a basketball game on Wednesday. Dad used to take me." His voice trailed off.

Cam stood and walked to the doorway. He rested his outstretched hands on the edge of the frame. "I'm not hearing any thoughts other than the proposal that's on the table. Miranda's not helping us and once we get you moved out of here, we're done with her. I'm overwhelmed with all of this, just like you are. I don't have any other ideas, so, I think, at least for the short term, you're coming to live in my house. Moving day is tomorrow."

Ilana nodded and Max didn't move. Cam walked out of the room leaving his siblings in silence.

PART 2

CHAPTER FIFTEEN

AT A LITTLE AFTER 9:00 a.m., three cars and a beat-up minivan lined up in front of the two-story brick house which had been home for Ilana and Max their entire lives. The trees were close to barren. Piles of leaves dotted the street. An occasional jogger or dog walker passed on the sidewalk, but, for the most part, they would have room to maneuver. Six people exited the vehicles and skipped up the cement steps. Cam took out a key and opened the front door.

Without any semblance of army-like precision, Cam and his mates descended on the house and began moving the boxes in which Ilana and Max had packed up their lives. The prior evening, Cam texted Miranda to inform her it would be best for her not to be around because he couldn't guarantee how his friends would act in her presence. She responded that she understood and when they arrived, there wasn't a trace of her for them to lob the verbal grenades each had practiced in their heads in the event she ignored Cam's suggestion and elected to greet them.

Within thirty minutes they had grabbed everything marked

for moving and placed it in the vehicles. Miranda had offered the kids some of the furniture but with little room to put it in the house, they only took a couple of small tables, Ilana's beanbag chair, and a desk for Max. Cam had made sure they were able to take a few tokens from their days before either parent died but, in reality, they didn't have much.

Marco placed the last box in his car, while Gabrielle and Sophia swept the house to make sure nothing of importance remained. They flashed thumbs up as they skipped down the front steps.

Cam stood on the sidewalk, silent, gazing up at his childhood home. Ilana buried her head in his chest, her body heaving. Max didn't bother to turn back towards the house. "Let's get out of here," he yelled to Cam as he jumped in the final car.

With a fleeting glance at the house, Cam and Ilana leaped in next to Max. The tires from the wheels of the four cars squealed as they pulled out from the curb and drove away.

———

THEY TOOK EVEN LESS time transporting the boxes into their new shared house on Ward Street. Ilana's stuff went into the third-floor room on the right, near the bathroom, while the group transported Max's to the bedroom to the left of the staircase.

The room in the middle now belonged to Cam. It had all his personal items in it, but with most thrown on the bed and some strewn on the ground, transferred during an express game of musical rooms the night before where he moved from the second floor up to the third. At the same time, the girls emptied their rooms on the top floor and moved to the middle floor, while Marco moved out of his room and in with D'Andre.

Once the boxes arrived at their appropriate destinations,

Ilana and Max tore into them and started to arrange their personal stuff and hang pictures on the wall. Ilana's pictures focused on her friends. Their heads bent toward each other with arms hanging over shoulders in varying displays of comfort and closeness. A couple of pictures of her mom and dad rested next to her bed on the small nightstand. An old pair of ballet slippers hung over a loose nail on the wall.

Max tacked to his walls varying sports pictures of his favorite Pittsburgh sports teams. A vintage framed picture of Willie Stargell hung near the window and a huge Sydney Crosby vinyl cutout clung to the wall behind his bed. He also put a small picture of his parents from a family trip to Canada near to his bed. Marco and D'Andre supervised to make sure all his clothes were hung in the closet rather than tossed on the floor.

Within hours, both of their rooms had become their own, reflecting their passions and the activities which motivated them and, before their dad died, filled their heads with comforting thoughts as they drifted off to sleep. Cam complimented both on how quickly they had cleaned out their boxes and set up their rooms. He assumed this would be the last time their rooms were not in a state of disarray.

After they finished, Ilana knocked on Cam's bedroom door. He nodded. "What's up?" he said.

"I'm leaving. I'm hanging out with some friends tonight."

"Okay. Thanks for letting me know." He smiled and raised his eyebrows. "By the way, do you have a curfew?"

She avoided the question for a moment. "Dad never took the time to give me one. He trusted me. I just had to text him if I was going to be out late."

Cam shrugged. "How about if you're out past eleven, you call me? We'll see how it goes."

As Ilana turned to leave, Max shoved his way past her.

"Same plan with me? We're watching a UFC fight at Nate's. I'll let you know if I'll be out late."

Cam shook his head. "Nope. She's a senior. You're a freshman. Home by eleven. That was my curfew when I was your age. Call me if you need a ride."

"Fine. I got a ride. I'll see you later." Max bounded out of the room. Thirty seconds later Cam heard the front door of the house slam.

Cam walked into the hallway and stretched. "First day being a dad," he said, even though nobody was near him. "I think I'm doing okay." He preened for a moment and then returned to his room. He made sure the volume was turned up on his phone in case he received any unexpected texts in the next few hours.

CHAPTER SIXTEEN

NONE OF THE CREWELL children had ever been to a lawyer's office. Yet, they sat in the leather, rounded-back chairs in the offices of Klein and Bohmback on the third floor of a small office building, snuck into a less than busy area of downtown.

The previous Friday, Cam had received a call from Morris Klein, who informed him that Cam's dad had hired him to draft his will. After expressing his condolences for his family's loss, Klein requested that Cam and his siblings come to his office so he could apprise them of his dad's intentions in his will.

"Is Miranda also coming?" Ilana asked while thumbing through a months-old copy of Better Homes and Gardens. Max slumped in his chair; the tie Cam had forced him to put on fell in between his legs.

Cam didn't bother to turn his head. "Nope. The attorney told me she would be on the Zoom call he was setting up."

"So why do we have to be here? We could have done this from the house." Max asked with a smirk.

"Dude, the lawyer said he wanted all of us here. It's not too hard for us to take an hour to show up. Don't you think dad would have wanted us to be here?"

Max bristled, but before he could respond the receptionist who had let them into the office reappeared. She was young, blonde, and sported a pleasant smile. "Mr. Klein is ready," she said. They stood. "Please, follow me into the conference room."

They complied and she led them into a large room with a long table surrounded by twelve leather chairs. Fluorescent lighting from a series of recessed fixtures cast a hazy glow over the room. A large, flat screen television mounted to the far end of the room was powered on but displayed no images.

They were left alone once the receptionist left the room.

Minutes later a tall, gray-haired man in a pin-striped suit entered holding a large brown folder, which he placed on the conference table. He eased around the corner, extending his hand. "You must be Cam. I'm Morris Klein. Your dad told me so much about you. How is law school?"

Cam grasped his hand. "It's great. Harder than I thought, but I'm learning a lot."

Klein moved down the row. "You must be Ilana. Are you still dancing? Your dad never stopped talking about what a great dancer you are."

Ilana's face turned an awkward shade of red. "I am. It's hard finding time with all of my schoolwork."

"I bet." Klein shifted a bit to his right. "Max. Wow. Your dad never told me how tall you are. Cam tells me you're playing a lot of basketball. Enjoying it?"

"Yes," he said. "I play at the park down the street. At least I used to." His voice trailed off.

"Impressive, nonetheless."

Klein walked to the head of the table. "We'll be starting the Zoom call." He looked at the one young adult and two teenagers. "Your stepmother, who is in California, will be on it.

Once she is with us, I will want to inform you all about your dad's intentions. Any questions before we start?"

They shook their heads and Klein picked up the phone to issue a series of instructions. In a few seconds, the screen jumped to life. He pushed a couple of buttons on his computer screen and Miranda appeared in the Zoom link. She smiled and waved. "Hi everyone," she said. "Kids, good to see you."

"Hi Miranda," Cam said. Ilana and Max raised their hands to shoulder level and waved. They said nothing to her.

"Miranda," Klein said from his seat, "thanks for joining us. How is California?"

"It's lovely. I'm taking some yoga classes, so I'm feeling much more centered."

Ilana turned towards Max and rolled her eyes. Cam bit his lower lip and shook his head.

Klein flipped open his folder. "We are here for the will reading of Henry Crewell. I have assembled all his named heirs, and instead of going through the formality of reading the will, I'll instead summarize and let you know how he wanted his estate divided. If anyone wants to read the actual will, my office will make it available to you or your representatives."

He gazed around the room and at the screen before continuing. "Please bear in mind that I am the attorney for Henry's estate, and I am also the executor for the estate. I do not represent any of you. If you have any issues with what I say or if you wish to contest his will, that is for you to decide and for you to obtain legal representation for that purpose."

He paused again. "Good. Let's start." He pulled out a typewritten sheet of paper from the folder and began to read.

"Henry came to me two years ago to do some estate planning. He had remarried a year earlier following the death of his first wife. He had three children. At that time the oldest was in college. The middle child was in high school and the youngest was in sixth grade. He informed me that he expected his situation to remain stable and he would stay married for a long time. His primary goal was to 'give something to his kids after he died.' But he also indicated that he wanted to make sure his wife didn't have to worry if he were to die younger than expected.

"Unfortunately, Henry died too young. He had, however, made arrangements to help his family in the event of an untimely passing. Henry worked for the University of Pittsburgh as a history professor. Under the rules of the University, any child of his who attends undergraduate school there will have his or her tuition paid for by the University. Henry, however, did not want to force his children to go to Pitt, so he put aside, in tax deferred plans, money to assist each child with paying for school. It would not be sufficient to cover all expenses if a student chose to attend another school, but it would help to cover a fair share."

Ilana and Cam looked at each other, but then turned their sights back to Klein, who addressed Cam and his siblings. "Your father has also provided for a yearly stipend for the three of you. Each will receive ten thousand dollars a year for the next ten years. He has also set aside certain sums of money for the maintenance of the kids and payment for activities beyond their education."

Klein turned his attention to Miranda. "Henry also wanted to make sure that you received a sufficient amount to assist in your living situation."

Miranda nodded as she bit her lower lip.

"He instructed me to set up a trust so that you can receive the income from the trust. Upon your death, the principle in the trust will belong to his three kids equally. The way the trust is designed, you should receive almost fifty-thousand dollars each year. The trust also has a provision which would allow you to seek a greater distribution should your circumstances dictate the need. You have already received all assets that were jointly held with your husband. Those never became part of his estate, so I won't list them here.

"Additionally, Miranda will receive the proceeds from the sale of the house, when the sale is completed."

Cam looked quizzically at Klein. "I thought my dad owned the house and it would be part of his estate."

Klein shook his head. "No. He asked that I put the house in both his and Miranda's name when they got married. 'Sign of good faith,' he called it."

Cam shook his head in exasperation.

"Don't worry, Cameron," Miranda's voice said from the television screen. "With the mortgage on the house, there's really not much equity."

"I'll bet," Cam said under his breath.

Klein stood. "Those were your father's desires for you," he said gesturing towards the kids. Lifting his head towards the screen, he said to Miranda, "He wanted to make sure you would have enough. With that, unless you have any questions, we're adjourned."

———

ONCE OUTSIDE, Cam walked ahead with his hands jammed in his pockets. Billowy plumes of condensed air escaped from his mouth with each breath. He walked with his eyes lowered to the sidewalk. Ilana and Max ran up and placed themselves on either side of him.

"That was fun," Ilana said, as she walked backwards in front of Cam.

"What do you mean?" Cam scowled.

"Well, dad's giving us a lot of money. Maybe I can buy some clothes."

"A lot of money? Miranda's getting more than all of us combined."

"So what?"

He shrugged. "She was with him for less than five years. She's already gotten a bunch of stuff. We're not even sure how much. We're not getting anything from selling the house."

"But dad made sure that we would be okay."

Cam scoffed. "Ilana, I don't think you know what you're talking about. Between the three of us, we get thirty thousand dollars a year. That sounds like a lot, but do you have any idea what the rent is at the house?"

Ilana stared back and raised her eyebrows.

"My share was over eight hundred dollars per month. And nobody has said anything about you guys and what your rent should be. That also doesn't include utilities. It costs a lot to heat a big house like ours. And food. How much per month is that going to cost us? Clothes? Your phones? Damn, it all costs a lot. That money will help, but I don't think it will cover it."

Ilana looked down. "I never worried about that stuff before."

"I haven't either." Cam kicked a rock down the sidewalk. "But I'm thinking about it now."

Cam gave the rock a huge boot, sending it careening into the street. They continued their walk without talking.

CHAPTER SEVENTEEN

PROFESSOR VOGEL STOOD AT the front of the class waiting for a response to a question. Her hands were on her hips and her head tilted to the side. Everyone in the large lecture hall understood she wanted more student participation. The dull silence and weary expressions plastered on nearly everyone's face suggested that the professor would remain disappointed for at least a while longer.

Contracts, even when taught by the most engaging teacher, tended to bore. Offer, acceptance, and consideration formed the basis of any contract, but explaining those concepts often involved detailed discussions about esoteric distinctions between alternative fact scenarios. Many law school students, under the best circumstances, tuned out when faced with slogging through figuring out why one scenario led to a valid contract, yet another almost identical set of facts, did not end with contract formation. To figure out the distinction, students had to parse the analysis of different appellate courts and determine which fact altered the outcome for the court.

Most of the time, the students were willing to analyze the

cases to decipher how the law developed in a particular area. Whether it was the carrot of good grades or the stick of intimidating professors, ordinarily, the students remained engaged so that a lecture moved forward with the utilization of the Socratic Method. While some teachers inspired, others resorted to intimidation to coax the students to work through the cases to discover nuances in the law.

Professor Vogel had no such skills. She had to beg for student participation during class discussions and often had to rouse students fighting not to fall asleep.

Vogel stomped her foot as no volunteers emerged to respond to her previous inquiry. She tried again by addressing the class, "Mr. Jones agrees to sell me land for four hundred and fifty dollars. At closing, he challenges the sale, claiming that all sales of property must be in writing and therefore we do not have a valid contract. I want him to go through with the sale of the land. Who wins?"

Again, no one in the class raised a hand to respond. She squinted and pointed at Marco. "Mr. Salazar, you're my attorney. What do you say?"

Cam, seated to Marco's right, placed an elbow in his side to remind him of the need to respond. Marco shifted and cleared his throat. "Professor, I believe I can win this one for you. In most circumstances a sale of land, according to the statute of frauds, must be in writing. An oral contract would not be enforceable. That requirement, however, is only for the sale of land over five hundred dollars. Given your sale is below that threshold, assuming I can prove your oral contract with Mr. Jones, you would be entitled to purchase the property."

"Thank you, Mr. Salazar. You can return to your state of semi-consciousness."

The class offered a patronizing chuckle.

Vogel shifted closer to the class and offered a maternal

smile. "First term finals are coming up in a week. They are a nice pre-holiday present for all of you. Participation in class has not been exemplary and it may not count towards your grade, but it is often predictive of the type of grade you will receive on my tests. You have already heard that my tests are commonly referred to as 'ballbusters.'"

The students laughed, more real this time. "I don't grade on a curve," she continued. "You'll receive what you deserve, and for some of you, I suspect you will deserve a bit of a comeuppance." She smirked. "Being forewarned is being prepared."

She returned to her lectern and began a discussion on the class's next case. Cam detected a text on his phone which was in his lap hidden by his computer. It said, "You are forewarned. The girls will still kick the asses of the boys in the Ward house grades challenge." It was from Gabrielle and included all the contestants from the house.

Cam grabbed his phone and texted, "Didn't you just hear Marco? He's killing it in contracts."

Sophia wrote back, "Perhaps, but you're three chapters behind in Con Law."

D'Andre was next to participate. He wrote, "The men of the house are superior, and we can't wait to prove it." A second later a highlighter hit him in the back of his neck. He turned and saw Kate smiling. She shrugged her shoulders before looking away.

The housemates ignored the last ten minutes of class, group texting about the other side's de minimus intelligence and talking up their own chances of winning. None had much of idea of what was happening in the lecture.

Kate's text was the last before the end of class. "I am sooooo confident in my girls and how well we are preparing for finals. I can't wait for the boys to run the house for a month. We are going to come up with such creative ways of abusing them. Love you boys."

They joined at the bottom of the steps of the lecture hall to walk home together. They each attempted to display bravado while their insides quivered at the thought of the upcoming week of first semester finals hell.

CHAPTER EIGHTEEN

9:00 P.M. ON A MILD Saturday night, the law students crowded around the dining room table, studying in near silence. They had promised to break at eight and go out for some food, but no one suggested stopping, so they continued pouring over their cases. None of them would be partying tonight as their first tests began the next week and they were undertaking their final preparations for the five exams they had to endure.

The weekend would be dedicated to intense review with limited breaks for food and other necessary bodily functions. Beyond that, they planned to review, and re-review, their case notes almost non-stop throughout the weekend. Their momentum was almost palpable, and nobody wanted to ruin the karma by suggesting they stop despite persistent pangs of hunger gnawing at their insides.

Cam's phone buzzed in his pocket, while six sets of eyes remained glued to computer screens. Contrary to his usual practice of allowing his phone to interrupt his studies, Cam had kept his phone shackled all evening. Hoping for some text that would lighten his mood, he instead saw that he was receiving a phone call.

The display indicated it was from his brother, so he answered, "Hey, what's up? How's the party?"

No one else at the table could hear the answer, but reacted when Cam's face turned a ghostly white and he started to shout. "Oh my god. I'll be there in five minutes. Text me the address. I'll call you back when I'm in the car."

Cam shoved his phone in his pocket as he threw his chair back. "Max passed out at a party. His friend found my number on his phone and said I needed to come right away. They called an ambulance."

Gabrielle slammed her computer. "I'll drive you. Let's go. C'mon."

They dashed for the front door. He yelled over his shoulder, "Ilana's at her friend's house. Will someone please pick her up?"

They ran out of the house not bothering to close the door.

Less than ten minutes later they pulled up in front of the house matching the address Max's friend had texted. A large group of kids scampered away from the house. Clearly, the party was over now.

The house itself exuded money. Rising three stories from the manicured lawn, it loomed over the street. Neatly pruned trees doted the front yard. Cam jumped out of the passenger door and rushed to the front door of the house. He entered without knocking.

A few kids stood at the edges of the marble foyer staring at Max, unconscious on an oversized area rug. Three girls sitting on the steps cried while hugging each other.

The first words Cam could make out came from an adult woman kneeling next to Max. "I can't find a heartbeat. Where's the ambulance?"

Cam dropped to his knee. "I'm Max's brother." He was screaming more than talking, but his fear and anger combined to make it impossible to control his volume. "Can somebody tell me what happened?" He stared at his brother's prone body.

"They were drinking. He came downstairs and passed out. We called the ambulance right away." The woman said.

Cam put his fingers on Max's neck and felt for a pulse. He put his cheek over Max's mouth and let his weakened breathing brush against his cheek. "I don't think we need to do CPR," he said, though not with confidence. "Is somebody outside to flag down the ambulance?"

As Cam stroked his brother's head, the door flew open, and two paramedics barged in. They placed themselves next to Max and, with Swiss watch precision, began to attend to him. One inserted an IV and the other checked his vital signs. Cam breathed for what felt like the first time with them in charge.

Ten minutes later they were loading Max into the ambulance. They closed the doors. "We're taking him to Presby," the taller one said. "We'll be using lights and sirens. Don't try to keep up with us. You know where it is?"

Cam nodded, flashing back to his dad's last days as a patient, and thanked the paramedics who jumped into the ambulance and pulled into the street. He ran over to his car and rushed inside. He said to Gabrielle, "They're taking him to the hospital. Let's move. I'll fill you in on the way."

CHAPTER NINETEEN

CAM AND GABRIELLE HAD to navigate the maze of hallways before finding the emergency room bay where the doctors were treating Max. They arrived no more than ten minutes after the ambulance, but Max already lay on a bed, his clothes strewn on the floor, cut from his body.

Cam almost seized when he saw six people attending to his brother, some working around his head, others near his arms and abdomen. The activity was frenzied as they put in a series of IV's and attached monitors to his body. Cam placed his hand against the glass window to support his body.

Gabrielle grabbed Cam's arm as the medical personnel worked in unison with complete focus on their patient. Cam stared at Max's body and begged for some sign of movement, gaining a modicum of relief hearing the constant ping of the heart-rate monitor.

They spent the next ninety minutes transfixed with the medical team's frenetic work, shielded from the room by a thin glass window. A young doctor, not much older than Cam, dressed in scrubs, left the room once the pace of activity slowed. He approached Cam and Gabrielle. "Are you family?" he asked, pointing a finger in Max's direction.

"I'm his brother. How is he?

"We did a blood alcohol test, and his level is .32. That's four times the legal limit. He's at the point where people stand a good chance of dying from consuming this much alcohol. We're pumping him with fluids. His vitals are looking okay. We're determining if he took any other substances. Also, we're checking him for head trauma. That said, we're optimistic."

"What can we do?" Gabrielle asked.

"You stay here until we have more information. We still have some work to do."

Cam and Gabrielle thanked the doctor who returned to the ER bay. They leaned against the glass, frustrated by their inability to do anything other than watch.

An hour passed before Max stirred as a doctor and nurse stood over him. He turned his head to his right leaning his body over the edge of the gurney and without warning, puked a copious stream all over the table and onto the floor. The nurse grabbed a clean blanket and wiped off Max's face and body. His eyes were now somewhat open. The doctor turned back to Cam and gave him a thumbs up, as if this was the result he had been expecting.

A few minutes later, the doctor waved Cam into the room. "He's quite groggy," the doctor reported, "but it's looking much more promising right now. Why don't you talk for a few minutes with him? We're going to admit him for the night for observation. He'll be taken upstairs soon."

Cam nodded and again thanked the doctor. He approached Max, whose face retained a little more color than the pasty white it had been for the past hour. His eyes, however, were rolled back in his head, unable to focus on Cam.

Cam leaned over and grabbed his brother's hand. "Dude, you had us really scared. That was beyond stupid."

Max didn't respond.

"We're going to make sure you're okay. They'll take you up to a room so you can sleep this off. We'll have a long talk in the morning."

The hospital attendant arrived with a gurney to move Max out of the ER. Cam took a step back to allow him to move Max. When he was rolled away, Cam turned to Gabrielle and collapsed on her shoulder. She rubbed his back while biting her lip.

———

CAM COULDN'T REMEMBER his body ever having to contort in the manner it did. He tried to sleep next to Max in a chair designed to reconfigure into a bed, but which only caused him to rest at an unnatural angle, his shoulder jammed underneath his body. He didn't worry about his comfort and accepted he wouldn't be sleeping much. He spent the few hours from the time they brought Max up to the room until the morning making sure Max was breathing and wondering how his dad would handle the situation if he were alive.

He stared at Max until his eyes opened, much more alert than the prior evening in the ER.

Cam eased into a seated position and stretched his arms. "How are you?"

Max slammed his eyes shut. "I'm so embarrassed. I'm sorry."

Cam had no idea where to start, so he said the first thing that came to his mind. "I thought you were dead. Twice I thought that. First when I saw you passed-out at your friend's house and the second time when I saw them working on you at the ER." Cam choked up and couldn't talk for a moment.

80

"I'm so sorry."

Cam leaned forward to put a hand on his brother's shoulder. "I know you are. How did you end up like that?"

Max took in a big gulp of air. "There was a party at the house where you found me, but we pre-gamed before going. We did a bunch of shots and then went to the party. There was no alcohol at the house. We did it all before."

"How much did you drink?"

"I don't remember."

"You're in ninth grade. You have no idea what you're doing."

"I think I proved that."

They laughed for a moment and then went quiet. The fluorescent lights buzzed above them.

"Why do you think you had to go drinking?"

He shrugged. "Everyone else was. Didn't you drink when you were my age?"

Cam shook his head. "This isn't about me. We can talk about what I did later. We need to find a way to get you through this year. This has been hard on you. It's been a crappy year for you. Is that the reason?"

"No. I don't think so. I just want to have friends and have something to do on weekends."

"But I'm responsible for you now," Cam said, pointing a thumb at his chest.

"I think this probably would've happened if dad was alive. It has nothing to do with you."

"Feels like it does."

They stopped talking for a few minutes. Max broke the silence. "I'm really sorry. I didn't want this to happen. I'm not going to drink anymore."

Cam scoffed. "Don't say that. What you say right now doesn't mean anything. We're going to discuss this a lot more at the house."

Max rolled his eyes. "I'm sure we will."

A few hours later, an intern came in to examine Max and informed Cam that he was fine and could go home. A counselor spoke to them about family alcohol training and suggested they enroll in a class the hospital taught. After receiving his discharge, they walked out of the room together. Cam put an arm around his brother's shoulder. "Let's go home and talk this out some more."

CHAPTER TWENTY

MAX STARED STRAIGHT AHEAD as they drove in silence. The trees on the side of the road whizzed by. Cam smacked the steering wheel as they neared their house and said, "I think we need to make a slight detour." He made a sharp right turn to head out of their neighborhood. In a few minutes, he pulled in front of the house where the party had been the night before.

Max recognized where they had stopped. "Oh no. I can't go. I never met the people who live there." He slunk down in his seat.

Cam chuckled. "I think you can, and you will. Come." He slapped Max on the thigh.

He gave Max a shove as he switched off the engine. "Time to face the piper."

When they approached the front door of the house, Cam took a step back allowing Max to knock unaccompanied. A short woman with dark hair in her late forties appeared and slammed opened the screen door. She engulfed Max in a hug. "Oh, my lord, you're okay. We were praying for you." She wouldn't let go as she started to cry. Max allowed her arms to remain locked around him and didn't move.

After a few more moments of being almost smothered, he extricated himself and forced a look into the woman's eyes. "I'm Max Crewell. I was at your house last night."

The woman smiled. "I remember you. Are you okay?"

He nodded. "Yes. I'm fine. I wanted to apologize for what I put you through."

She grabbed his hand. "That is so thoughtful. We were so worried. You don't know how much I appreciate you coming here to let me know you're okay."

Cam stepped forward from the sidewalk and introduced himself. "I'm his brother, Cam."

"I'm Dolores Mackenzie." She touched Cam on his cheek.

"I want to apologize for how we scared you. I'm also sorry I was rude last night. I never said hi, let alone thank you."

"You have nothing to apologize for. You were concerned about your brother." She grabbed Cam's hand with her empty one. "We didn't know what happened to him."

Cam looked down. "When I got here, I didn't understand what was happening either. I assumed he was drinking here, and you supplied the alcohol. You have no idea what thoughts were going through my head while he was in the hospital. I was tempted to call the police and tell them what supposedly occurred here."

The woman put her hand to her mouth. "I can imagine why you were thinking the way you were. You can rest assured we didn't have any liquor available for the kids. I'm just glad he's okay."

"So am I."

Dolores looked back and forth between Cam and Max; her eyes scrunched together. "I hate to snoop, but where are your parents?"

"Um, they aren't living anymore." Cam hesitated for a moment. "I guess I'm in charge."

"Wow. You got your hands full, don't you?"

"I'm realizing it more every day." He put a hand on Max's back. "He's a good kid. Everyone makes mistakes, but this one has to have some consequences."

Dolores nodded. "I guess we all need to take some responsibility for what happened."

They said their goodbyes, but not before she gave both another big embrace. As they walked back to the car, Cam kicked Max in the butt. "Now you go home and study."

"Can I go out tonight?"

"I wouldn't count on it, mister. We'll have to decide how long you're grounded."

CHAPTER TWENTY-ONE

RAIN SPLATTERED AGAINST THE windows as an occasional crack of thunder sliced through the silence in the house on a late Tuesday afternoon. First semester finals were only a few days away, so like every other day during the past week most of the group hung around the dining room table, trying to study.

Marco and D'Andre had left an hour earlier to play basketball at the church down the street. They needed a break from the constant studying. They had asked Max, two days removed from leaving the hospital, if he wanted to join them. Max, who never displayed any ill effects from the binge drinking episode, hesitated at first, concerned he couldn't keep up. He agreed to go after they suggested the game on most nights wasn't competitive as the teams were littered with overweight, middle-aged professionals who specialized in slapping rather than possessing serious ability to play.

Those who remained planned to study for a while, and then order some takeout and watch a movie. They promised to avoid their typical late-night specialty of watching reality shows while sipping cocktails. Rather, they intended to get to sleep early, wanting to build some reserves to continue their push. Ilana, who had her own looming exams, studied in her room, intending to join when the food arrived.

As they entered the REM phase of studying, where the mind takes over and awareness of time drifts away, a small tap emanated from the front door. Nobody flinched as it wasn't loud enough to pierce their study fog. The second knock was much louder and broke the trance. Cam was closest to the door, so he announced with only the slightest hint of sarcasm, "Nobody move. I got it."

A small-boned woman in her late forties, dressed in an unflattering pantsuit and carrying a brown folder close on the color wheel to the shade of her outfit, stood motionless on the porch. Cam opened the screen, and she took a step back. "Can I help you?" he asked.

The woman studied the outside frame of the door and then turned her focus to Cam. "I am looking for Mr. Cameron Crewell."

Cam smiled and pointed to himself. "I'm Cam."

"Good afternoon, sir. My name is Helen Cartwright. I am a case worker with the County Children's and Youth Services. Is this your home?"

"It is." He stood straighter and removed his hands from his pockets. "Why do you ask?"

"I am here based on a report my Agency has received from Presbyterian Hospital. Does a Max Crewell live here also?"

"He does."

"Is he related to you?"

Cam nodded. "He's my brother."

"I see." She opened her folder and began to take notes. She raised her eyes to examine more of the house. "May I come in?" She stepped inside without waiting for Cam's response.

"Don't mind me," he mouthed as she sidled by.

The women seated around the table turned to face Ms. Cartwright standing in the middle of the room with her folder open. Even with her two-inch square heels she didn't make it to five feet tall.

Cam stepped in front of her. "Ms. Cartwright, can you tell us why you're here?"

She ignored the question while she jotted on the paper. Her eyes lifted when she finished writing her notes. "It has been reported that Mr. Maxwell Crewell, age 15, was admitted to the hospital with alcohol poisoning three nights ago. Is that accurate?"

"Yes, it's true."

"It also was reported that he has no legal guardian. Is that true?"

"No. I'm watching over him?"

"I see. Where are your parents?"

"My dad died a couple of months ago. Our mom died a few years back. We have no other close family relationships. So, he's living here with me."

"Oh my. I'm so sorry for your loss." She pointed at the women seated at the table. "Who are they?"

"They also live here."

"How many people live here?" She stood poised to memorialize the answer on her pad.

Cam's face flushed red. "Well, six of us go to law school. And Max. And my sister, Ilana."

"Oh, you have a sister also. How old is she?"

"She's almost eighteen. She's a senior in high school."

Ms. Cartwright bit the tip of her pen. "You have eight people living under this roof? Two in high school without any adult supervision?"

"We're adults. They're doing fine, considering the circumstances."

"How do you supervise the high schoolers?"

"We manage. It hasn't been that long, but we're figuring it out. We have it under control."

She scoffed. "Apparently."

Ms. Cartwright strolled around the room, eyeing its contents. She picked up a bong sitting on the windowsill and stroked it. "Do you think this is the best environment for the kids?"

"Absolutely. They have nowhere else to go. They're doing fine."

Cartwright nodded. "Please understand Mr. Crewell, it is my job to look out for the welfare of kids. I'm glad we were made aware of this situation so we could investigate it. I am concerned that this house may not be the best place for your brother and sister."

"What are you saying?" Cam said, his voice getting louder.

"Given that these kids have no legal guardian and given this does not appear to be an ideal environment for them, I'm going to recommend further investigation. A court file will be opened, and a Family Court Judge will be assigned who will make the decision as to what is in the best interests of these children."

"You're saying someone else might be put in charge of them?"

She nodded. "I believe that under these circumstances a court appointed guardian may be best here. I will get back to you with further requests."

Cam stood speechless. Sophia approached and said, "Ma'am, we are all doing our best to protect these kids. Taking them away will only do more damage."

Ms. Cartwright grabbed the handle to the front door. "I'm

not sure much more damage could be done beyond ending up in the hospital poisoned by alcohol." She opened the door. "You will hear from my office."

Cam tried to say something as she left but couldn't find any words. They stood in silence, staring at the front door.

CHAPTER TWENTY-TWO

THE GROUP REMAINED IN silence after Ms. Cartwright left, gloom permeating the room as the wreckage from her visit hovered like the black clouds outside. As they were just starting to try to regain some of their composure, the door burst open. D'Andre, Marco, and Max entered.

The boys carried water bottles and their shirts were soaked with sweat. D'Andre spun a basketball on his finger. He flung the ball to Cam. "Dude, your brother can hoop. We dominated at the church. Didn't lose a game. I played pretty well. Hit a couple of threes, but your brother, man, he got game."

"It's true," Marco broke in. "We had him covering the other team's big man. They had a couple of big dudes, but your boy didn't back down. He'd grab a rebound, lead the break and then pass to one of us for an easy basket. We played for two hours straight without having to give up the court."

The three ball players exchanged fist bumps, oblivious to the mood in the room. D'Andre gave Max a shove forward. "Tell your brother what we talked about." When Max wouldn't respond, D'Andre coaxed him more. "Don't be shy, little dude. Tell him."

A grin appeared on Max's face as he looked down. "These guys," he said, his thumbs pointing to D'Andre and Marco, "told me I should try out for the high school team. I didn't think I could make it. I'm only a ninth grader, but they said I should." His smile gave away the pride he felt by being pumped up by the boys.

Cam didn't respond.

"Well, what do you think?" Max asked again.

Cam crossed his arms and rolled his eyes. "I'm not sure that's so important right now."

Max pouted. "What do you mean, 'it's not so important right now?' What's more important?"

Cam turned his back, but responded, "Can we talk about this another time? I got things I have to do."

Max stepped forward. "I want to talk about it now. What's the big deal?"

Cam wheeled back around, his face a devilish red. "Fine, you want to talk about it now? Let's talk."

Max's eyes opened wide, and he took a step back. "Well, I think playing on the school's basketball team would be good for me. I might have a chance to make it."

"Great, you want to play, you play. Let me ask you a question. Does a parent have to sign a form to allow you to play?"

He shrugged. "I guess so."

"So, who's going to sign the form for you?"

Max paused for a second. "I guess you will. Won't you?"

"I would, but I'm not your legal guardian. You don't have anyone to sign for you."

"I don't understand."

Cam took a deep breath and grabbed Max by the arm. "Let's sit. We have to talk."

He called for his sister to come downstairs and placed himself and his siblings at the table. The rest of the housemates stood listening, but not saying anything as Cam explained the visit from Ms. Cartwright.

Cam had regained his equilibrium by the time he finished recounting the story. He still had no answers to the many questions Ilana and Max raised, which could be summarized into one overriding concern, "What's going to happen to us?"

Cam's inability to respond to their inquiries did nothing to quell their fears of living with an unknown guardian. He tried to assuage them, but without answers or an understanding of what they faced, he couldn't alleviate their stress.

Recognizing none of them had any answers, Sophia stepped forward with a thought. "I know a good place where we might be able to get some help to figure this out. I think I know the right person to ask."

She took a few minutes to explain what she was thinking, which allowed a bit of the overwhelming pressure to escape the room. They at least now had a plan for where they could turn to next.

CHAPTER TWENTY-THREE

THE LEAVES SPUN IN circles on the ground as a brisk breeze stirred up chaos in front of the law school. Cam and Sophia hustled through the doors, yet instead of heading for a classroom or to the library like usual, they took the elevator to the third floor where the professors' small offices were located. Both had come here before for office hours, but now felt like they were entering a forbidden area of the school.

A quick walk down a narrow hallway led them to a cluster of doors. After a moment of hesitation, they found the right one. Cam knocked three times and took a small step backward.

The evening before, he spent an hour composing an email to Professor Hawkins, a family law professor, outlining his problem and requesting help. He sent it only after everyone in the house reviewed it and suggested revisions. She responded minutes later, telling him he should stop by her office in the morning.

"Come in, Cam," the professor said, as she waved from behind her desk. The odor from the remnants of a tuna fish sandwich hit them as they entered.

With no classes to teach today, she sported jeans and a white chiffon blouse. Her sandy blonde hair was pulled behind her ears like she was twenty-five, which wasn't that far from her actual age. Tenure was within her reach, which if she continued without hitting obstacles, would make her the youngest full professor at the law school.

The office was spartan, and with three people inside, there wasn't much room to maneuver. Sophia attempted some small talk, but Hawkins smiled and turned back to Cam. "Your email gave me a flavor of your predicament. Tell me more."

Cam cleared his throat. "I told you a little bit about my situation when I wrote to you last night, but, short version, it appears as if CYF has discovered us, and they want to investigate our household. I have no idea what's happening, but I don't want my brother and sister living in somebody else's house. They don't want it either."

"How can I help?"

He shrugged. "I'm not sure where to start. I don't know what rights we have or if we have any rights. I just want to talk to someone who can give me some advice." He shrugged. "By the way, we both have you next semester."

"Really looking forward to it." Sophia interjected, offering a weak smile.

"That's good," Hawkins said. She locked eyes with Cam. "I've thought about what you sent me. I'm not sure how much I can help."

"Why? They shouldn't be allowed to just come in and mess up our lives. We haven't done anything wrong."

Hawkins nodded. "Of course not, but that's not the way they look at it. Their mission is to do what's in the best interests of the kids. At this point, living in a house with six law students, they might argue, is not in their best interests."

"It didn't look good when the case worker came to our house, but I'm sure us living together is what's best for them."

"Perhaps, but it's a bit out of the ordinary."

"Professor, I'm not going to sit back and let this happen. If I need to hire a lawyer, I'll do that."

Hawkins lowered her head and stared out over her glasses. "Cam, you have any idea how much money it would cost to retain a lawyer? You'll have to go through discovery and the Department might want to do more inspections. There will be hearings and preparation time for those hearings. Any decent lawyer will cost you many thousands of dollars."

Cam slunk down in his chair. "I don't have that kind of money."

The professor nodded her head. "Thought that might be a problem." She bit her lower lip and tapped her pen against the desk. "There might be a solution," she said almost to herself. "Most of the time, in the Family Law course I teach I do a semester-long case study. The term ends with a mock trial with the students having to play the roles of the aggrieved parties. What if we use your situation as the case study?"

"I'm not sure how that will help me."

"Maybe it won't be a mock study, but they can represent you for real."

"I'm not following."

"The class can be your attorneys. In certain situations, law students can appear in court if a licensed lawyer supervises them. I could be that person. With fifteen students doing the work of your attorney, I think we should be able to deal with any court filings and cover any hearings. This could be a fantastic, practical teaching opportunity."

"Do you think it could work?" Cam leaned forward in his seat.

"Maybe. We might be biting off more than we can chew, but it also might be the best way to handle your situation."

"Professor," Cam said, "I don't have any other options. If you think this could work, I will accept any help. This is pretty important to me."

"I'm sure it is." She reached forward and patted his arm. "We'll organize this when the class starts next semester. Focus on your tests for now and then we can set this up when you come back after the break."

Cam leaned back in his chair. "It's not like we don't have enough pressure with finals. Throw in a little life-altering threat from a governmental agency. It all adds up to lots of fun."

Cam and Sophia stood and reached for the door.

"Cam, you're facing an uphill climb," the professor said. "I can't help you with your finals, but I hope we can have your back when it comes to the threat from the government. See you in a couple of weeks." She waved as Cam and Sophia walked out.

CHAPTER TWENTY-FOUR

FOR EACH PRIOR CONTRACTS CLASS, empty seats were interspersed between the students who elected to show up for the lecture. For the first time all semester, everyone decided to attend. No one was late and people were seated long before the start of class. Of course, today was the first semester final and failure to show up would guarantee a failing grade.

Computers hummed, and a limited number of hushed conversations sprung up around the room. A few students stretched, raising their arms above their heads, trying to release stress from their bodies. Others just shook their heads as if to release any negative thoughts trapped inside. The scene resembled feeding time at the monkey cage with the animals doing random movements for no discernible reason.

They all understood how much rode on this test. Their core courses, Contracts, Torts, Civil Procedure, Property Law, and Criminal Law ran the entire year. The grade for each class was a mix of the test this semester and the final held at the end of the year. Nothing else mattered. Brilliant case analysis during class had no impact on a final grade. Not coming to class all year also didn't have a negative impact on grades. Everything depended on performing well on the two tests. Screw this first one up and an A would be necessary on the final just to pass.

Third year students enjoyed scaring the first years by telling of others who bombed their first semester tests and dropped out, never to be heard from again. Apocryphal perhaps, but spreading the story served the purpose of spooking the newcomers. The stress of not knowing how they would perform had gnawed at them pretty much from their first day in class. This was their first of their five tests, but once they walked out of the lecture hall in two hours, they would be able to detect the faintest light at the end of the long first year tunnel.

Cam sat near Kate and behind Sophia. Gabrielle, Marco, and D'Andre were on the other side of the room. Professor Vogel entered as the clock hanging in the front of the class ticked close to 9:00 a.m. She walked to the front of the auditorium and stood next to the lectern. Sophia turned and mouthed "Good luck." Kate grabbed her shoulder. Marco flashed a thumbs up to Cam.

Cam thought he detected a bit of a smirk on Vogel's face when she said, "We will begin in a few moments. This exam will test your knowledge of all the relevant cases we have studied in class. I've come up with four equally weighted questions. I'm not just looking for issue spotting. Sound analysis of what the law is that governs the fact situation and how it applies will please me. Entertain me a little with your intelligence. It won't hurt."

Perhaps wanting to add a little tension, perhaps hoping someone would acknowledge her humor, she paused for a moment. No one responded. She shrugged and continued, "When I say start, please open the Contracts portal to find the test. Hit the 'Submit' button once you have completed your responses. The portal will automatically grab everyone's test after one hundred and twenty minutes. Please remain until the end, respectful of your classmates, even if you finish early."

She took out her phone and tapped a button. "The test is live. Good luck."

Each student stared at their computer, first pulling up the test and then reading the initial question. Soon, the only sound in the room was the clicking of computer keys.

If a random person sat in the back of the classroom, he would be unable discern anyone's progress on the exam or how well someone might be answering a question. Each student appeared diligent in typing their responses and no one, at least initially, gave any outward sign of panic.

Despite the absence of signs of overt alarm, some of the people in the room were bombing. It happened every year. Thoughts of "Please don't let me be the one who fails," and prayers of "I'll be a better person if you let me do well," snuck into their heads as each tried to push away these extraneous thoughts and focus on crafting an engaging and accurate answer.

The class's collective nervous energy became more evident as the test wore on. First, there were occasional head shakes and quick smacks of foreheads, and next muffled sighs and groans as the time remaining ticked away. These superfluous sounds only contributed to the escalating pressure in the room.

Sophia turned back to Cam and rolled her eyes. He nodded but returned his attention to his screen. Gabrielle never wavered, always focused on her exam and remained unaffected by the nervous activity in the room.

A few students finished with more than fifteen minutes of exam time left and made a show of slamming their computers shut to let everyone else know they were done. A couple of people still working on their exams groaned to express their frustration with their classmates' lack of consideration. With five minutes left, some pounded away at their keyboards with increasing ferocity, needing to complete their responses for the last question. By the end, most leaned back in their chairs still trying to review their responses but lacking sufficient energy to do much more than fix typos.

After two hours of grinding through the test, a series of dings pierced the near quiet of the room as the portal closed and electronically collected everyone's exams. "Good luck on the rest of your tests," Vogel yelled, as the students gathered their backpacks and trudged out of the room. A few students mumbled their thanks, but most left without saying a word, too drained to respond.

In the hallway, Cam's housemates gathered. "That was quite the ballbuster," Gabrielle said while shaking her head.

"I just threw out some word salad for that third question," Kate exclaimed. "I had no idea how to analyze that fact scenario."

Too tired to add any additional analysis of the test, they stood together unable to find a better way to express their feelings.

Sophia laughed, "That was lovely. So nice to feel incompetent early in the morning." She tilted her head to the ceiling. "Oh, I forgot, we have the Civ Pro test tomorrow. Time to head to the library."

"This sucks," D'Andre said, as he led the shuffling group toward the study rooms.

CHAPTER TWENTY-FIVE

GABRIELLE STARED AT HER Civil Procedure book as if the cases would jump into her head without any effort on her part. It wasn't working.

Her computer displayed her class notes arranged in organized paragraphs and color-coded by topic. The imposing wooden library shelves housing row-after-row of books loomed over her. The hushed silence had helped her focus for the first two hours of study, but now the quiet suffocated her train of thought and the words on the page held little meaning. She scoffed under her breath at someone at a nearby table slurping from his Yeti. Unlike when she was cranking through the cases earlier, every sound or movement now distracted her. She twirled her hair, staring out the window at other students leaving the building.

She leaned over to Kate who also appeared to be reaching the point of diminishing returns. "You want to call it a night?"

Kate nodded her head and slammed her computer closed. "We are outta here."

Sophia, seated alone at a neighboring table, perked up

when her two friends stood. She waved and mouthed, "I'm coming too. Let's stop at the coffee shop." The other two nodded while grabbing their backpacks.

Gabrielle waved at her three male roommates across the room. "Later boys," Gabrielle said as they walked away, not showing any concern that her volume was significantly above standard library levels. "Don't study too late. You'll be too tired for tomorrow's test."

The boys ignored the taunt and turned back to their computers. At least they were staying longer than the girls, more concerned about the optics than whether they were being efficient with their studying.

Fifteen minutes later the three women sat at a round table in the back of their favorite coffee shop across Forbes Avenue from the library. Three hot chocolates each with no whipped cream, steamed in bone-colored porcelain mugs, rested in front them. They looked straight down at their drinks, gathering energy to engage in conversation, their reserves limited from weeks of non-stop studying and having taken earlier in the day their second of five exhausting tests.

Sophia blew a drawn out, cleansing breath into her mug and shook her head. "We all knew law school would be tough and that this week would be challenging, but I never thought the pressure would be so intense."

"So much harder than college," Gabrielle said. "Can you believe we thought we had it so rough then?"

Kate nodded and leaned her head back to stretch it out. "You remember all the papers we had to write? We always waited until the last minute to start. There were a lot of late nights." She sighed.

"This feels different," Sophia added, shaking her head. Her hair swayed. "In college we knew some law school somewhere would take us and the clock would start over again. This time, it's permanent. Who knows if we'll be able to find a job if we screw up? I could be back filling boxes in my dad's warehouse."

"Doubtful," Kate scoffed. "You're the one who's always on top of everything. Remember your color-coded calendar freshman year? You plotted out every course you had to take. You knew what jobs you would get during the summer. You had a planned path to getting into Law School. And boom, here you are now."

"I copied your system freshman year," Gabrielle said. "Still using it. It's what's kept me organized this semester. Freakin' godsend that system of yours."

Sophia stared over their heads. "We're two tests down and three more still to go. I'm wasted. Like someone sucked all the energy out of me. How will we feel when this is over?"

"Totally spent." Kate said. "But it's going to be so awesome." She paused. "We need to have a blowout right after we're done with finals. One that is bigger than the one we had Junior year. Remember waking up the next morning with bodies scattered all over the living room."

Gabrielle nodded. "You're right. That was great, but we need to do something even better. Have a huge party that everyone remembers when we graduate."

Sophia pouted. "But we got the high schoolers at the house."

"Damn, you're right. Will Cam care?" Gabrielle shook her head in frustration.

"You bet he will," Sophia said. "Remember the rules we agreed to when they moved in? I do, because Cam made us repeat them like forty times. No parties. No more smoking. No men staying overnight. I gotta say, we're pretty cool to have agreed to all that."

Kate nodded. "It has cramped us, but what else could we have done?"

"Maybe we should receive some recognition for changing our lives the first semester in law school," Gabrielle said.

"He has. He's always thanking us. So do Ilana and Max." Sophia said, trying to insert positivity.

Kate nodded. "They've been pretty awesome. I don't think I could have handled their situation. I would have blown a gasket. Been seeing a shrink. Doing coke. Who knows what I would've done? But I would be doing some bat-shit crazy stuff."

"Considering what they've been through, they seem to have it together pretty well."

"True, but what about us? We've played by Cam's rules all semester, which means we haven't had any parties. Not one. I need to blow off some steam."

Gabrielle shook her head. "So true. I haven't been with anyone for months. Like I told you before--me so horny. I think I'm going to explode."

Kate laughed. "You still thinking of that guy we talked about early in the year?"

Gabrielle nodded. "Hell yeah."

"Well, let's do this," Sophia said. "We'll have a small gathering after the last final. It won't be a party, per se, just some people getting together, drinking, and doing whatever. But it won't be a party." She smirked. "I bet your guy can be convinced to come and maybe you can let him know what you're thinking?"

A big grin crossed Gabrielle's face. "Good plan. We just need to figure out how to make it happen, or I might just explode."

CHAPTER TWENTY-SIX

LIKE MOST OF THE LIMITED times when he got a few minutes to himself, Cam rested on his bed. Ten minutes earlier he had returned from his third final exam. His Criminal Procedure text rested next to him, unopened, despite it looming as the next test. He stared at his ceiling unable to muster the energy to open it.

The bedroom window framed the sun as it descended in the sky. The evening beckoned. The Civil Procedure final, which like the other two finals under his belt, had sapped his limited reserves of energy, yet he still hadn't eaten anything since early in the morning.

His stomach rumbled, but he was too wiped out to decide what to make. He placed his hands behind his head, instead, reviewing the questions on the earlier exam. His body jolted with anger for failing to take enough time to study pendant jurisdiction, the subject of the third and longest question.

The hum of the ceiling fan distracted him, and he stretched both hands upwards trying to touch the blades, ignoring his computer which also remained unopened. He reached as far as he could, which eased some of his lingering tension. A mumbled grumble escaped from his mouth as he lowered his arms and opened the computer.

A loud knock rapped on his door as he pulled up his case notes. He rolled his eyes and yelled, "Come in. I'm not doing anything important."

Max, dressed in green shorts and a sweatshirt, and glowing from sweat, entered and tossed a green tank top in Cam's direction. In violation of house rules, he bounced a basketball in the doorway.

"What's this?" Cam asked, catching the shirt and examining it by holding it from the top. He ignored the dribbling infraction.

A huge smile appeared on Max's face. "It's my varsity jersey. Coach just handed them out. I made the roster."

Cam leaped off the bed and grabbed his brother by the shoulders. "Holy crap, you made the team! That's a big deal! I wasn't sure you could do it."

Max shrugged. "I did." He yanked the shirt out of Cam's hand to examine the back of it. "Coach gave me number eleven because I'm the eleventh man. He says I'm not going to start, but maybe I'll get some minutes if I work hard at practice."

"Damn, dude, you're only in ninth grade. This is so impressive. By senior year you'll be starting. You'll make All-City. Maybe you'll play in college. Receive a scholarship. Grow a little, you can play in the NBA."

"Funny. Maybe I'll worry about this year before planning out my basketball career. Our first game is next week. You coming?"

"Of course, I'll be there. Wouldn't miss it."

"Thanks." Max paused and took a breath. "I told myself not to expect anything, but then I started to think I had a chance. It's very cool. It would have hurt bad if Coach cut me now."

Cam reached over and rubbed Max's head. "This has been a messed-up year for you. Dad would've been proud. He loved basketball. Remember how good he told us he was when he was our age? Never saw a lot of skills when we played in the backyard."

"He didn't play a lot with me. Probably because he married Miranda by the time I was old enough to really play." He tugged at his T-shirt. "This is the first good thing to happen to me for months." His voice cracked.

"I know."

"I miss him a lot." He plopped onto Cam's desk chair. "I lie in bed and think about him. I see us all together, with mom. Then, I can't picture either of them."

Cam bit his lip. "I do the same thing. Sometimes when I'm studying, I look up and see them. It's kind of distracting."

Max nodded but remained a bit lost in his thoughts for a moment. "Everything's hard. I'm having trouble in class. You're not going to be too happy when I get my grades for this semester."

"You can have a pass for now."

"I can't sleep. At least not too well."

"I assumed that. Some weird noises are coming from your room at night. It sounds like you're having some wicked dreams."

Max shrugged. "Sometimes I wake up with my heart racing, covered in sweat. It takes a long time to fall back to sleep. It's really hard waking up when I'm supposed to."

"We noticed. Sometimes we have to drag your ass out of bed."

"Thanks for that. I would never make it to school if you didn't."

D'Andre poked his head in the room as Max finished his thought. "We hitting the library later?"

Cam nodded. "Yup, let's go around eight. Hey D, guess who made the hoops team?" He tilted his head at his brother.

D'Andre wheeled towards Max. "Dude, you made the team? That's awesome!" he shouted. He picked up Max in a bear hug and lifted him off the floor. "I knew you could do it."

He dropped him back to the floor and they bumped fists. "I'm off for some studying, but we're celebrating when I come back." Cam shot him a look. "And we will be celebrating in an age-appropriate manner." He bolted away.

Max forced a smile. "Your friends have been really good to me. I'm not sure how to say it to them."

"You'll figure it out. This has been a weird year for all of us." Cam stopped. "I heard what you were saying before." He paused. "I'm supposed to be in charge, but I have no idea what I'm doing. I understand you're still grieving for dad. What I'm trying to say is, if you need to talk, I'm always here for you. And... if you need to talk to somebody more qualified than me, we can figure that out also."

"You mean like a shrink?"

"Yes, like a shrink."

"Maybe. I'll try to figure things out on my own for now. I'll let you know how that's going."

"Good. By the way, congrats again on making the team."

Max smiled and left the room bouncing the basketball down the hallway towards his room.

CHAPTER TWENTY-SEVEN

CAM TRUDGED UP THE front steps to the house so weary he wasn't sure he would make it. Thoughts of getting into bed and falling asleep rumbled through his head. The last of his first semester finals was over and he had nothing to worry about. No cases to review, no pending research papers, and no more ball-busting finals looming on his horizon.

The rest of the housemates had finished their last tests earlier in the day and had made vague suggestions about going out later that evening. He hadn't responded to their texts, ambivalent about hanging out with a bunch of other law students who would be unable to avoid discussing the minutia of every question on the five exams they had completed during the week. He wanted a little solitude away from everyone, including his brother and sister.

As he grabbed the door handle, he felt the rhythmic thumping of bass vibrating through the wood surface of the porch. He imagined Marco with a beer in his hand raised over his head, bouncing to the beat. He rolled his eyes, wanting to ignore his housemates and head immediately upstairs.

When he entered the front room, he saw a group of class-mates who waved at him. Many others milled around the living room and by the dining room table, too many to count. A keg sat on a plastic mat near the door; the smell from spilled beer attacked his nostrils.

To his right, Marco preened in the horizontal mirror on the wall near where they hung the coats, fixing his hair. Cam looked left to catch D'Andre prancing down the stairs like a disco superstar, as his three women housemates shimmied close behind. The crowd hooted which caused them to gyrate even more.

In front of him, the warped wooden table, most of the time stationed at the center of the room, was pushed up against the far wall. A couple of stacks of Solo cups sat on one side, with paper plates, already strewn, placed on the other. Plastic bowls filled with chips and pretzels rested in between. Marco, wearing only shorts, moved next to speakers on the bookshelf. He fiddled with his phone and then the volume jumped. He smiled, nodded his head, and jumped in the middle of a group of people already jumping in time to the music.

Cam bolted towards the three women as they made their way down the steps. He stared at them, still lugging his back-pack. "I thought we said no parties." He had to scream to make sure they heard.

Kate glanced at Sophia and giggled, "This isn't a party. It's a get-together. We're having a few friends over."

Cam scoffed. "A get-together?" A few friends? You're joking, right?"

"Listen Cam," Kate said as she guided him to the kitchen where there were a few less people. Sophia followed. "We need to blow off some steam. This has been a long semester." She pouted.

"You've been planning this for a while, haven't you? You never said anything to me."

She smiled back at him. "What would you have said?"

"I would have told you that you agreed there wouldn't be any parties. I would have reminded you that Ilana and Max still live here." He looked around. "Where are they, anyway?"

Sophia stepped forward. "Don't worry. They're not here. Staying at friends' houses tonight. Marco made the arrangements and dropped them off. Mrs. Cartwright will have nothing on us, even if she's conducting surveillance right now on the house."

"Dammit, you should have told me about this." Cam turned away to head back out of the kitchen.

Kate called over his shoulder, "Go upstairs and change. Come back down. It'll be good for you."

———

CAM SULKED on his bed for a while, the noise from the party rising through his floor. He pondered his exams, alternatively rehashing his answers and then trying to adjust his thoughts to anything but his finals.

The worst part of law school, the tearing down of their prior personas to lay the groundwork for teaching them to think like lawyers, was over. He was now confident in his ability to make it through law school in one piece. It took some rigidity on all their parts to make it through the semester, and for the first time in months the stress of law school didn't haunt him. Maybe letting loose a little was the right idea, given they hadn't had a chance to do so for months.

Cam jumped off of his bed and darted for the steps. He took them two at a time and at the bottom, D'Andre was waiting with an overflowing beer. "Thanks man, I could use this," Cam said, taking a healthy chug. D'Andre slapped him on the back. "Time for some catching up."

The music pulsated and bodies danced in the living room. Drinks sloshed all over the wooden floor, but nobody cared. The dancing was communal, no partners. Everybody moved with the beat. There was little unoccupied space on the ground floor of the house.

Classmates poured beer in the living room, shots in the kitchen and a few utilized the downstairs bathroom for other forms of stress reduction. Nobody talked much because the music made it difficult, but most people had no interest in small talk. They were all just letting loose and releasing stress before parting ways for the semester break.

After midnight, as the crowd thinned and people waved goodbye, D' turned down the music which allowed for some conversation. Gabrielle, down to a cut-off t-shirt and skimpy shorts, and covered in sweat from hours of free-form expression on the dance floor, walked over to Cam, who sat on the staircase resting his head against the wall.

"Nice party," she said, her red hair falling, covering her eyes. She leaned over, placing her head a few inches in front of Cam.

"We needed that," Cam responded.

Gabrielle smiled and grabbed Cam's hand. "I know something else we need." She pulled him into a standing position.

He squinted his eyes at her while running a hand through his hair.

"I think it's time," she said, biting her lip. "Your brother and sister aren't here, so no more excuses."

Cam stared into her eyes and shrugged. "You're the boss."

She held his hand as they jogged up the stairs.

CHAPTER TWENTY-EIGHT

THEY AGAIN ENCIRCLED THE dining room table, but sat gendered with the girls on one side and the boys on the other. There were no books or notes, only computers with their tops raised. Eyes remained above screen level, focused on the others.

Kate brushed her hair off her face and stood. "One semester of law school is now under our collective belts. We didn't know each other at the beginning of the semester. For the past four months we have lived together and gotten to know each other. You could say we became a family." She nodded to Max and Ilana off to the side, seated against the wall. Max sat closer to the boys and Ilana to the girls. "But before we expanded and before we really knew each other, the boys claimed they were smarter than the girls, while we knew we had the goods over all of them." She leered at the guys.

Marco waved his hand. "We know what happened. We bet on ourselves. Whose grades will be better. The loser has to be the slaves of the winners for the next month. Let's get on with it."

"Good idea." Sophia said, patting her computer. "School posted grades ten minutes ago. I'm so ready to check mine."

Cam rose to interrupt. "Everybody's ready. As we agreed, each person will check their grades and send me their cumulative grade point average. I will total for each side and declare the winner." He scanned the room and found no objections.

"Ready, go." He took his seat and pulled up the school's portal on his computer.

They clicked away on their laptops for the next five minutes, always avoiding eye contact. No one offered any clue, positive or negative, as to their results, with no groans of despair or shouts of joy.

They texted Cam their GPA's and he entered the results onto a spreadsheet. After completing his calculations, and reviewing them twice, he stood and nodded.

"Wow. It's tight," he said. "Without getting into too many specifics, it was almost too close to call. What I will say is that everyone in the house did amazing. We put in the work, and I think our grades prove it. Given the results we've achieved, it's clear that once we take our finals in the spring, there will be a bunch of members of the Law Review sitting in this room."

They turned to each other to offer congratulations. D'Andre shouted, "Enough already. Who won?"

Cam looked down at his computer. "You won't believe how close this is. Looks like it came down to a plus or minus grade for one person because the difference between the two sides was less than one point. Without belaboring the issue, the guys have the higher grades."

The boys jumped in the air and began a series of chest bumps, hugs, and, back smacks. They didn't taunt the girls but made no effort to hide their glee. After a few minutes of over-the-top celebration while the losing side stared on, they took their seats.

"Great. You won," Gabrielle said. "What's our first task?" She bowed her head.

Cam looked back and forth between D'Andre and Marco. They couldn't control their smiles.

"We had a bunch of thoughts of what you should do," Marco said, "but we couldn't decide."

D'Andre tapped Marco on the shoulder. "Marco thought the first thing you should do would be to clean all of our bedrooms."

"You got to be kidding," Sophia said. "None of you have cleaned anything since we moved in."

"Of course, we haven't eaten yet," Marco added. "Maybe we need them to make some dinner."

The girls rolled their eyes.

With deliberation, Cam closed his computer and cleared his throat. "I think what my friends are trying to say is that we could have had you do any number of tasks to complete your obligations under the terms of the bet. It's a simple contractual analysis. But Marco, D', and I talked this through, and we have a different plan."

The girls crossed their arms and waited for Cam to continue.

"Instead of having you make us dinner tonight or cleaning our rooms, we had a different idea to satisfy your obligations." He paused to gather his thoughts.

Kate jumped up and waved a finger at Cam. "We're not doing any of that..." She couldn't complete her sentence.

Cam shook his head. "We're not suggesting anything sordid. What I'm saying is we decided that if we won the bet, we would call it off because we believe you have already paid off your obligations."

"What are talking about?" Gabrielle asked.

"Our arrangement since the beginning of the school year,"

Cam said, "has changed. All of you have taken in my brother and sister without complaint. None of you has said a negative word about the situation, even though it has caused a major disruption in your lives. Marco, D', and I agree you have been so cool about this that you have long ago paid off your obligations."

"Are you serious?" Sophia asked. "You're canceling the debt?"

Cam nodded. "We are only going to make you do one thing." He pointed to the door and Marco opened it revealing a delivery woman with bags of food. "All we want you to do is eat dinner with us tonight. Our treat."

Kate stood and gave Cam a hug. "You've got to be kidding. We had such better ideas of what to do if we won the bet. It would have been so humiliating for you. But you would have looked good in the outfits we had picked out for you."

"So true." Gabrielle said. "This is so cool of you."

Sophia and Kate brought plates and glasses to the table while the boys spread the food out. Within seconds they were diving into it.

"This could be our last good meal before classes begin," Kate said. "Let's enjoy it."

Gabrielle leaned over to Cam, her mouth inches from his ear, and whispered, "I don't care what you say, I'm still willing to be your slave girl."

Cam smiled and shoved some humus and pita into his mouth.

CHAPTER TWENTY-NINE

THREE BODIES CONSUMED THE COUCH, slumped with heads resting on pillows and legs dangling, tangled together. Popcorn kernels dropped on their laps, with stray pieces scattered on the floor. The room was dark except for the glow from the screen mounted on the wall in front of them.

The familiar dialogue, at least for those who were over sixty, spewed from the television. They listened, enraptured. "A toast to my big brother George: The richest man in town."

Cam raised his cup and yelled, "To George Bailey." Max and Ilana raised their cups, and they all took swigs.

The movie continued, "Teacher says, 'Every time a bell rings an angel gets his wings.'"

A few minutes later, the film finished, and Cam tapped the clicker so that the countdown to New Years show was on. He turned down the volume. "Dad would be happy knowing we watched It's a Wonderful Life again. How many times have we seen it?"

"Every New Years eve. That was his tradition." Ilana said. "Like clockwork."

"Well, last year," Cam said, "we didn't finish it until three in the morning because he waited until Ilana and I got home after hanging out with our friends."

They laughed. "And he kept adding movies to the list," Cam said. "His newest Christmas favorite was Home Alone. He thought it was so funny. Every time."

Ilana sighed. "I would give anything to be able to watch movies with him now. To hear his laugh or his silly comments trying to give us some background about the movie."

"This was a weird New Years. Just the three of us," Max said. "It's nice hanging out with you and all, but last year I never would have thought this would be how we spent our next New Years."

Cam nodded. "I bought a cheap bottle of champagne. It's in the fridge. Should we open it?"

"You didn't let us drink anything all night," Ilana said. "Why stop now?" She pointed at him. "You've been drinking beer non-stop."

Cam nodded at Max. "I think we have good reason to be careful. I'm over twenty-one and haven't been in a hospital for drinking, yet. But a few sips to celebrate shouldn't be a problem."

He walked into the kitchen and returned with a bottle and five glasses.

"There's only three of us," Ilana said.

"I know," Cam responded. "The extras are for mom and dad. I think they would like to have some champagne with their kids."

"What about Miranda's glass?" Max asked.

"Put it in the basement," said Ilana.

"Filled with vinegar," Cam added.

They laughed while Cam poured the champagne into the glasses.

"I hope Miranda's drinking alone tonight," Ilana said.

Cam handed out the glasses, leaving two on the coffee table in front of them. "Let's not worry about her. I want to say something." He lifted his drink.

"These aren't really champagne glasses," Ilana said, holding the oversized water glass in her hand."

Cam scoffed. "We're poor law students. We haven't had a chance to stock our house with appropriate stemware yet."

Ilana bit her lower lip. "Sorry, you were saying?"

Cam stood and motioned for his brother and sister to follow his lead. "I wanted to say as we start a new year, that this has been a hard time for all of us. You've been put in a situation that would drive anyone crazy. Living in a new house, with new people. But I can't imagine anyone else handling this as well as you have. And I can't think of anyone else that I would want to share this challenge with."

He hugged his sister and then his brother.

"We also need to thank you," Max said. "You've made a lot of sacrifices since dad died."

"Also, everyone else in the house," Ilana added. They've made so many accommodations for us. How can we ever thank them? By the way, I miss all of them and wish they were here to celebrate."

"You know they went home to their families," Cam said.

"I know. It's just... they're part of our family now."

Cam put his arm around Max. "They have been remarkably chill, haven't they?"

Max nodded.

"It's so weird," Ilana said, "Just the three of us. No mom. No dad." She paused. "No Miranda."

"There's something okay about that," Cam said. "It's cool having the three of us together. Dad would have wanted us to stick together. We will, won't we?"

Ilana buried her head into Cam's heavy navy sweatshirt. "Do we have any choice? I don't see anyone else here. I think we're stuck with each other."

Cam rubbed his sister's head and pointed at the television screen which projected images from Times Square. "It's time. The ball's falling."

They stood together with glasses extended above their heads.

"Three, two, one. . ." they said in unison. "Happy New Year!"

They hugged and stood in silence. "Well," Cam said, "hopefully, next year will be a better one for all of us. I guess it's time to go upstairs."

They put their glasses on the table promising to clean up in the morning. As they headed towards the stairs, a ringing sound came from the kitchen.

"That's the microwave," Max said, "Anybody getting more food?"

They shook their heads while the microwave continued to sound.

"Anytime a bell rings, it means an angel gets his wings," Ilana whispered.

They looked towards the sound. Cam inched forward. He whispered, "Dad?"

The dinging stopped. They stood still with hands touching each other in the near darkness. They didn't move.

CHAPTER THIRTY

KATE STOOD BY HER BED, placing binders and books into her backpack. She examined each compartment making sure she had all her supplies, and everything was in its appropriate place. This followed the same tradition she had undertaken since second grade. With the new semester beginning in the morning, she flitted back and forth from her backpack to her desk. Once satisfied her school supplies were in proper order, she placed the pack next to the door and nodded her head in satisfaction.

She straightened the few wrinkles in the duvet cover on her bed and readjusted the pillows, so they rested in a perfect triangle extending from her headboard. The two posters over her bed ended precisely at each end of the bed and she walked over to her desk and began to examine the series of notations on the calendar hanging next to the shelf of books.

Noting that an assignment for contracts did not have yellow highlighting, she grabbed a marker to rectify the oversight.

"Hey," a voice called out from her door, "can I ask you a question?"

Kate turned and smiled. "Of course, Ilana. What's up?" She motioned for her to enter, who complied by almost tiptoeing into the room.

"Do you know where my brother is?" she asked.

"Is that what you wanted to ask?"

"No, but maybe I should talk to him first."

Kate approached her. "Is there a problem?"

Ilana's cheeks flushed red, and she turned away. "No," she said into her shoulder.

Kate grabbed her forearm and guided her over to the bed. "What is it?"

They sat. "It's nothing. I just need some advice."

"About what?"

Ilana looked down and then turned her body toward Kate. "There's a dance at school. I don't have a huge desire to go, but everyone's going. There's this guy, Devon, I kind of want to go with him, but I've never had an actual conversation with him."

"Got it. I've been there before and understand the issue." She flicked a strand of hair out of Ilana's eyes. "I think we should keep your brother out of this until we get it figured it out. He might not be the best one to advise you on this."

Ilana smiled. "That's what I was worried about."

"No need to worry now. I got you covered." She ran her hands down her legs to smooth out any wrinkles. She tapped Ilana's leg with her hand. "Spill."

"My problem's not what you think it is. I'll figure out a way to talk to Devon and get him to ask me to go. If not, I'll ask him. Not an issue."

Kate scrunched her eyes. "So why are we talking? I mean, I love it, but why?"

"It's kind of embarrassing, but I don't think I have the right clothes to wear. I'm not even sure what I should wear. I thought I would talk to Cam about buying something for the dance." She stopped for a moment. "It's just that I don't think he'll get it."

Kate bounced up and down on her bed. "Sweetie, there's no way that your brother, who I love very much, will get it. He's a guy. Have you seen what he wears? It's a different T-shirt with one of three pairs of cargo shorts. He's about seven years behind and he's not catching up."

She stood and grabbed Ilana's arm to drag her to the closet. "The good news is, you've come to the right place." She threw open the door to the closet.

Ilana let out an audible gasp. "Holy crap, this is amazing." She dragged her hand along a long row of dresses, skirts, blouses, and pants in a variety of colors and textures, organized with precision and thought. She looked at the top shelf running the entire length of the closet filled with additional folded shirts and accessories.

Kate leaned forward and allowed her head to be smothered by a couple of the dresses. She took a long, full breath. "This is why they let me have this room. It has the biggest closet. I have a bit of a problem. My mom and I love to shop and every time we do, I end up with something new. Sophia and Gabrielle are sharing the other room. They have two tiny closets. Can you imagine if I had to be in that room?" She rolled her eyes.

Ilana's eyes roamed over the clothes. "You have such good taste."

"No way." Kate threw her hand forward. "Well, compared to some people, maybe I do. The other two are in here all the time borrowing my clothes. I love lending them out. What I'm saying is, I think we can find you something in here. I've got pretty much every situation covered."

"You do. You'd let me wear something for the dance?"

"No doubt. You go talk to that Devon. Get him to beg you to go. Once you've accomplished that task, come back to me. We'll pick out the right outfit and he'll have to tell you how amazing you look. You'll have a great time. Maybe you'll marry him."

Ilana laughed. "You might be getting a little ahead of yourself."

"Never underestimate the power of the right clothes."

Ilana stepped forward and engulfed Kate in a hug. "I never will again." She put her head on her shoulder. "Thanks."

CHAPTER THIRTY-ONE

PROFESSOR HAWKINS LEANED AGAINST the table at the front of the small classroom. In her mid-thirties and dressed more like a student than an instructor, she projected an air of casualness, but also managed to combine it with an aura of competence.

Only twelve students were enrolled in the class, and it was the first time any of them had sat in a large lecture hall without ninety other students present. They gave her their full attention, understanding that they couldn't hide like they often tried to in their larger, full-year courses.

"Let's jump right in. Welcome to the Family Law Seminar. I presume you all received the syllabus and reading assignments for the first day of class?"

Each student nodded.

"Good. Most times when I teach this course, I provide a packet of materials for a mock hearing we do the last day of classes. It helps you see the real-life implications of what we are doing in class and the issues you'll be learning. This semester will be somewhat different and, likely, more advanced."

The students leaned forward in their seats. Cam squirmed in his.

"One of the students in this class," the professor said, "is dealing with a significant legal matter in his life that touches on many of the issues we grapple with in this course." The heads in the room rotated from side-to-side as they checked out their classmates trying to guess which of their classmates was dealing with a significant legal matter. With only four other males in the class, Cam felt like most of the class was staring at him.

"He came to me for some assistance, and I offered him the opportunity to be the guinea pig for the class. Not a good choice of words, but in any event, he agreed. He has signed the appropriate forms which will allow you, the students, to serve as his attorneys in his legal matter."

A spate of muttering enveloped the room as the students whispered to each other. Professor Hawkins held up her hand. "I know you have a lot of questions and in a moment the student will address you as if he was coming to your office to seek representation. He will present his problem, and want an attorney, or in this case a bunch of attorneys, who will help him figure out how to navigate the maze of dealing with a family court matter."

She paused as the students began typing notes on their computers. "First matter, this is a real case, and you will be acting in the capacity of lawyers-under my supervision. So, because of that, attorney-client privilege will attach. What does that mean in this context?"

A hand in the back row shot up. She pointed to an African American woman dressed in business casual attire, who said, "Whatever our client tells us stays here. He's our client and he needs to be able to speak without reservation with us. We are duty bound to keep the conversation confidential."

The professor nodded. "Good. You can't talk about this

with your friends or family. That's what it's like to be a lawyer. Often, we can't tell our spouses the details of our cases to protect the privilege. Keep your thoughts about this case to yourself. If you violate privilege, you will harm your client and violate your ethical obligations. Also, your grade will suffer."

She saw there were no questions, so continued her instructions. "You are sitting in your law office and in comes your next potential client. Treat the rest of the class as an initial meeting. Get to know him and obtain as much of the necessary information as you can."

She nodded at Cam who stood and walked to the front of the classroom. The class gave him their full attention. "I know most of you here," he said, "but my name is Cam Crewell. I am a first year. I need your help."

A young man in the first row looked up from his notes. "Mr. Crewell, please tell us why you need our help."

Professor Hawkins grinned, but said nothing.

Cam reached into his backpack and pulled out a folder containing a pile of papers. "I was served with this complaint. It says the County is going to split up my family. I want to stop that from happening."

A woman in the second row asked, "Why do they say they should be able to split up your family?"

For the next fifteen minutes, Cam gave a history of his family, talking about his mom's death, his dad's remarriage, and then his dad's death. He explained his current living situation, emphasizing his belief that it was in the best interests of his brother and sister to stay where they were. He ended by saying, "I don't know what to do, but I need your help to make sure that Max and Ilana don't get moved somewhere else."

He sat back in his seat, while Hawkins retook her spot at the front of the classroom. "Excellent job of getting as much out of your client as possible. The first meeting with your client is vital. You need to get the relevant information. The client needs to feel that you are competent and care about his situation. You allowed him to say what's on his mind without much interruption, which is the best way to accomplish those goals. Now, you need to evaluate how to handle his case. Any thoughts?"

There was a pause as the students looked over their notes. Sophia then raised her hand. "According to the complaint Mr. Crewell has provided, there is a final hearing on May 15th. That gives us about four months to prepare. Not a lot of time, but we have a lot of talent in this room. I think we need to divide into groups. First, a group to research the law to determine if Cam has a good argument why the status quo should be maintained. This group would also be responsible for drafting the appropriate pleadings and filing necessary briefs with the court outlining the law. The second group would be the trial attorneys--those who will handle the hearing and present Cam's case. I think this would be a smaller group of 3-4 attorneys with the rest doing the research and supporting the trial team. How does that sound?"

Hawkins looked around the room to gauge the reaction. Not finding much, she said, "I think that's a good plan. Let's break into two groups. The first will be the trial lawyers and the second, the research and brief writing lawyers."

Within a minute, groups had formed on each side of the room. Sophia, Gabrielle, and Marco were among the four students joining the trial lawyer group. Eight others sat in a circle on the other side of the room. Cam sat alone in his seat, a member of neither group.

"Excellent," said Hawkins. "I want the research group to draft the Answer to the Petition filed by the Commonwealth. We must file it within thirty days from the date Cam received it, which gives us only fifteen days to complete it."

She turned to the trial lawyers. "I want you to begin strategizing. You need to outline a plan for the hearing. What witnesses to call. Outline their testimony. Figure out what research you need from the other lawyers and start coming up with a list of exhibits. Four months may seem like a lot of time now, but it will be here quickly. Also, you don't have near as much experience doing this as the County lawyers have."

Hawkins moved to the front of the classroom. "Each class will begin with a brief lecture on substantive family law matters pertaining to this case. The rest of the class time will allow you to work on the substance of our case. This is now a law firm with one client. Time is your enemy. You need to learn the law and out-prepare the other side. Your client's entire life depends on your abilities and effort. This is not a drill."

She glanced over at Cam who could only offer a weak smile.

CHAPTER THIRTY-TWO

THE SHEETS WERE STREWN, almost falling off the bed. Cam slept on his back, his snoring shooting up towards the ceiling interrupted only by an occasional grunt. The fan above his head spun as if in response to his heavy breathing. Two hours until his first class of the day and the unwelcome alarm would not sound for another ninety minutes.

Despite his stern warnings never to interrupt his sleep unless, "You're on fire, the zombie apocalypse is about to begin or Emma Watson is downstairs asking for me," Ilana bolted into his room and jumped on his bed. She screamed, "Wake up!"

Cam rolled over and pushed her away, so she jumped on him and smacked his back. "Wake up, Cam. I got news."

Cam grunted. He strained to get to a seated position, putting two pillows behind him to support his weary body. He scratched his neck and yawned. "Okay, why are you violating one of my sacred rules?"

Ilana bounced on her knees; a smile stretched across her face. She extended her arm placing her phone inches in front of Cam's face. "Look what I got."

He grunted and grabbed the phone from her. "What am I looking at?"

She shook her head and grabbed her phone out of his hand. "I'll read it to you." She cleared her throat. "Dear Ilana Crewell," she jammed a thumb in her chest. "That's me."

"I know who Ilana Crewell is. Get to the point."

She nodded and continued in a formal tone, "'On behalf of the Regents we are happy to offer you admission to the University of Wisconsin to begin your education this fall.'"

She jumped off the bed and turned towards Cam. "It continues by telling me how wonderful I am and what an amazing addition I would be. Blah, blah blah. You know the drill. Want to know something else? I got another one just like it from Pitt!"

Cam leaped forward and engulfed her in a hug. "Those were your top two schools. You're in! It has to feel great."

"It does, but I..." She turned away from Cam.

He grabbed her shoulders. "Wait. What's happening? Why did you just lose your enthusiasm?"

Ilana put her hands in her lap. "I don't know what to do. I kind of always pictured myself going to Pitt. Dad taught there. You're here. Max's here. When dad taught, I knew the school would pay my tuition."

Cam interrupted, "They will still honor the tuition pledge-- even though dad's not teaching there anymore."

Ilana bit her lip. "But Wisconsin has always kind of been my dream school. Big 10. The lakes. The winters. Great academics."

"It's going to be up to you. Your decision. You're going to have to decide which is best for you."

"But Wisconsin will cost lots more money."

"I get it. But you know dad put some money away for your

college. It's yours. We may have to take out some loans, but we'll figure it out."

"Cam," she said, almost to herself, "I'm going to college next year."

He put his arm around her. "Dad would be so proud of you right now."

She nodded but didn't say anything further.

CHAPTER THIRTY-THREE

THE CHLORINE SMELL FROM the school's pool just down the hallway mixed with the lingering odor of game-used uniforms in the locker rooms to coalesce into a mustiness which hung over the gymnasium. Constructed in the middle of the prior century, the gym retained some of the charm from that period, while avoiding many present-day comforts that newly constructed high schools packed into their sporting venues, like individual seats instead of bleachers for the spectators or hot water in the showers for the participants.

Half-expecting to find the all-white, high-socked, set-shot taking team from Hoosiers running the picket fence on the court, Ilana and her housemates, minus her older brother, squeezed together in the midst of a packed crowd, cheering on the Dragons, Max's High School basketball team.

With little resemblance to the type of team they had imagined, the Dragons played an in-your-face, trash-talking, and high-flying style of basketball. Through the first half, the team had three dunks including a no-look, alley-oop pass to a streaking forward who slammed the ball through the hoop over an overmatched defender.

The Dragons led by seventeen points at intermission and when the team returned from the locker room, Max took his spot on the last seat on the bench where he had been plastered for the first half. This was the fourth game for the undefeated team, which was beginning to look like the favorite to win the City League championship.

In none of the games so far had Max come close to getting on the court. Hours before game time he had told everyone in the house not to come, assuming he would continue his streak of non-playing. He had no interest in worrying what they would be thinking as his butt remained plastered to the metal bench.

It was a Friday, so despite his entreaties, most members of the house decided to venture over to the school, having little desire to push through any more case review. Plus, the games took less than two hours, so their evening wouldn't be shot, and they would have time to go out after.

Nothing changed in the second half. The Dragons continued their domination despite fierce effort by their opponents who were simply overmatched. Ten minutes remained in the game, yet the outcome was not in doubt. With a lead of thirty-five points, and the real possibility of inflicting unnecessary humiliation, the Dragons' coach, dressed in a navy suit, began to substitute, allowing the starters to return to the bench to the fans' loud cheers. Even with five new players on the court, Max, the eleventh member of an eleven-player squad, remained glued to the same spot on the bench, no closer to his coach.

The players on the court wanted their chance to shine so the intensity level didn't decline. The Dragons continued to outperform the other team and raised the lead to forty.

With four minutes remaining, and perhaps out of some level of boredom, Kate and Sophia started rhythmic clapping and began to chant, "We want Crewell! We want Crewell!" Within a few moments, most of the fans in the stands were echoing the chant. "We want Crewell! We want Crewell!"

Seated on the bench with his elbows on his legs on the other side of the court, Max lifted his gaze a few inches and scanned the crowd. He shook his head in a meager attempt to stop the chant, and then put a white towel over his head when no one stopped, which only increased the intensity of the chanting.

With two minutes left, the ball went out of bounds, so Kate and Sophia stood and turned to face the crowd. They motioned for everyone to stand, which many did. The cheering became more deafening.

"We want Crewell!"

The Dragon's coach shrugged his shoulders and walked over to Max to tap him on his shoulder. Max rose and jogged to the scorekeeper, who hit the buzzer to signal his entry into the game. When he strode onto the floor, the crowd erupted.

Both teams missed shots after play resumed with Max not getting a chance to touch the ball. The Dragons possessed the ball with under thirty seconds remaining. The coach signaled in a play, which did not alter the disorganized way the team passed the ball around the perimeter without attacking the basket.

The clock ticked under ten seconds.

"Crewell! Crewell!"

Max stationed himself in the corner while the ball rotated in his direction. He readied himself for the pass. When it came, he received it and then launched a high arcing three pointer. The buzzer sounded as the shot swished through the hoop.

Most of the players were already walking off the court by

the time the ball went through the basket and didn't react. Everyone from the house, however, exploded as if the shot had won the NBA championship. They high-fived and hugged each other, jumping up and down in unison.

They waited in the stands for the post-game speechifying to end. Once completed, Max's teammates grabbed their gear and headed towards the locker room. Max detoured and walked across the court towards the housemates.

They yelled, "Great game," as he approached. D'Andre threw his arm over his shoulder. "Nice shot."

Max blushed. "It was important to go up by forty-two."

Gabrielle tapped him on the arm. "You got into the game. Broke the hymen, as they say."

Everybody took a step away. "Good analogy, Gab," Sophia said. She turned back towards Max. "I thought you looked great out there."

"Yeah--for the minute I was out there. Next game, I'll be back in my usual spot. I'm not complaining. We've got a good team."

As they continued their congratulations, Cam jogged up from the entrance door. "How was the game? Looks like you won big."

Max glanced at his brother, but turned to D'Andre. "Can we get some food? I'm hungry."

D'Andre nodded, but raised his eyebrows towards Cam. "Did I miss something?" Cam asked.

Max scoffed while moving away from his brother. Cam stepped in his direction and grabbed his arm. "What did I miss?"

Max cheeks turned red. He wiped his face with the towel he was carrying. "Not much," he spit out. "Just my first time in a game. I'm sure you had somewhere more important to be."

Cam's body slumped. "I was studying. Got stuck at the library. Had to review three cases." He stared at Max.

"Whatever. It's not important."

"You told us not to come."

"Well, you're the only one who listened."

Max turned away from Cam and started to walk with D' Andre. Sophia put her hand on Cam's arm. "Don't worry. He just wanted you to be here."

Cam shuffled behind the group. "I would have been, if I could." His voice trailed off.

CHAPTER THIRTY-FOUR

THE KNOCK ON THE DOOR, though tentative, still resounded through the living room because nobody was making a sound. The three women sat on the couch, while the guys took seats around the table. Cam stood and glanced at his housemates who gestured to him to open the door. He smoothed his hair and pressed his shirt with his hands.

Upon opening the door, Cam waved in the young gentleman, whose eyes widened when he saw six people in the living room awaiting his arrival.

"Hi, I'm Cam. I'm Ilana's brother. You must be Devon."

Before he could respond, Cam grabbed his elbow and led him into the house. Devon stood three inches taller than Cam. His sandy brown hair rose to a crest in the front, but the women focused on his azure eyes, like the color of the sky on a clear day, bright and determined, as he headed their way. He wore a thin cut, black suit with a narrow black tie, contrasting with his barely off-white shirt. His dark leather shoes gleamed while tapping on the floor as he walked across the room.

Cam pointed to a chair facing the group and Devon dutifully placed himself in it. He waved at everyone and said, "Hi, I'm Devon, you can call me Dev. I'm here to pick up Ilana."

Cam took the seat in the center of his friends, in front of Devon. He picked up a yellow pad on the table next to him and flipped over some pages. "Ilana is upstairs getting ready. She's been told to stay there until we ask you a few questions. Okay?"

Devon squirmed. "Sure. Fire away."

Cam looked at his notes. "What grade are you in?"

"Twelfth."

"Plans for next year?"

"I just got into Penn. Looks like that's where I'm going."

"Impressive. Plans with my sister for tonight?"

Sophia jumped out of her seat. "Cam," she shouted, "not appropriate." Cam pouted and Sophia continued. "What Ilana's brother is saying is that he hopes you have lots of fun tonight. What time does the dance start?"

Devon looked at his watch. "Eight. We're picking up a few friends before. One of them is having an after-party. Is it okay if Ilana goes?"

Cam was about to speak, but Sophia shot him a look and said, "Of course. You have a great time."

Marco leaned forward to add, "But not too great of a time, understand? We all were in high school at some point. We know what can happen."

"Yes, we do," D'Andre said after standing and pulling his shoulders back. "All of us care very much about Ilana and we assume you understand what that means."

Devon turned his head from side-to-side to make eye contact with the six housemates. "I understand what you are saying. I will make sure that Ilana has a great time at the dance tonight, but I will also make sure that it's done in an acceptable manner. I hear all of you." He smiled as he nodded at each person.

Cam stood and approached Devon, putting a hand on his shoulder. "Good. I think we are all on the same page. You've done well. We will now get Ilana down here. She's very excited."

He looked at Kate who bolted upstairs taking the steps two at a time. Thirty seconds later she stood at the top of the steps and pronounced. "I present the lovely, the stunning, the beautiful, Ms. Ilana Crewell." She swept her arm outward, and Ilana appeared to begin her descent.

Ilana took each step with deliberation and like in every coming-of-age teen movie all eyes followed her path. She wore a thin black dress, off her shoulders and tight-waisted that flowed outward from her hips. A small strand of pearls, which Cam recognized as their mom's go-to party wear, encircled her neck, providing the outfit with an accent of maturity.

Cam noticed Devon's eyes not deviating from Ilana's path down the steps but put aside the mixed emotions that caused him. Ilana eased over to her date and whispered, "I see you've met the fam."

Devon nodded. "Thanks for warning me. Interesting situation you got here." He took a step back. "You ready to go?"

Ilana bounced on her toes. "I am. Let's head out." They turned towards the door and as they walked out, they gave an over-the-shoulder wave and headed down the sidewalk.

Gabrielle leaned into the door to shut it, exhaling a deep breath of air, and exclaimed, "They grow up so quick, don't they?"

"Soon they will be out of the house, and we'll be left with nothing but the memories," Sophia said while hugging Gabrielle.

"What time do we start texting her to make sure she's okay?"

Kate asked. "I can't believe how much worrying you have to do when you're a parent."

D'Andre grabbed Kate by the arm. "Let's not worry now. It's time to study. The kids will be home when they get home."

Cam fell backwards onto the couch. "I'm not going to be able to study until she gets home. I'm going to be a mess."

PART 3

CHAPTER THIRTY-FIVE

WEARING WHAT APPEARED TO be the same brown pants suit as the last time she graced their house, Helen Cartwright, her face devoid of any expression, or makeup, as one would expect of a family court investigator, again stood on the front porch. With her yellow pad pressed up against her chest, she forced a smile when Cam opened the door. He let her in without saying a word.

"Thank you, Mr. Crewell," she said after she was inside. "As you know, I am here for the second required in-house visit. You are prepared?"

"We are. Let's get this finished," Cam said, trying not to sound too dismissive. He walked away from her towards the kitchen. She followed a few steps behind. When they stopped next to the table, Cam motioned to determine if she wanted to sit. She shook her head.

"Mr. Crewell, I am here to do a second assessment of the living conditions at your residence. You have agreed this is a proper time for the visit."

Cam nodded. "Yes, I've agreed. It still doesn't mean that I'm happy about it."

"I gather you are not."

Cam scoffed.

"First, I want to see the living conditions in the entire house. Your brother and sister's bedrooms would be a good place to start. I also want to inspect all the common areas. Finally, I will interview Max, and then Ilana. You are not allowed to be present for these. I am hoping that they will speak without reservation with me about their living situation."

"They are hanging out in the basement. I can show you their rooms and then they can talk with you. I think you'll find everything we are doing here is in their best interests. All of us are concerned about their well-being."

She looked up. "Cam. Can I call you that?" Cam nodded his assent. "I'm sure you are concerned for them; they are your brother and sister. What I am here to assess is whether this situation is the best possible one for them. Bear in mind, you are not far above the age of majority, and you are still in school. You have concerns and responsibilities that may detract from your ability to take care of your siblings. This is true even before we deal with the fact that there are five other young, single adults who reside here."

"I understand your concerns. My primary concern is that you don't prejudge this situation. I realize this is not typical, but lots of times typical is not in the best interest of kids."

Mrs. Cartwright tilted her head in Cam's direction. "Rest assured, I have not prejudged anything. It is my responsibility to complete a final report that will assist the court in making its determination."

Cam walked towards the staircase. "Let's get started." With his back towards his guest, he mumbled under his breath, "Mi casa es su casa."

The tour through the third-floor bedrooms proceeded without incident. Cam noted to himself with a modicum of pride how Max and Ilana had pulled the covers up on their beds and made sure all clothes were off the floor and put away. Perhaps a first since they had moved into the house.

The vibe in Max's room typified a young, high school student. A desk for his books situated across from his bed. His sports equipment in bags on the floor. A few cardboard boxes lined the shelves indicating at least a small passion for gaming. The hint of well-worn gym shoes hovered near the closet. Cam looked upwards in thanks when Mrs. Cartwright avoided opening the door.

Cam couldn't imagine Mrs. Cartwright finding any issues in Ilana's room. Everything appeared in order with her dance shoes lining the bottom shelf of her bookcase and every item meticulously organized on her desk. In contrast to Max's room, there were no pungent odors, just a hint of the hair and nail products she applied each morning.

On the second floor, she poked her head in each of the bedrooms, but took no notes. She had no one to speak to as Cam had made sure all his housemates would be gone for the visit.

"Do you want to see more?"

"Yes, but I am most interested in speaking with your brother and sister. Where would be a good location for the interview?"

Cam bit his lip, but replied, "I'll get them. Please meet me downstairs.

A few minutes later, Max sat across the dining room table from the diminutive woman. She shooed Cam out of the room with a backward wave of her hand. Ten minutes later, the scene was repeated with Ilana taking questions from the same seat

Max had. Cam fretted in the kitchen during the questioning, frustrated by his inability to hear or participate.

When she completed the interviews, Mrs. Cartwright appeared in the kitchen. "I am done with the housing inspection and the interviews of the affected adolescents." Cam's head jerked backward at her nomenclature. "Once I have reviewed and collated my notes, I will be done with my investigation."

"You know, this is the best place for them, don't you?"

"It's not my decision. I only gather information. The final decision is made by others."

"But your report has an impact. Putting them somewhere else will screw them up. It would be a horrible decision to move them."

"I understand your feelings, Mr. Crewell," she said, her eyes downcast while she walked towards the front door. "Please also understand, I take a dispassionate view of any situation and evaluate it in the context of comparing the present living conditions with available alternatives. Ultimately, we look to secure a permanent solution that allows for growth and to protect the safety of the adolescents."

She yanked the handle of the front door. "No final decision has been made. We will let you know of our evaluation in conformity with the court rules. Thank you for your time."

Cam leaned against the door after closing it. Her words rang in his head. Affected adolescents. Permanent solution. We will let you know of our evaluation.

He couldn't expand his chest to get enough air into his lungs. He put his hands on his knees and lowered his head between his legs. He was so dizzy he thought he might fall over.

CHAPTER THIRTY-SIX

DAVID SIMPSON STOOD AT the front of the auditorium waving his hands, attempting to get the throng of students to take their seats. For the past two hours, he had taught a Con Law seminar on the history of Due Process and an advanced corporate taxation course for third year students, and now he had to pretend that he was excited about heading up the school's mock trial competition. His only hope was to get the crowd under control so the orientation could proceed, and he could get out of the building.

The mock trial competition was a rite of passage for many of the first-year students and a major developmental milestone for those who wanted to become litigators. Despite its importance, Simpson had little interest in shepherding them through the process. A warm bath and a glass of Chablis seemed a better reward for the effort he had put in, not only in teaching his classes but in organizing the event.

He put a smile on his face, and yelled, "Have a seat people. We have lots to get through."

A minute later, the sixty students in the room found their places and the din in the room lowered.

Simpson cocked his head to one shoulder and then to the other, while shaking his arms at his side like a sprinter warming up before a race. The room quieted. "I'm glad to see so many people. We are here to give you the preliminary instructions."

A couple of students in the back grabbed their backpacks and headed out the back doors of the auditorium.

"Too much pressure for them, I guess," Simpson said. The remaining students responded with a smattering of chuckles.

"As most of you know, the mock trial competition is a long-standing tradition here. Many of the city's finest litigators cut their teeth in this event and used it as a steppingstone to success in their professional careers. We expect extensive preparation, intelligent presentation, and some wicked cross examination."

Simpson took a step backward and looked at his notes. "Any first year can participate. The packets with the case materials will be emailed to you later in the week. The event will take place in six weeks with four rounds of competition. If you score high enough, you advance. If your score is low, well, you don't. There will be one team that will remain undefeated at the end of the day."

He scanned the room. "Each team will have two lawyers, who will split responsibilities for opening and closing statements. Each lawyer will also have one witness to handle on direct examination and one on cross. All teams will be required to find two people to serve as witnesses. Each round will take one hour. So, the winner will have to prevail four times over the course of the day. It's grueling, but also should be fun and serve as a tool for learning. Any questions at this point?"

With no one raising a hand, he continued, "Now to the good part. In past years we have awarded a thousand-dollar scholarship to the winners. Not bad, but this year, the prize has improved. So let me introduce our guest, Mark Taylor, the managing partner at the firm of Broadside, Taylor, and Sanders in New York City."

Simpson clapped his hands as he pointed to a forty-ish man in the front row who stood and walked to the front. His grey, pinstriped suit accented his shoulders and waist while his fiery red tie hung without a hint of movement, right on his belt. His dark hair cut to lay with a clean line right above his ears resulted from a styling costing more than all of their textbooks.

"Good morning," he began, "I am Mark Taylor. A few years back I graduated Pitt Law School." Nobody in the room could articulate why, or for that matter, how, but Taylor had their attention. He stood without moving, with only minor modulations in his voice, yet the room remained quiet, and the students listened without distraction. He had, as they say, a presence.

"I am a litigator at the firm of Broadside, Taylor, and Sanders in New York and handle what my firm refers to as 'significant litigation.' I'm responsible for anti-trust and corporate malfeasance matters for the most part, but my job is to make sure our clients are well-represented when a case ends up going to trial." He paused for effect.

"My first experience questioning a witness was during my first-year mock trial competition here, an event I am proud to say I won. I also still remember every round in vivid detail and can say with confidence that it was a significant impetus for my success."

He stopped to scan the room. "This year, due to my insistence, my firm decided to sponsor the competition. Many of the younger lawyers from the firm will fly into Pittsburgh to judge the trials. We will be responsible for determining which team is the winning team. What is new this year is the prize the winning team will receive. Given my belief that the winners of the event will become confident, successful litigators, our firm will offer each a summer internship, paying a competitive New York salary and offering the perks that summer clerks have come to expect."

An excited murmur overtook the auditorium. Taylor raised his hand. "I have huge expectations for the talent in this room. I can't wait to see it in action."

He strode over to Professor Simpson, shook his hand, and turned to exit through the metal doors on the side of the auditorium.

The students grabbed their backpacks to leave. In the back row, Cam turned to Gabrielle and said, "Let's go home and review last year's course materials. We've got to be prepared. I want that internship. Think about what working for a mega New York law firm for the summer would do for our resumes. No more worries, baby."

Gabrielle yanked his arm. "I'm so ready to start."

They grabbed their bags and sprinted up the steps, taking them two at a time.

CHAPTER THIRTY-SEVEN

A MAELSTROM OF ACTIVITY SWIRLED around Cam as he sat in the center of the classroom, alone. To his right, a group of three gestured wildly with all appearing to want to talk at once. None gave any indication of listening. On his left, near the window, another group stared at each other saying nothing, waiting for someone to take charge and offer instructions. Behind him, a third group stared at yellow pads, heads locked downward, not offering any indication that they were doing anything substantive.

Cam lowered his head toward the desktop and tapped it three times. He looked around the room once more before standing. He walked over to Sophia's group near the window and said, "Have you finished your witness outlines?"

No one would meet his gaze or offer a response. "Who's questioning which witnesses?" he asked louder. Again, he received no response. "Do you have any idea what you're doing?" his volume rising higher.

He shuffled over to the group charged with doing legal research and writing court briefs. "Our pretrial statement is due next week. Our trial brief is due the following week. Can somebody tell me how far along you are with them?"

Like the other group, no one would make eye contact with him. He threw his hands up in the air and turned towards the last group in the back of the classroom. "Maybe the evidence team can give me an update." He pointed at them. "Anyone want to tell me how you're progressing?"

The lack of response raised Cam's level of exasperation even higher. Professor Hawkins took notice of the confusion spreading through the classroom. She called from the front of the class, "Cam, take your seat. Lawyer groups, let's get everyone together and have a team discussion."

While the students moved their chairs back into position, Cam slammed his yellow pad onto his desk chair and yanked his chair back creating a loud screech that echoed off the cement brick walls. Cam ignored the stares from his classmates.

"You have a client who is asking you questions and, from what I observed, nobody gave him any answers. How is a client going to react when his lawyer won't answer his questions?"

Seeing no response, Hawkins muttered, "About the same way a professor will react when nobody answers her questions."

She turned to Cam. "Explain to the lawyers what you are feeling."

Cam looked around the room. "I'm scared. Really scared. I know this is just a class for everyone, but for me this is real. My life, and the lives of my brother and sister are in your hands. You aren't getting paid for your work like real attorneys, but I feel my case deserves your attention and energy. It doesn't look like I'm getting either." Cam looked at his yellow pad, even though he had nothing written on it. "My hearing is five weeks away and we are nowhere close to ready." His voice trailed off.

Hawkins sat on the edge of her desk. "Does anybody have anything to say?" She waited, but no one volunteered. "Listen up. Being a lawyer is difficult. You have many constituencies you have to address. Other lawyers in your firm, judges, juries, not to mention opposing counsel. You have to balance the demands from each of these groups trying to please perhaps your most important constituency, your clients.

"You'll hopefully have lots of clients. Some big cases, many small cases, but to each of those clients, their case is the most important thing in their life. And you know what will trip you up? It's those little cases you ignore. You'll work for hours and hours on the big case and then forget you have a brief due in a smaller case. That won't fly. You have to treat all of your clients like they have the most important case you are handling. If you are able to do that and keep on top of all of your work, you just might be able to avoid waking up at three o'clock in the morning in a cold sweat."

She paused, noting she had everyone's attention. "Your client here is telling you he is not happy with how you are representing him. You don't want phone calls from clients asking what's happening with their cases. You should've kept them updated so there was no need for them to call you.

"You have an unhappy client. Now you have a chance to make it right with him. He's not firing you, but you only have a short amount of time to fix this. I hope for his sake you are able to give him the attention he needs. For your sake because your grade in this course depends on your performance representing your client. Next class, you will have answers for your client that you weren't able to give today."

She forced a smile as she looked around the room. "Class is over. Get out of here."

CHAPTER THIRTY-EIGHT

"HOLY CRAP," CAM SAID, while smacking his laptop. "Six depositions, pleadings, exhibits. They gave us a lot of material."

Gabrielle leaned over Cam to examine his screen. Her hair fell across his arm and her magnolia scent interrupted his thoughts. She scrolled down to scan more of the case materials. "You're right. It's a butt-load," she said, biting on the pen clenched in between her teeth.

"Let's make a list," said Cam, "of everything we need to do to get ready for this competition. The case is not too complicated and everything we need is in the packet, so we shouldn't have to do too much extra research."

Gabrielle nodded, still examining the materials. "One of us has to give the opening statement and the other the closing argument. I suggest I open and explain what the case is about. You take the closing because you're much more argumentative than I am."

"Brilliant." Cam rolled his eyes. "I won't argue that point. What else?"

"We each have to direct one witness and cross another.

They have a doctor and a fact witness. We have two fact witnesses. We can figure out who does which one the next time we go through the materials?"

"Sounds good. I just want to make sure we divide this up evenly, so we are doing the same amount of work."

"We'll have to argue objections, but I suspect we each should handle the objections relevant to whatever witness we are handling. Does that work?"

"Sure, you make it sound simple, but we have so much material to review and index."

She nudged him. "You're right, but if we understand the division of labor, we'll be able to slog through it all much easier." She ran her hand along the edges of her hair. "I think the only other issue is witnesses."

Cam tapped her on her arm. "We have to find people willing to pretend to be the people testifying. It's a lot of work for them also, being responsible for all of the materials relating to their testimony."

"And," Gabrielle leaned forward, "who we pick is important. We need witnesses who will convince the jury they are giving real testimony. That's part of how the judges will evaluate us."

A sly grin crossed Cam's face. "I think I can find the perfect people to be our witnesses. The judges will find them quite credible. Plus, they owe me a few favors, so I should be able to convince them to do this."

"I'll trust you on this one. Just don't screw it up. If we have some losers as our witnesses, we'll have no chance."

"Hey," Cam nudged her, "I need this as much as you. I'm going to do everything possible to make sure we have the best chance of winning. I promise you I will know these materials better than anyone."

"I think we're idiots trying to do this. It's not like we don't have enough work without taking on this competition."

"We've got three weeks. Let's start with these depositions." He tapped the top of his computer.

They pulled their chairs closer and turned their attention to the materials. Each adjusted the screens, leaned back, and began to read.

———

THE ROOM WAS DARK, save for the glow from their computers. Two hours had passed during which they had read through a chunk of the mock trial materials. At times, Cam let out a series of exasperated sighs, realizing the materials were denser and more complicated than he had expected.

"We bit off more than we can chew," he muttered more than once. Gabrielle, like a bulldog tearing through a rawhide bone, didn't waver from their task, paging through the materials and making an occasional note on her computer. After a while, she also became a bit distracted and couldn't maintain her focus on the depositions. She let her hand fall onto Cam's thigh and offered a gentle squeeze. Three times Cam pushed away her hand and pointed to his screen. Gabrielle nodded and directed her attention back to hers.

Once they realized they wouldn't be able to review everything in one seating, Gabrielle again dropped her hand onto Cam's thigh. This time Cam didn't offer any resistance. Gabrielle moved her hand under the bottom hem of Cam's shorts and gently rubbed the inside of his thigh.

Cam threw down his pen. "I think we've done enough for tonight. Don't you?"

Gabrielle locked eyes with him and nodded. "You're the boss."

Cam grabbed her hand to yank her up. He licked his lips and threw her onto his bed. He leaned over, kissed her parting lips, and rolled on top of her. A barely audible yelp of delight escaped her lips.

CHAPTER THIRTY-NINE

FOR THE LAST COUPLE of months, Cam hadn't spent a lot of time in the lounge in the basement of the law school. Remodeled a few years earlier from its original dank prison vibe, it now had comfortable, secluded areas and expansive tables so that students had space to study or to hang out with friends in between classes.

Back in the early fall, Cam had spent hours in the lounge, sometimes studying, at others killing time because he didn't need to be anywhere else. Since Ilana and Max moved in, however, he rarely spent time there, most days rushing home after his classes to help them.

So far, he had been able to spend the entire day in one location because after school Ilana had three hours of dance and Max had a long basketball practice. Kate had dinner responsibilities so Cam hung in a corner of the basement trying to figure out what work he should focus on and what could wait for another day.

As he put one textbook away and grabbed another, Marco

nabbed a chair and slammed his water bottle on the table. Cam rolled his eyes at the intrusion.

"Don't mind me," Marco said, leaning back in his chair.

Cam nodded and returned to reading. His fingers hovered over the computer keys as he organized his thoughts to take some notes. Just as his fingers touched the keyboard, Marco said, "You should have seen what Olivia did in class today."

"Dude, I'm trying to get some work done."

Marco held up both hands. "Got it. You need some quiet."

A few minutes later, Marco tapped Cam on the arm. "Hey, look over there. It's Deanna Briggs. Remember how I said the next time I saw her I would go over and talk to her?" He leaned back and watched her head for the stairs. "Damn, she's leaving. I'll talk to her when she comes back."

Cam stared at Marco in disbelief, who remained oblivious to Cam's annoyance. The energy in the lounge picked up as more students arrived with the end of the last class of the day. Cam shook his head and began to pack up his computer. "I'm not going to be able to focus on what I have to do. I need to find another place to study."

"Relax," said Marco, "why don't you just hang here for a while?"

Cam shoved his chair back and slung his pack over his shoulder. "I got too much to do. I'm going somewhere else."

Marco grabbed his stuff and ran after Cam. He caught up to him as he reached the stairs. "What's the matter?" Marco said.

"I have to study." Cam kept walking.

Marco followed him as they left the law school. "Hey, slow down?" Marco said as Cam huffed down the sidewalk.

"I got too much going on," Cam said, without stopping.

"We all got a lot."

Cam stopped and shook his head. "I'm not questioning how

much you have to do. I'm just worrying about what I got. Here's a partial list: Next week is mock trial. Gabrielle has us putting in two hours a night getting ready for that."

He stared at Marco to see if he wanted to offer a response. He offered none, so Cam continued, "Week after, finals. You're done once you finish your finals. You can relax. Me? I got a hearing the following week where some judge is going to decide whether my sister and brother have to go live somewhere else. So, I'm pretty confident I got more going on."

They kept walking until they reached the five-story undergraduate library. Cam motioned at the door. "I'm going to study here tonight. At least I won't know anybody, so nobody will bother me."

Marco stood silent. Cam paused with his hand on the door. "Hey man, I'm sorry. The pressure's just mounting. Every hour of every day. We'll talk later back at the house." He threw his hands up in the air and turned to enter the library.

CHAPTER FORTY

MARK TAYLOR LOOKED LIKE he had just stepped out of a salon. The grey specks on his purple tie set off the pinstripes on his tailored suit. His hair seemed perfect, like it had just been dried with a Dyson, impossible because only forty minutes earlier he had landed at the airport. Of course, getting picked up at home by a private limousine and being dropped off at the door of his firm's private jet made it easier for him to avoid the type of travel weariness suffered by those who had to fly commercial.

His team of young lawyers and support staff, in suits of various shades of grey and blue, stood behind him in a neat arc. In contrast to their boss, they did not have the status to command limo rides to the airport. For most of them, it was their first time in a private plane, and they enjoyed the convenience of the county airport and the luxury onboard.

They also learned a lesson in punctuality as one wayward lawyer looked on as the plane taxied down the runway, having arrived five minutes late for departure. Taylor laughed as the attorney waved his arms as they departed, announcing,

"Remember his face, because that's probably the last time you'll ever see it."

Cam and Gabrielle sat in the second row attired in their only suits. Theirs cost about one fifth as much as the clothes Taylor's associates were wearing. Taylor's suit was on a level well beyond that.

Energy surged through the room as the teams, which included the witnesses and the lawyers, milled about. As the decibel level reached a crescendo, Taylor lifted his hands and motioned for the crowd to calm.

Without thinking, Cam and Gab complied and took their seats. As the room quieted, Gabrielle's leg pulsated up and down.

"Let's get started," Taylor said to mild applause. He smiled. "I'm glad you want to get to the festivities. It's going to be a long day. You all ready?" This time everyone roared signaling their desire to begin.

"Today is the big event," he continued. "The first annual Broadside, Taylor, and Sanders mock trial competition. We have thirty teams signed up to test out their litigation skills. There will be four rounds. With that many teams in the competition, we will have fifteen trials in the first round, seven in the second round, two in the third, and the finals will pit the last two teams left standing.

"I have brought thirty attorneys, paralegals and support personnel from my firm who will act as judges and jurors for the early round trials. They will score each team on how the lawyer functions, meaning you will be graded on your openings, direct examinations, cross-examinations, closings, objections, and legal arguments you make during the trials, as well as your general courtroom presence. Your witnesses will also be graded as to how believable they are and how knowledgeable they are of the trial materials and the specific facts related to the witness they are portraying. In my experience, the best prepared teams, and I emphasize the word 'team,' will be the ones who progress and advance in the competition."

He glanced around the room and found everyone hanging on his every word. "Please be respectful of your judges and jurors. Of course, failing to heed this warning will be to your detriment and most likely will result in being a spectator in the later rounds, rather than a participant."

A few catcalls echoed through the auditorium.

"One more thing. I will rely on the members of my firm to evaluate you and make sure that the best prepared teams advance. However, given that the members of the winning team receive summer clerkships at my firm, with full compensation that all interns will receive, I will make sure that the most accomplished team receives that benefit. I will be the judge of the final round of the competition. I will allow the jury to have some input into the final verdict, but truth be told, that decision will be mine."

He looked out into the crowd. "We have a lot of non-participants here today who will be watching the trials. We welcome them and hope that even if the person you are rooting for happens not to advance, you will remain for the final rounds.

"I also want everyone to recognize how much work each of the participants has done to prepare for the competition. The case may seem somewhat simple, but the lesson is that when you come to trial, nothing is easy. You have to comprehend all of the material and be ready for any contingency which might arise. You also have to make sure that you are the best prepared lawyer in the courtroom."

He paused for a moment to adjust his tie. "I can't wait to find out what the teams have dreamed up as compelling argument or what cross-examination you will spring on an unsuspecting witness." He took a step backwards and yelled, "Are you ready to start?"

A thunderous "Yes," echoed off the walls.

"Good. I think we are prepared to begin." He looked at his watch. "The first round begins in fifteen minutes. You have your room assignments. Please let the judge and jurors get settled. Gather your witnesses and your evidence. Our competition coordinator will send an email fifteen minutes after each round indicating which teams will be moving on to the next round."

A young woman with blonde hair stood and waved to a light round of applause.

"You will then have fifteen more minutes before the next round begins. I would suggest the teams not advancing stick around for the later rounds. You will learn something by watching how the other teams put on their cases."

He started to walk away from the podium and then smacked his head. He turned and leaned back into the microphone. "I forgot to mention-- everyone, witnesses, lawyers, anyone's family who is here to watch is invited to the banquet at the end of the competition. You all will be very tired, but my firm will make sure that you are well fed. There, we will celebrate the winning team and award them their certificates. It should be exciting." He paused for the last time. "Good luck everyone and kick some butt."

Scattered applause spread as everyone rose at the same time. Cam turned to Gabrielle, "Can you find our witnesses?"

She nodded and pointed to the back of the room at Max and Ilana alone and standing out as the youngest participants in the competition. "They better be ready."

Cam slapped Gabrielle on the back. "They better be. If not, we'll be watching the second round as spectators."

CHAPTER FORTY-ONE

CAM EXITED THE BATHROOM by slamming the door open and spotted Gabrielle pacing in the small, well-lit alcove down the hall. Ilana and Max relaxed in chairs twenty feet beyond her. He jogged up to her, his forehead dotted with specks of sweat.

She motioned for him to stand closer, but his stores of energy prevented him from stopping. She grabbed his elbow and pointed to a chair. He rolled his eyes, but complied, plopping into one of the faux leather seats. With a big huff, she dropped into the chair next to him. "Seven minutes," she said, "until we find out the results. Let's debrief our performance."

Cam squinted up towards the bright fluorescent lights, ignoring Gabrielle's entreaties. She smacked his arm. "Hey, pay attention," she said. "If we somehow make it through to the next round, we have a lot of places where we can improve."

Cam shook his head in an obvious attempt to clear the cobwebs. "That was brutal. The trial took less than an hour, but my hands are shaking, and my pits are soaked." He raised his hands above his head and shook them. He let out a large breath causing his cheeks to quiver. "The pressure today is more intense than a normal day of studying. We're thinking and responding every second. How do real lawyers do this?"

Gabrielle nodded. "It's challenging, and we made a lot of mistakes, but I can suggest a bunch of ways we can improve in the next round--if we make it through."

"It's just so hard to focus. If we aren't eliminated, then we have to repeat everything again. All that pressure..." He let his voice trail off.

"I hear you," she said, but ignored his complaints. "Here's a partial list of what we can change: First, you can't read your closing. I know you know it. Act like you do. The judges will ding us big time if we rely too much on our yellow pads."

She glanced at the notes she had jotted on her phone. "Second, I need to do better on my cross. Yours was pretty good. You only asked leading questions. I choked and asked my witness why something happened, and she just took off with her answer. Pretty much used up all my time. I can't let that happen again.

"Third, our witnesses need to be better. Your brother looked like a deer in headlights. He mumbled through his answers. I mean, he knows his material cold, but his presentation was so boring. He needs to take some acting lessons before the next round." She chuckled.

Cam nodded, but didn't respond to her thoughts. "I'll talk with Max," he said, without looking at her. "What else you got?"

She shook her head. "I got a whole list, but we don't have any time; the notifications should be coming any minute."

As if summoned by the gods, their phones dinged at the same time. They lifted them and scanned the text for a second before letting loose with a scream. "Oh, my god!" Cam said. "We made it to the next round! We're starting in fifteen minutes."

Gabrielle's face glowed, her cheeks flushed with excitement. "Damn. There were a bunch of teams that were worse than we were. Losers." She grabbed her backpack. "Okay, that was our freebie. The teams remaining are the ones that cared and took some time to prepare. We won't be able to get by on our good looks and charm anymore. Time to pick up the intensity."

Cam jumped up and down in front of Gabrielle, shaking his arms at his sides. "I'm ready for the next round. Winning has energized me. You grab our stuff and I'll meet you at the next courtroom. I'll get our witnesses and give them a pep talk."

Gabrielle turned towards the classroom where their trial would take place. Cam scampered over to Ilana and Max to inform them they still had more work to do. When he did, she hugged him. Max, on the other hand, offered no response and continued to look at his feet. After a moment, with much grunting and huffing, he dragged his body out of his chair, and with obvious deliberation, followed his siblings down the hall.

CHAPTER FORTY-TWO

THE MORNING AND EARLY afternoon passed quickly as Cam and Gabrielle, and their team, continued to advance in the competition. Neither was thrilled with their performance, but the act of moving forward was sufficient to alleviate their concerns so far.

A quick wave of exhaustion passed through Cam as he left the classroom where the third round of competition had finished less than a minute earlier. Cam needed a bathroom badly. D'Andre met him outside of the door and started talking even as Cam continued his brisk walk down the hall. "Dude," he said, as he grabbed Cam's elbow, "I have some thoughts about what your team can do to improve."

Cam knocked his elbow away. "I can't listen to anything until I hit the head."

Cam broke away and dashed towards the men's room bending over a bit because of the sharp pain emanating from his bladder. D'Andre jogged close behind imitating Cam's awkward gait.

The bathroom was beginning to reek of too many people using the facilities for too long without an appropriate cleaning. Ignoring the stench, D'Andre sidled up to the urinal next to Cam. As they each relieved themselves, D'Andre turned his head and said, "That round was way too easy. You two did great, but your competition still sucked. I'm hoping the judges don't downgrade you because your opponents were so mediocre."

Cam scoffed. "We were good. Gabrielle killed her cross and I think I nailed my closing."

"Perhaps," D'Andre said as they walked to the sink. "I'm praying your scoring is good enough to put you in the top two and into the finals. To win, everything has to be perfect. Your team isn't quite there, yet."

Cam looked at him perplexed. "What are you saying?"

D'Andre threw away his paper towel and then put a hand on Cam's shoulder. "Nothing against your brother, but he's not putting out much energy. It's a snoozer whenever he's talking. The witnesses I've seen on the other teams are much better. He needs to step up his game or you're done."

"I'm aware of what he's doing. How can we fix it? We can't change our witnesses."

"He's just a little shy. I think I can help bring out his inner beast."

"Do whatever you can. I'm fried right now. I need a few minutes to myself to recharge before we find out if we made the finals." D'Andre opened the bathroom door. "Thanks man," Cam said, "I appreciate whatever you can do."

———

D'ANDRE FOUND Max sprawled on a chair down an empty corridor. His shirt was untucked, his hair askew and his eyes barely opened, but he managed to shoot D'Andre a smile as he approached.

"You looked whipped," D'Andre said as he eased into the adjoining seat. "Like you just played a triple overtime game and lost on a last second three-pointer."

Max nodded.

"You might have to do one more round." D' raised an eyebrow. "Are you ready?"

Max shook his head.

"Why so down? This ain't so bad. You're just answering questions."

Max sat up a little. "This isn't my thing. I'm just making stuff up. It doesn't feel real."

D'Andre let out a small chuckle. "It isn't real. At least not for you. But for your brother, it's all real. You know what he gets if they win, don't you?"

He bit down on his lower lip. "I want him to win."

"Good. Then let's talk about what you can do to help." Max sat up a bit. "First, you have to show that you are the witness. This dude has gone through a lot. Kind of like someone else I know." D'Andre placed an elbow in Max's side. "You have to emote a little. Show the judges that this guy would be hurt by what they're trying to do. I think you can relate to that too, can't you?"

Max kept nodding. "I understand his situation, but so what?"

"You just have to show a little emotion when you're testifying. You know the material cold. Don't just speak it in a monotone. Give the judges some entertainment."

D'Andre stood and leaned over Max placing both hands on his shoulders. "Your role here is important. The team can't win without you. You may not be the quarterback, but you can help to determine the outcome. You're the little placekicker. You have to make the winning kick, or your team loses. The team needs its kicker."

D'Andre's phone dinged and he pulled it out of his pants pocket. His face broke into a huge smile. "Guess what? Your team is in the finals. It's up to you to nail that game winning kick." He yanked Max to his feet. "Now, tuck your shirt in. Fix your hair."

Max complied and D'Andre turned him in the direction of the location for the finals. As Max walked down the hallway, D'Andre chanted, "Nail that kick. Nail that kick." Max didn't look back, but raised one hand above his head and extended his fist towards the ceiling.

CHAPTER FORTY-THREE

STANDING AT THE FRONT of the large auditorium did not diminish Mark Taylor's apparent stature. Most professors who lectured from the same podium seemed to be swallowed up by the enormity of the space. Not Mark Taylor. Somehow, he managed to make the space appear smaller, and therefore, himself larger. The gleaming mahogany paneling lining the walls towered over most mortals, but now it seemed to draw back to offer Taylor a little more room to address the throng which had gathered for the final round of the mock trial competition.

Cam sat next to Gabrielle on the stage which had been reconfigured to a courtroom setting. Two counsel tables faced the judge's bench and the witness stand. To the right, a jury box, filled with twelve professionally dressed men and women holding pens and yellow pads, waited for the trial to begin. A throng of observers filled most of the seats.

Taylor, now dressed in a different suit than he had worn earlier in the morning, this one a grey pinstripe, tailored to his large shoulders and narrowed waist, motioned for silence.

When the audience members sat back and calmed, he addressed them. "We are now ready for the final round of today's competition. I want to thank all the participants and those who came out to support their family and friends. It's been an amazing day. I can't imagine that the quality of the advocacy has been any better than what these first-year law students have displayed. I would expect this level of work in a federal courthouse, but we are all lucky enough to watch it here."

He was interrupted by heavy applause but picked up right where he had left off when it slowed. "I expect more amazing lawyering in this final round—and some great acting by our final set of witnesses." He pointed to the first row of the auditorium where Ilana, Max, and another man and woman, a few years older than them, waited. A small burst of clapping erupted, but then subsided.

"In a few minutes we will start. Plaintiff will give the first opening. The defense, the second. Plaintiff will put on its two witnesses and the defense will cross each. Then the same procedure with the defendant's two witnesses. Defendant will close and then plaintiff will wrap everything up by giving its closing. Just the way it's done down the street in court.

"As I said earlier, at first glance this appears to be a simple case, but with every case the lawyers have to develop mastery over the facts and be able to present it in a digestible manner to the jury. We are not evaluating which side might win at trial, but who makes the best presentation and which team advocates best for its side."

He took a breath. "That's a lot, but our teams have already been through so much." He turned to the jury box and bowed. "What a nice group of associates. Very smart. However, for now they are not attorneys, but are jurors. They will evaluate each lawyer and witness. We will all consult at the end of the trial and decide which side wins. It's that simple."

He picked up a gavel and rapped it three times causing a sharp wooden sound to echo off the walls. He looked over at Cam's competitors and asked, "Is plaintiff prepared to open?

A woman dressed in a navy blue, two-piece suit and a cream-colored blouse stood. "Plaintiff is ready to open."

Taylor nodded. "Please proceed." He offered a smile, which counsel returned with a similar nod of her head.

Cam leaned over his yellow pad ready to take notes. He touched Gabrielle's wrist while she scribbled on her pad. She didn't respond.

Marjorie Mupple walked over to the rail in front of the jury box and placed her left hand on the edge. She posed for a moment wanting the jurors to return her gaze.

"Everything is theatrical with this woman," Cam thought. His mind drifted for a moment to the time in Contracts when she started to cry while discussing a case involving a young woman who was snookered out of money by a devious con artist. Cam remembered the nauseous churning in his stomach as she performed for the class. The renewed agitation in his stomach signaled he would have to suffer through a bit more during this trial.

"Ladies and Gentlemen of the jury," she began, "on July 13th of last year, the life of our client, Steven Planeff, was savagely altered by the willful negligence of the defendant, Arnold Dawgoner."

Mupple turned and pointed right at Max, who for a moment forgot he was playing the role of the defendant. Max's face turned a crimson hue, but he didn't twitch, so no one in the audience could detect his moment of embarrassment.

"Today you will hear how Mr. Dawgoner's failure to take even the most remedial steps to train his dog, led to the grievous

176

injuries my client suffered." She backed away a step and turned to the person now seated alone at the counsel table. "Good afternoon, my name is Marjorie Mupple, and along with my partner, Andrew Kitchner, we have the privilege to represent Mr. Planeff." Kitchner half-stood and nodded at the jurors.

She turned back to the jurors. "On what started out as a beautiful day last summer, Mr. Planeff walked down a street in his neighborhood, minding his business. He was listening to music on his headphones, and he wasn't bothering anyone. Without any provocation, Mr. Dawgoner's dog, who was running through the neighborhood unrestrained, attacked him and ripped a large wound in his arm and then bit him again, ripping flesh from his leg."

She spread her arms out from her body. "The dog latched onto his leg pulling him to the ground. He kicked at the dog and was able to escape, but not before suffering very serious injuries.

"You will hear from Dr. Helena Troy, a surgeon, who will tell you about the extensive treatment Mr. Planeff had to endure to help him recover from this incident and the permanent injuries he has received as a result.

"Mr. Planeff is suing Mr. Dawgoner for negligence because he was careless in how he took care of his dog. He never trained the dog and even though the dog had been involved in other incidents, he took no precautions to prevent this type of incident from happening again. This was an accident waiting to happen.

"Mr. Planeff is here to today seeking compensation for the major injuries he suffered, including the permanent limitations he now has to his arm and leg, and for the emotional distress he suffered and continues to suffer.

"In addition, our local legislative body has enacted a municipal ordinance which requires a dangerous dog to be taken from its owner to protect innocent people in the neighborhood. We will prove that Mr. Dawgoner's dog has been involved in other incidents and the severity of this attack requires intervention. We will be seeking a verdict from you establishing that Mr. Dawgoner has violated this ordinance which would require removal of the dog from his home. "

She paused and looked at the jury. "We accept that this is harsh but given the history of the dog and the injuries it has caused, in addition to the compensatory damages I have outlined, the evidence will prove to you that this is the appropriate outcome.

"On behalf of my partner, we thank you for your time and attention today to listen to the claims of our client."

She stepped back and nodded before returning to her seat.

As she pulled her seat back to the table, Cam whispered to Gabrielle, "She was good. You'll be better."

Before she could react, Judge Taylor asked, "Is the defendant prepared to open?"

CHAPTER FORTY-FOUR

FOR THE TEENSIEST OF MOMENTS, Gabrielle's legs froze. She wanted to forget the imperfect openings she gave in the prior rounds. In practicing for the competition, she wrote and re-wrote her opening a hundred times, never satisfied with her presentation, always finding some phrasing stilted or awkward. Cam had implored her that her opening was excellent, and she should let it breathe and not worry any more about it. Yet, Gabrielle ignored his advice and for nights spent hours in the basement saying it to the walls and suitcases stored in the dankness.

Despite the amount of time she practiced, her openings in the first rounds were subpar—at least by her standards. She stammered at times, didn't maintain eye contact with the jurors and fumbled with her papers. This time, for the finals, she promised herself she would do it right.

She pushed any negative thoughts out of her head and approached the jurors. "Members of the jury," she said, while standing erect before them. She took a mental picture of herself from their point of view and liked what she saw—a confident litigator ready to explain why her client wasn't liable to the plaintiff. "Arnold Dawgoner's actions had nothing to do with why Mr. Planeff got hurt. And Mr. Dawgoner's dog, who has a name, which is Pickles, also isn't to blame."

She smiled before continuing. "On behalf of Mr. Dawgoner, my name is Gabrielle Moore, and along with Cameron Crewell, we will prove to you that this is a case of misidentification and that neither Pickles, nor our client, had anything to do with why he was hurt."

Gabrielle took two steps to her right and pulled a clicker out of her right jacket pocket. Without making it obvious, she pressed a button, and the screen near the jury box jumped to life displaying a large photograph of a black and white dog with its tongue out, looking like it was smiling for the camera.

"This is Pickles. He is a two-year-old rescue that Mr. Dawgoner adopted when he was six months old. Since that time, he has taken care of the dog, trained him, and been responsible for the dog. Despite what Mr. Planeff says, the dog doesn't cause problems and no legitimate complaints have been filed against Mr. Dawgoner regarding the dog.

"On the day of this incident, Mr. Dawgoner was napping while Pickles played in his fenced-in yard. At some point in the later afternoon, the police came to his house and informed him that Mr. Planeff reported that Pickles had attacked him. Mr. Dawgoner will tell you what he told the police officer—that Pickles was in the yard the entire afternoon and there was no way he attacked anybody.

"What you haven't heard yet, however, is that there was an eyewitness to what happened to Mr. Planeff. This person's name is Isabel Sawit, who is a young lady who was walking in the neighborhood, blocks away from where Mr. Dawgoner lives. She will tell you that a dog did attack Mr. Planeff, but it was a different dog than Pickles. She will tell you that the attacking dog was not Pickles and therefore this incident could not have been the fault of Mr. Dawgoner."

Gabrielle walked the edge of the jury box, letting her hand drag along the rail. "What you will conclude is that Mr. Dawgoner trained Pickles, Pickles is a friendly dog who did not attack anyone, and that this incident was in no way caused by any negligence of Mr. Dawgoner."

She pushed the clicker again and a slide appeared with the words, 'Not negligent.' "When you hear the evidence in this case, it will be clear that Mr. Dawgoner was not negligent, and when you have the opportunity to deliberate, we will ask that your verdict be in favor of Mr. Dawgoner."

Another adorable picture of Pickles appeared on the screen after she put her hand back in her pocket. "Please save this wonderful dog who did nothing to anyone. On behalf of our client, we thank you for your time and attention."

As she turned to return to counsel table, two jurors smiled at her. After she took her seat, Cam whispered, "Awesome job. Short and to the point. Well done."

Gabrielle leaned back over to Cam. "Let's get ready to do some serious cross-examination."

CHAPTER FORTY-FIVE

IN THE FRONT ROW, Cam's classmate, Roger Berman, sat next to Max. Berman leaned forward, his back erect, and stared straight ahead, his gaze locked on the judge. Given that they were on opposite sides of the case, neither Roger nor Max said a word to each other. It was a bit awkward perhaps, but they weren't sure if they should acknowledge anyone from the other side of the competition.

"Plaintiff calls Steven Planeff," Andrew Kitchner announced, his dark grey suit hemmed above his black wingtips. He adjusted his red striped tie as Berman walked to the witness stand. By the time he was seated, Berman had transformed into Planeff, even displaying a slight limp to compensate for his injured leg. He grimaced as he extended his arm to adjust the microphone.

"Please tell the jury your name," Kitchner said, standing at the far edge of the jury box.

"My name is Steve Planeff. I live on Oak Street. It's in the same neighborhood where Mr. Dawgoner lives." He pointed in the direction of Max, who responded with a "who me?" look, once again forgetting, at least for the time being, that he was Dawgoner.

"Mr. Planeff, please explain what happened on July 13, of last year."

Planeff nodded. "I was walking down the street that day—going to visit my mom. I had my headphones on. I was on Maple Street. It's one block away from where the defendant lives." He stared straight at the jurors. "I didn't do anything. I'm not sure where that beast came from, but he must have been flying down the street. He attacked me from behind. Took a chunk out of the back of my arm. About ripped my shirt off."

"So, what did you do?"

"I tried to get away, but the dog kept coming at me. I kicked at it and pushed it away, but then he took a chunk out of my leg." He raised his pants leg to show his "wounds" to the jury. They leaned forward and squinted as if trying to examine the damage the dog had done.

"Finally, I managed to get the dog off of me. I hobbled away and then had to go to the hospital."

Kitchner held up one finger. "Before we discuss that, were you able to identify the dog and who its owner is?"

The witness nodded. "At first, I had no idea who the dog was. He ran off while I was bleeding on the sidewalk. I don't think I had ever seen it before. While I was at the hospital, my girlfriend walked around our neighborhood trying to find the dog. After an hour, she found it in Mr. Dawgoner's yard. He lives less than a block from where that dog attacked me. She called me and told me it matched the description I had given her of the dog. She took a picture and sent it to me. After I looked at it, I told her it was the dog that attacked me. After I got out of the hospital, we reported the attack to the police. Later, I went in-person to make sure I had the right dog. I did."

Again, the screen came to life and another picture of

Pickles appeared. In this one, Pickles bared his teeth and appeared to be snarling. "Mr. Planeff, is this the dog that attacked you?"

"It is."

"Did you find out who the owner of this dog is?"

"I did. Like I said, we went back to the yard where my girl-friend found the dog and were able to find out who owned it."

"And who was the owner of the dog?"

Planeff jerked his body in Max's direction and pointed at him. "That is the man who owns that savage dog." Max didn't flinch, but the back of neck burned red.

Kitchner looked up at the judge and announced, "Let the record reflect the plaintiff has identified the defendant as the owner of the dog that attacked him." He waited a moment. "Let's turn to the extent of your injuries from this incident. Please tell the jurors where you were hurt."

Planeff turned back to face the jury. "The dog ripped my triceps muscle in my right arm. He tore through my left calf. Both required surgery."

"We will be hearing from your doctor as the next witness. How has your recovery been?"

"Well, it's been almost a year since the surgeries. Both my arm and leg still hurt. I can do activities at home like showering or washing the dishes, but anything more strenuous is difficult."

"Can you give us a few examples?"

"Sure. I used to run three miles a day. I can't do that anymore. I used to bike. That hurts too much now, and my arm is sensitive, and it feels weird if anybody touches it. That bothers my girlfriend."

"One final question—did you do anything to cause the dog to attack you?"

Planeff shook his head. "Absolutely not. That dog came out

184

of nowhere and attacked me. I was only walking down the street minding my own business."

"Thank you, sir. I have no further questions."

Gabrielle stood and walked to the front of her counsel table so that Planeff's gaze would follow her and move away from the jurors.

"Sir, didn't you see this dog coming down the street before it attacked you?"

"No. The first thing that happened was the dog biting the back of my arm. I never saw it coming."

"Didn't you raise a stick at the dog and threaten it?"

"I'm not sure how many times I have to say it, but I didn't do anything to that dog. He did everything to me. You don't see any bite marks on the dog, do you?"

"Sir," Gabrielle said as she grabbed a paper off her counsel table, "let me show you what's marked as trial Exhibit one. This is a statement you signed at the hospital, isn't it?"

"Yes, I wrote it out while bleeding in the waiting room."

"I understand. You put down on paper what had happened right after this incident happened?

"I wanted to make sure I didn't forget anything."

"Exactly." She turned to the jury, but addressed the witness. "Please look at the third paragraph. Please review the high-lighted portion and read it to the jury."

He complied. "It says, 'I was over on Elm Street when this black dog attacked me.'"

"Sir," Gabrielle began, as a map of the town appeared on the screen. She directed a red laser pointer at the streets. "In your direct testimony you said that this incident occurred on Maple Street, but in your statement, you said this happened on Elm Street."

"I think I may have been mistaken when I wrote this. I realized where I was after my girlfriend and I went back and found the dog.

Gabrielle smirked. "You would agree that Elm Street, where you said the incident occurred in your statement, is three blocks away from Maple, where you are now saying this attack occurred?"

"I suspect I wasn't quite positive at the time I was in the hospital where it happened. But after I got out and retraced where I walked, I'm quite confident that what I just said was accurate."

"And with regard to your identification of the dog, you said in your statement that it was a black dog. Clearly, Pickles is not a black dog." The original picture of Pickles highlighting his white and black coat again was on the screen.

"There is a lot of black on this dog. Yup, that's the dog who bit me."

"Sir, again will you read the highlighted portion in the fourth paragraph?"

"It says, 'I was minding my business and was attacked from behind by an unknown dog. He bit my arm and leg and then while I was lying on the sidewalk, he ran away.'"

"Thanks. That means you never got a good look at the dog and would be unable to identify it."

"No, I told you what dog attacked me. It was Pickles. No doubt about it."

"Sir, the only reason you say that is because you found Pickles in his yard. You weren't able to give any type of accurate description of the dog after the attack."

"No, it couldn't have been any dog other than Mr. Dawgoner's dog that attacked me."

Gabrielle said, "No more questions." She turned her back to head to counsel table.

CHAPTER FORTY-SIX

MARJORIE MUPPLE, PRIM AND composed as always, glasses perched on the tip of her nose, rose to say, "Plaintiff calls Doctor Helena Troy."

A young woman in the first row with straight auburn hair pulled back behind her ears stood and walked to the witness box to take the oath. After doing so, she sat and put on a pair of glasses, solely, at least to Cam's way of thinking, to make her look smarter. The green scrubs she wore added to the illusion that she was a real doctor, and the only surprise was the lack of a stethoscope draped around her neck.

"Please identify yourself for the jury," Mupple requested.

"My name is Helena Troy. I am a medical doctor and a surgeon."

"Will you describe for the jury the training you received as a doctor and a surgeon?"

"Sure." She smiled at the jurors acting as if she had testified hundreds of times as an expert witness before. "I am a graduate of Harvard and then went to Medical School at Cornell University. I had my internship in general surgery and a specialized residency in trauma and related treatment. I moved to Pittsburgh after my residency and have been in practice as a surgeon for the past twelve years, often moonlighting on weekends in local emergency rooms. I have done hundreds of surgeries on my patients ranging from minor cosmetic type surgeries to much more complicated surgeries like the ones Mr. Planeff needed."

Mupple turned to Cam. "Does defendant have any questions regarding Dr. Troy's qualifications as an expert witness.

Cam rose and said, "Defendant will reserve its questions on the doctor's qualifications until after the completion of her direct testimony." Cam couldn't attack the witness's credentials directly as she clearly had sufficient training as a surgeon. He, however, wouldn't concede to the other side that she was sufficiently qualified to be an expert witness.

The courtroom stilled for a moment while Mupple turned back to the witness. "Is Mr. Planeff a patient of yours?"

"He has been since he came to Shadyside hospital after being attacked by a dog last July."

"Please explain your course of treatment for Mr. Planeff."

The witness nodded. "Sure. I examined him in the emergency room. He had serious dog bite wounds to his left triceps and right calf. That afternoon I performed surgery on both. I repaired muscles and attended to nerve damage in both locations. I reattached a partially severed section of the gastrocnemius muscle in his calf. I cleaned out both wounds to make sure they were sterilized and to reduce the chance of infection. Ultimately, I had to put in thirty-seven stitches in his arm and forty-two in his leg."

"What was your follow-up treatment for him?"

"He had an appointment to make sure his wounds were healing. Two weeks after the surgery, he returned so I could take out the stitches. I saw him four other times for follow up to make sure the wounds were healing without issue."

"Doctor, with a reasonable degree of medical certainty, do you have an opinion as to what caused his injuries and the need for his surgeries?"

"I do. It was the dog bites he suffered when he was attacked by the dog."

"As a result of these injuries, does Mr. Planeff still have problems or need further treatment?"

"He does. He continues to have pain in both areas. He will continue to have functional limitations, including the inability to lift anything over ten pounds and has difficulty with anything beyond walking, meaning he can't run the way he used to or participate in athletics like before."

"Are these limitations permanent?"

"Most likely they are. He will continue to need physical rehabilitation, but even with that, he likely will not regain the full functional abilities he had prior to this incident."

"Finally, Doctor. Have you submitted a bill for the services you rendered for Mr. Planeff's treatment?"

"I have."

Counsel sought permission to approach the witness, which the judge granted. He handed her a piece of paper and asked, "I'm handing you what is marked as Exhibit three. Is this a copy of your bill?"

"It is."

"Are the services enumerated on the bill fair and reasonable, and necessitated by the injuries caused by the dog bites?"

"They are."

"Thank you, doctor. The other side may have some questions for you," counsel said, turning to Cam.

"Mr. Crewell, you care to cross this witness?" the judge asked.

Cam stood. "Absolutely." He walked to the front of the counsel table closest to the witness. "Doctor, you didn't see when Mr. Planeff was bitten by a dog, so you cannot offer any testimony to identify the dog that may have bit him."

"That's true. My job was to fix him up after this happened."

Cam nodded. One small concession in the books. "Looking at your operative notes, you would agree he suffered no complications following the surgery."

"None that are in my notes, correct."

"The surgeries took a total of one hour and thirty-five minutes."

"That is true."

"Because they were relatively simple."

"Nothing is simple when you operate. There are always risks, but here the surgeries went well."

"According to your medical records, you examined Mr. Planeff four times after his surgery. One of those times was to take out his stitches."

"That is true."

"The last time you saw him was nearly one year ago."

"True."

"And he has no appointments with you in the future."

"Yes. I am unaware of any additional appointments he may have scheduled."

"So, any opinion you are offering regarding his physical condition is based on how he presented when you last saw him and not on his present condition."

"I have no reason to believe that his condition has changed since that time."

Cam pondered whether to press the doctor and seek a more definitive response. He elected to move on. "You were paid to offer your opinions here today."

The doctor smiled. "I think it's more accurate to say that I am being compensated for my time in coming to court."

"And you were also compensated for writing a report and for reviewing Mr. Planeff's medical records."

"That is correct."

Cam let out a long breath. "That's all the questions I have for this witness."

Judge Taylor looked to plaintiff's counsel. "Do you have any more evidence?"

Mupple stood. "No, Your Honor. Plaintiff rests." She smiled.

Taylor glanced at his watch. "Let's give everyone a break and take a five-minute recess. We will resume precisely at 4:30. Please be in your seats." He stood and rapped his gavel. The sound of people standing, and random conversations echoed through the auditorium.

———

CAM AND GABRIELLE remained at counsel table putting papers into piles. "Give me your honest assessment," Cam said.

Gabrielle stopped what she was doing and shook her head. "The other side is pretty strong. They haven't made any mistakes. They are like lawyer cyborgs—always moving forward, eating up what's in their path. We're doing fine. So far I don't see much difference between the two sides."

Cam nodded. "I agree. I think we're holding our own with them. Given how many times we've practiced with our witnesses, we're going to do fine. I'm not worried about us."

They both looked over to Ilana and Max. "I think it's going to come down to witness performance. Their witnesses were good. No glaring errors. We need ours to do even better than they have so far. What do you think?"

Can glanced over to his siblings. Ilana offered a smile and a quick wave. Max stared at his shoes, his right foot vibrating up and down at a rapid pace. Cam thought he could feel how hard Max's heart was pounding.

"If my brother isn't able to control his nerves and give the judges something to hang their hat on, we're in trouble. Maybe we should have used some law students for our witnesses like you suggested."

"Don't second guess now. We're this close to winning. Let's just funnel some positive energy over their way."

They both closed their eyes and clasped their hands together.

CHAPTER FORTY-SEVEN

THE MOCK TRIAL COMPETITION wasn't prominent on Ilana's radar before today. They had asked her to be a witness weeks ago, giving her sufficient time to attack the materials and memorize everything relevant to her character. Like most things in school, she was able to digest the information quickly. The practice sessions gave her confidence that she knew her materials, and since witnesses were not allowed to refer to any of the written materials, rote memorization, one of her strengths, was a requirement.

With each passing level of the competition, Ilana realized that the lawyers who survived grasped the materials as well as she did, and she could no longer bluff her way through an answer. In the last round a lawyer caught her making up a fact that wasn't included in the course materials and made her look bad in front of the jury. Ilana wanted to help Cam and Gabrielle, so she needed to avoid any similar gaffes.

She walked up to the witness box. Her head spun a bit as she looked out at the auditorium filled almost to capacity.

After she adjusted the microphone, Gabrielle asked, "What is your name?"

"Isabel Sawit," Ilana said, turning to engage with the jurors as they had instructed her to do.

"Ms. Sawit, how old are you?"

"I'm fourteen."

"Where do you live?"

"I live on Oak Street. It's about two blocks from where this happened." Ilana was clearly older than the witness's stated age, but more than any other witness was able to present as someone with the attributes of a person in the witness's cohort. Ilana was also demonstrating as much composure as the other witnesses. At counsel table, Cam sat enraptured by his sister's maturity.

"Did you witness an incident last July involving Mr. Planeff getting bit by a dog?"

"I did."

"Please tell us about it."

"I was walking down the street and I saw this big dog attack the man."

"Where did this attack take place?"

"I was walking to visit my friend, Megan. She lives over on Main Street. So, it was like two blocks away from Megan's house."

The map of the town again appeared on the screen. "Isabel, can you mark on the exhibit where you were when this happened? Please put an X where you were."

Ilana complied and the red X appeared on the screen.

"Now," Gabrielle continued, "would you please put a Y where attack took place?" Ilana again marked the exhibit and the Y appeared near to where she had placed the X.

"What street did this occur on?"

"It was Elm Street. That's where it happened."

"Did this happen on Maple Street?"

Ilana squished her eyes together. "Oh no, it was definitely on Elm. I remember that distinctly."

"So, were you able to observe what happened?"

Ilana nodded. "I was."

"Then please tell us what you witnessed." Gabrielle took a step back as if to give Ilana space to tell her story.

As she reengaged with the jury, Ilana smiled and said, "I was walking down the street. It was a very pretty day. I looked across the street and there was this big, solid black dog running down the street. It was loose, but it wasn't bothering anybody. The guy who got bitten saw the dog running. He picked up a big stick and shook it at the dog as it ran by. I think he scared the dog, and then the dog bolted at the man and bit him."

"What happened next?"

"Well, the dog wasn't leaving, so the man started kicking the dog. I think he probably could have gotten away, but he was kicking the dog. Then the dog jumped up and bit the guy again. Got him good on his leg, so he stopped kicking him. The dog then ran away."

"Isabel," Gabrielle said, pointing to the map, "how close was this to the defendant's house?" She had a laser pointer zeroing in on where the defendant lived.

"Oh, it was two or three blocks away. A long way, I would say."

Gabrielle stepped forward. "Now, Isabel, look at the picture of Mr. Dawgoner's dog, Pickles." His cute picture was now on the screen. "Is this the dog that bite, Mr. Planeff?"

"Oh, no." Ilana feigned indignation. "The dog that bit that guy looked nothing like that dog. The dog that bit him was all black. That dog has a lot of white." She pointed at the screen.

Gabrielle was walking back to counsel table when she said, "No further questions, Your Honor."

Kitchner stood at his table and, with deliberation, picked up a piece of paper. He walked towards Ilana, never dropping eye contact with her. Gabrielle stiffened, knowing the onslaught about to happen.

Kitchner placed the paper in front of Ilana, but she wouldn't look at it. "I'm showing what has been marked as Exhibit two This is a statement that you wrote on the day of this incident, isn't it?"

"I think it is."

"Please look at it. That's your signature on the bottom, isn't it?"

"Yes."

"You received a phone call asking you to go to the police station that day and they asked you to write out a statement. True?"

"Yes, that's what happened."

"You wrote out the statement immediately after this incident occurred."

"Yes."

"When the events were fresh in your mind. Correct?"

"Yes."

"And what you wrote that day, is significantly different than what you are saying today."

"I wouldn't say that."

Kitchner smiled as he leaned against the witness stand. "Well, let's go through it. First, you said in the first line of the statement that the incident occurred on Maple Street, not Elm Street like you said today."

"That's what it says, but now I'm sure it happened where I'm saying it happened."

Kitchner stared at her for a moment. "You also gave a description of the dog that attacked Mr. Planeff in the second paragraph of the statement. I have highlighted it for you. Will you please read it for the jurors?"

Ilana picked up the paper and cleared her throat. "It says, 'the dog that attacked the man was approximately 60 pounds. It was black and white and was wearing a red collar.'"

Once again, the mean looking photograph of Pickles was on the screen. Kitchner moved forward and asked, "Isabel, isn't the dog in the picture about sixty pounds, black and white, and wearing a red collar?"

Ilana shrunk down a bit. "Probably?"

"Plaintiff has no further questions of this witness."

CHAPTER FORTY-EIGHT

MORE BORED THAN TIRED, Max was ready to end this drudgery. At first, the concept of helping his brother and testifying sounded like fun—a chance to play a role and watch a trial unfold. Cam never, however, told him how much time he would have to set aside not only to practice, but also in having to spend an entire day at the law school. Max understood there could be multiple rounds of the competition, but nobody warned him he would spend the day mainly watching the same trial over and over, like Groundhog Day, before he got a turn to testify, which lasted about four minutes.

He hadn't much paid attention so far during the preliminary rounds, mostly trying not to fall asleep when the other witnesses testified. It wasn't easy. He had listened to, or at least sat through, the entire trial three times already, and although each one played out somewhat differently, it was still just a dog bite case. No deaths, no destroyed lives, just some guy whining because a dog had bitten him. Hopefully, Cam would have more exciting cases when he became a real lawyer.

"Call your final witness," Taylor said, with perhaps a hint of exhaustion, or perhaps, an eagerness to crown a champion.

Cam rose. "Defendant calls Arnold Dawgoner."

Still not used to being called that name, Max hesitated for a moment before rising and walking to the witness stand. He took the oath and adjusted his tie which had become misaligned while he fidgeted during the other witnesses' testimony.

Cam stood at the edge of the jury box and wanted to get right to business. "Will you please introduce yourself to the members of the jury?" he asked.

"My name is Arnold Dawgoner. I am the owner of Pickles."

"How old are you?"

"I'm twenty-seven and I live alone, except for Pickles. He's my dog."

"Tell us a little about Pickles."

"I got him at the shelter when he was a puppy. He had been living in a house in West Virginia with twenty other dogs. They told me he was abused."

"Objection, your honor. Hearsay," Mupple said, standing to address the judge.

Taylor looked towards Cam. "Counsel, how do you respond?"

"We are not offering it for the truth of the matter."

The judge scratched his chin. "Seems like you are and want the sympathy of having an abused dog. I will sustain the objection." He turned to the members of the jury. "You will disregard the last question and not consider whether the dog had been abused when he was a puppy." He turned back. "Please proceed counsel."

Cam nodded. "How has Pickles been as a dog?"

"He's great. He was a handful as a puppy, but he's pretty well-behaved."

"Do you have a backyard?"

"Yes, and he plays in it a lot."

"Ever have a problem with him escaping from the backyard?"

"One-time last year, apparently someone opened my back gate. I didn't realize it and I left him in the yard, but because the gate was open, he was able to wander down the street."

"So, what happened?"

"He ran up to someone and jumped on them. They said he bit them, but there wasn't any sign of a bite. Pickles wouldn't do that. Pickles is a good dog."

"Any other problems with Pickles?"

"No. Like I said, he's a good dog. He likes people."

"Do you remember the day of this incident?"

Max nodded. "I do. I remember Pickles playing in the yard, and me working in my kitchen on my computer. I was focused on my work, but I was aware of Pickles hanging out in the yard. It was right outside of the window, and I remember hearing her bark a couple of times when two police officers knocked on my front door."

"What happened?"

"They said some guy was reporting that Pickles had attacked someone. I told them that Pickles had been in the yard the whole time, which he had."

"What did the police do?"

"They came into my yard and played with Pickles. They took a couple of pictures of him. They said they were going to file a police report."

"What happened with the report?"

"I never saw it and never heard from them again."

"Thank you, sir. I have no further questions, but the other side might."

Marjorie Mupple was already on her feet, waving some

papers before Cam had returned to his seat. "Mr. Dawgoner, your dog Pickles has attacked other people before and has had more than one brush with the law before his encounter with my client, didn't he?"

"Objection," Cam nearly yelled, "Compound question. Argumentative."

Judge Taylor looked at Mupple. "Slow down counselor. One question at a time."

She inhaled and asked, "Pickles has been involved in more than the one incident you identified, hasn't he?"

"That was the only one where Pickles actually touched someone."

"That wasn't my question. There have been at least two other reports of Pickles attacking someone, correct?"

"I wouldn't say that."

She walked to the witness stand and placed two pieces of paper in front of him. "I show you what has been marked as Exhibits Four and Five. These are other police reports where Pickles had attacked someone."

Max shook his head and gently put the papers down. "These are reports made up by my next store neighbor who claimed that Pickles had done something. He had no proof. He was only trying to get back at me because I had reported him to the Magistrate because his sidewalk was cracked and dangerous."

"They say that Pickles had attacked two members of his family."

Max shook his head. "He made them up. He had no proof of anything. Nothing ever happened with these complaints."

"Let's talk about the day of this incident. Isn't it true that you told the police you had been napping before they arrived?"

"I had for a little."

"Your statement to the police indicated that you had napped for an hour and a half before they arrived. True?"

"Perhaps."

"And in that time, you had no idea what Pickles was doing?"

"He was in the yard."

"You don't know if he had escaped the yard and then was able to return to the yard before you awoke?"

"Not a chance."

"You didn't have any cameras in the yard, so you can't say what Pickles was doing during that time?"

"It's true. I didn't have cameras to record what was happening in the yard."

"Mr. Dawgoner, will you admit that your dog wasn't well-trained?"

"No, I wouldn't say that. He's a great dog. Never would hurt anyone."

"Again, sir, would you look at the police report in front of you. Doesn't it say in it that Mr. Dawgoner has indicated that he never trained his dog well?"

"That's not what I meant, ma'am," Max said, with extra emphasis on the word 'ma'am.' "What I meant was that I didn't take Pickles to any dog obedience school. He won't rollover on command, but he understands his boundaries and wouldn't do anything like what happened to Mr. Planeff."

Mupple moved closer to Max, cutting off his view of Cam. "C'mon Mr. Dawgoner. You never trained your dog. He's attacked other people. He attacked Mr. Planeff. Something needs to happen with that dog, doesn't it?"

In the other mock trials, Max had been asked similar questions which suggested that Dawgoner hadn't taken care of Pickles or properly trained him. The other times, Max sloughed off the implication and just said that Pickles was a good dog. This time, however, he wanted to say more. Maybe because it was late in the day or because he had answered too many questions already, but this time something inside of him compelled him to say more.

"Ma'am," he began, again the extra emphasis he placed on the word made Cam squirm in his seat. "You don't understand. I have taken care of Pickles since rescuing him when he was just a pup. We spend every day together and he is my best friend." He spoke slowly and stared at Mupple who didn't dare to interrupt. "You don't know anything about Pickles. He has never hurt anyone, yet you want to take him away from me. You're distorting the truth only because you want your client to win." Max's cheeks flushed red.

Max didn't appear to be anywhere close to being finished. Mupple raised a hand in a vain attempt to get in a question. "We don't want anything bad to happen to Pickles," she began, but Max wasn't ready to cede the floor to her.

"That's exactly what you want to do," he said. "You want to take Pickles away from me and I would never see him again." Max tried to say more, but the words got caught in his throat. He looked down and shook his head. He said quietly, "Everybody who's important to me always leaves."

Cam stared at his brother watching his emotional outburst. Max's eyes were moist. His reaction was visceral. This was about way more than just an imaginary dog.

Mupple wanted to regain control and ask a question but hadn't formulated one first in her head. "You don't, have you, ever..." she began.

Max took Mupple's stuttering as an opportunity to keep speaking. "Pickles is an amazing dog. Please, don't take him away. It wouldn't be fair." Max's eyes were now wide open. He stared over Mupple's head.

At this point, Mupple threw her hands up in the air. "Plaintiff has no further questions."

The auditorium sank into silence. Cam rose and said, "The defendant rests."

Judge Taylor looked out at the audience. "The parties will now give their closing statements. Under the rules of this court, defendant will give the first closing. Plaintiff, because he has the burden of proof, will close last. We will take a five-minute break." He rapped his gavel.

Cam leaned back in his chair and let out all the air in his lungs.

CHAPTER FORTY-NINE

"IS THE DEFENDANT PREPARED TO CLOSE?" Taylor asked.

Cam rose and said, "We are."

Taylor motioned for Cam to address the jury.

As he stood in front of the jury, a sense of weariness from doing back-to-back-to-back trials since early in the morning coursed through Cam. The muscles in his neck tightened like steel cables and an achiness pounded at his temples. At the same time, a wave of adrenaline spread through his body providing him with a needed boost. Recognizing that he wanted to muscle through to the end of the day, he reminded himself not to rush.

"Ladies and Gentlemen," he began. "Thank you so much for your time and attention during this trial." He smiled and a couple of jurors in the front row grinned back at him. "This case is about responsibility, and I think as you understand from the evidence in this case, Arnold Dawgoner takes full responsibility for his dog Pickles."

Cam took a couple of steps back. "He may not have taken

him to obedience classes. He may not have taught him special tricks, but he understood the dog and didn't let the dog do anything harmful to others. Yes, one time the dog got out and wandered down the street, but we don't have any evidence that the dog hurt anyone on that occasion, or any other occasion for that matter.

"Yes, the plaintiff has suggested that the dog had attacked other people but didn't present any evidence Pickles had ever hurt anyone before. In addition, the plaintiff's testimony identifying Pickles as the dog who supposedly attacked him also fell apart.

"First, the plaintiff has changed his story entirely as to what happened from when he wrote his statement in the hospital. There he said that the dog was a different size and different color than Pickles and it was only after his girlfriend found Pickles in his backyard, did Mr. Planeff change his story so his description matched that of Pickles. That's just not credible.

"Don't let him change his story without repercussions." Cam paused to gather his thoughts. "The problem is that the dog which attacked Mr. Planeff ran off. He wasn't apprehended at the time of the incident. We aren't disputing that a dog attacked him. The dispute here is that they have no good proof Pickles was the dog that attacked him.

"The problem is Mr. Planeff's attempts to frame Pickles for the acts of another dog have significant effects for both Pickles and his owner. The ordinance governing ownership of a dog mandates that dogs found to have attacked and significantly harmed a person must be taken from its home and destroyed. If you rule in Mr. Planeff's favor, they will take away Pickles and destroy him.

"You have seen the bond between Mr. Dawgoner and his dog. Please don't cause more harm here. They have provided no evidence that Pickles is the dog who attacked Mr. Planeff. For these reasons, we ask that you find in his favor and save Pickles."

Cam retreated to counsel table and received a glowing smile from Gabrielle. They sat motionless waiting for the plaintiff's closing.

"Mr. Kitchner, it's your turn," the judge said.

Andrew Kitchner rose and strode to the jury box. He still looked fresh as if this was the first time he had made this closing today. He placed a couple of papers on the stand in front of the jurors.

"On behalf of Mr. Planeff, we also thank you for the time you have spent listening to our case. Mr. Planeff was savagely attacked by a dog and suffered serious and permanent injuries." He turned and pointed at Cam and Gabrielle. "They concede that a dog attack happened. They don't dispute it. Also, the defendant has not, and cannot challenge the extent of injuries our client has suffered. The only issue in dispute is which dog attacked my client—and the evidence clearly establishes that Pickles was the dog who caused the damage.

"First, Mr. Planeff's girlfriend, based on the description given to her, found Pickles in Mr. Dawgoner's backyard and positively identified him as the dog who attacked Mr. Planeff. She took a picture of the dog and Mr. Planeff later agreed it was that dog who had attacked him."

Kitchner paused and grabbed an exhibit. "This is the statement that Isabel Sawet gave less than two hours after the dog attacked Mr. Planeff. In fact, her testimony actually helped the plaintiff more than it did their side." He waved at Cam and Gabrielle without even turning to look at them.

"Here's what she said." He held up her statement for the jurors. "First, in her statement she indicated that the attack had occurred on Elm Street and not Maple Street, like she had said in her direct examination. This is vital because it not only destroys the credibility of her testimony on direct, but it completely buttresses what Mr. Planeff said in his direct testimony. The attack occurred near to where Mr. Dawgoner and Pickles lived, making it much more likely that Pickles was involved in the attack.

"It's clear she witnessed Pickles attack our client near to Mr. Dawgoner's home. I understand why she would feel some sympathy for the dog and his owner, but her story has not been consistent because she is only trying to protect the dog.

"Second, and more important, her description of the dog when she wrote her statement matched that of Pickles. She said he was a sixty pound, black and white dog wearing a red collar." The menacing picture of Pickles, which included him wearing a red collar loomed again from the big screen. "I mean, Ms. Sawet went right to the police station and gave a perfect description of Pickles without any prompting.

"Third, this is not the first time Pickles has attacked another person. Even Mr. Dawgoner acknowledged one other incident where a person had reported Pickles for attacking them. But there were another two police reports which are in evidence. Maybe it's because Mr. Dawgoner never got Pickles any formal obedience training, but it's clear, Pickles does not respect boundaries and is a danger to people."

Kitchner shook his head. "The local ordinance is clear: If a dog is a danger, it must be removed from the home. We may not like it, but it is the law. The facts in this case are clear. Pickles attacked Mr. Planeff. Your verdict should not be swayed by sympathy and should be based on the facts. And if you base your verdict on the facts, there is only one outcome you can reach and that would be finding in favor of Mr. Planeff."

He paused before saying, "Thank you."

THE JUDGE WAITED a few minutes for everyone in the auditorium to stretch and then return to their seats. He spoke to those gathered. "At this point in a trial the judge would ordinarily read the instructions of the law to the jury. I don't think it will be necessary in this instance, nor do I think you all would want to sit through a paragraph-by-paragraph recitation of the law of assault."

A small burst of applause spread through the auditorium. Taylor smiled. "Instead, given this is a mock trial, our mock jurors will gather all of their ratings for the lawyers and witnesses. The scores will then be totaled, and then we should have a winner. Let's take a fifteen-minute break and when we resume, I will announce the winners to you."

Without any prompting, a large round of sustained applause burst out. Cam lowered his head as much out of exhaustion as in appreciation. As the clapping ceased, Cam realized he would have to wait a bit longer before finding out if all their hard work had been worth it.

The sound of people getting out of chairs and milling about spilled over them. Cam and Gabrielle rose and walked over to opposing counsel. They held out their hands. Cam said, "You tried a great case. Good luck."

Their opponents offered positive remarks about their performance at the trial and returned the good wishes. They then separated and went back to their respective tables, plopping into their seats to await the verdict.

CHAPTER FIFTY

IN A FEW YEARS, after they passed the bar exam and became real litigators handling cases ranging from minor motor vehicle accidents to the most complicated antitrust lawsuits, they would sit in quiet courthouses waiting for juries to return their verdicts. They would soon realize that few events in life are more gut-wrenching than waiting for a jury to make its decision.

Most juries take hours, and sometimes days, to decide on the outcome of their case. While they perform this function, lawyers pace empty hallways re-litigating every choice in their heads, picking apart every question asked and second-guessing each decision made. Logically, they understand they had done everything humanly possible to try their best case, and the jury's decision reflected the facts of the case and not the talents of the lawyers. Despite this, attorneys' evaluation of their own performance generally coincides with the jurors' final decision. Winning becomes paramount and lawyers wait for verdicts negotiating with whatever deity happened to be listening, willing to exchange almost anything for a positive result.

The four acting attorneys endured this process waiting for the mock jury's decision. They sat without talking, each trying to appear calm and collected, but nonetheless dying on the inside as every minute ticked by.

Without drawing attention, Taylor returned to his seat at the head of the proceedings. Once the throng realized he was back in place, the room quieted. He still rapped his gavel to ensure order. "We have a verdict," he announced while holding a set of papers.

Taylor looked up at the audience. "These are our jurors' rankings, which we have tabulated, and, in a minute, I will give you the results." He then motioned to those gathered and thanked them for making the event a success. Seeming to enjoy having everyone's undivided attention, he then thanked the jurors for their time, while reminding the crowd that they were his associates and didn't really have any choice.

The churn of anxiety ate away at Cam's gut as Taylor delayed giving the verdict.

Please, just give us the results.

"Now, let's get into the substance of the finals," Taylor continued, acting oblivious to the participants' need for finality. "First of all, I think it's obvious that as the rounds went on, the quality of the presentation improved. What does this teach us? Experience is a great teacher. Yes, there is clearly some natural talent on display here, but hard work, practice, and actually getting into court will help forge seasoned litigators.

"Let's go over some of our jurors' thoughts. Constructive critiques are always helpful, and every trial is a learning opportunity. First, they were unanimous that the lawyers did a professional job in presenting their cases. Yes, this was 'only' a dog bite case, but even in the most mundane case, the lawyer needs to make a comprehensible demonstration to the jury."

He turned his attention to the lawyers. "You all made excellent presentations in your openings and closings. You were poised and summarized the evidence to make it understandable for the jury.

"Your questions of the witnesses were also first rate. The direct examinations were to the point and allowed the witnesses to shine. Virtually every question on cross was leading and did not provide much opening for a witness to filibuster.

"And with respect to the exhibits, you all did exactly what you needed to do. You laid the proper foundations and utilized the exhibits in a way that enhanced the witnesses' testimony, rather than interfering with it. Well done."

He grabbed the verdict forms and waved them in front of him. "So, let's turn to the results."

Gabrielle reached out and grabbed Cam's arm, while Taylor continued. "It was close. Damn close. In fact, the jurors scored the lawyers even. The result came down to the witnesses' scores. And again, we can learn a lesson here..."

Oh God, the results, please. Cam forced himself to remain still so that his appearance did not betray his turmoil.

"Witnesses are the ones who tell the story. It's not really about the lawyers, but about the people who can communicate to the jury what happened. You need to prepare them and let the jury feel the emotion of their testimony. One side did this just a little bit better than the other, and because of that, that side is the winner."

Taylor raised a finger. "Yes, I will be telling you who the winner is in about one minute." The audience groaned. "But before we get to that, we have decided to give out a second-place award because we were so pleased with the effort everyone put in and believe more prizes were warranted. So, although they will not be clerking for my firm this summer, we have decided to give the second-place winners a gift certificate to The Eatery, the newest, swankiest restaurant, so I am told, which has recently opened down the street.

"And the winners of that fancy dinner are..." He held his thoughts for a moment. "...the plaintiff's team and their attorneys, Marjorie Mupple and Andrew Kitchner." They rose to exuberant applause and approached Taylor who met them in front of the judge's bench. They hugged each other and then posed for pictures.

At the same time, Cam leaped in the air with his hands stretched above his head and grabbed Gabrielle in a bear hug. After a moment of jumping around together, they separated and tried to regain a modicum of decorum so as not to interfere with the presentation to the other attorneys.

After directing the other lawyers back to their table, Taylor turned his attention to Cam and Gabrielle. "This obviously means that the winner of the first Broadside, Taylor, and Sanders' moot court competition are the defendants and their attorneys, Cameron Crewell and Gabrielle Moore."

Cam and Gabrielle stood, turned to the crowd and half-bowed in their direction and then walked to the judge's bench. Taylor shook hands with them and then turned to address the audience. "They have prepared for weeks. They have studied the law and have learned the facts. They have endured four rounds of competition and have beaten some extremely strong teams. These are your well-deserved champions."

He grabbed one of each of their hands and raised them above his head. Cam and Gabrielle accepted the congratulations from the crowd who clapped and whistled.

Within a few seconds, the commotion died down and people began to head for the exits.

Cam reveled for a brief second in the victory, savoring the moment when their hours of preparation were rewarded, but Gabrielle's body-engulfing hug knocked his mind back to the present. Their celebration was quickly interrupted as Ilana and Max, soon joined by Sophia, Kate, D'Andre, and Marco, came over to offer congratulations.

The attention was gratifying, yet somewhat overwhelming. They had won the competition. Cam didn't have to worry about where he would be working in the summer, but now he had to focus his energy on other pressing tasks.

He accepted everyone's good wishes, but then reached for his backpack which was under their counsel table. "Guess what everybody? Finals start next week."

Everyone groaned. D'Andre slammed his books over his shoulder. "Let's hit the library for a bit before the celebratory banquet. We have two hours, so we can knock off a few cases before coming back down."

They nodded and followed him out of the auditorium without uttering a word.

CHAPTER FIFTY-ONE

THE GANG RETURNED TO the basement of the law school to find it transformed into a festive environment. Large, round tables, covered with table clothes filled the open space. Each was set with dining ware for twelve. They wouldn't be using paper napkins for the first time in months.

They claimed seats at a table by stowing their backpacks and made sure to save two for Ilana and Max for when, or if, they returned. A couple of their friends came over to offer congratulations to Cam and Gabrielle. Taylor appeared wearing a third suit for the evening celebration and the large throng quickly found their places.

The lights dimmed as Taylor strode to the microphone someone had placed on a makeshift dais. "I hope no one needs to use the facilities," he said, noticing that someone had placed the podium a few feet in front of the men's bathroom. "We are here tonight to celebrate not just the victors, but everyone who participated in today's amazing competition.

"First, I want to thank all of the family and friends who showed up today. It's tough enough having to cross-examine a witness, but it's much harder with people in the crowd watching your every move.

"Second, let's thank all of the students and friends who agreed to be the witnesses for our trials. They had to memorize all the materials and then subject themselves to withering questioning. I'm not sure why anyone would agree to that, but they did. So, let's ask them to stand and show our appreciation."

Ilana and Max, who had just snuck into their seats, stood with twenty others witnesses. They sat even as the applause continued.

"We had four rounds of trials," Taylor continued, "and the advocacy improved each round. This may have only been a dog bite case, but all the advocates attacked it like it was the biggest case they would ever handle. Which, I may add, is how you as attorneys should handle everyone one of your cases—like it is the biggest case you will ever handle.

"Before we bring up our winning teams, there are two awards I will hand out. The first one is for the best witness. This is given to the person who most adeptly handled the materials and who portrayed that person's witness most compellingly.

"The winner of the best witness award, as decided by my team, won primarily by their testimony in the finals. This person may have sleep-walked through the first few rounds, but found their rhythm in the finals, giving a sense of drama and depth to the proceedings. And the winner is—Max Crewell."

Max stood to a round of applause and dragged himself up to the dais and took the best witness certificate from Taylor. He spun in a circle when he realized he had forgotten to shake Taylor's hand. He grabbed Taylor's hand to the laughs of the crowd and returned to his seat.

Taylor didn't fail to make a point of Max's faux pas. "Everyone in a courtroom should be in the moment when moving. I've have seen lawyers trip over their bags and immediately lose credibility with the jury. I'm sure Max will learn that lesson in time."

He reached down to pick up the next certificate. "The winner of the best advocate award could go to any of four finalists. I am so impressed by all of them, but we had to pick one out of that group and this person won by the consistency of his performance and never having an awkward moment during any of the rounds of the competition. The winner is--Cameron Crewell."

Cam jogged to the front of the crowd to accept the award. "I guess," Taylor said, "the Crewell family is collecting certificates tonight." He handed Cam the paper. "I will be seeing you again in a moment."

Taylor started talking as Cam turned to return to his seat. "Wait, no need for you to leave," Taylor said, forcing Cam to make a full circle. "Well, now you're walking like your brother."

Cam blushed, but stood next to Taylor, who waved at Gabrielle to join them. She complied and stared straight ahead, her red hair hanging still like her body.

"I present you with the winners of today's competition. Cam Crewell and Gabrielle Moore outlasted twenty-nine other teams and are now the winners. They each will receive a full paid summer internship at my firm with all the perks of that position. Like the other twenty-five interns we will hire for the summer, they will have the opportunity to receive an offer of full employment upon graduation. I hope the effort has been worth it."

Gabrielle and Cam shook hands with Taylor, who announced, "By the way, the second-place team can pick up their gift certificates at the end of the evening."

Cam smirked as he returned to the table. At the beginning of the day, he probably would have been happy to finish in second and win a fancy dinner. Would have looked good on his resume. This, however, was so much better. Now, people would recognize him at school and would always look at him as a winner. His money worries were pretty much in the rearview mirror as he was now so close to receiving a permanent job offer when they graduated.

He couldn't contain his smile as his friends pounded him on his back and mussed his hair. Max had a similar look on his face when they then went over to him to offer their congratulations.

PART 4

CHAPTER FIFTY-TWO

WHILE IN COLLEGE, CAM learned how to budget time and manage his life, at least to the extent a college student must to take control of his life. Only after he dropped out of school and then managed to get himself back in, did he figure out that studying the day's materials before class produced much better results than just showing up to. This was a significant improvement over the first time he tried college, when he considered just getting to class a success.

College had also given him his first real brush with handling his own finances. Again, they were baby steps, but he learned how to make sure that at the end of the month he had a couple of dollars in his wallet even after paying for food and his share of the utilities. He learned that even with a parental safety net in place, it was ultimately up to him to make sure he was where he was supposed to be and paid whatever financial obligations he had.

Law school had upped the ante on all counts. Coming to class unprepared was an invitation for disaster. Maybe because students who didn't prepare refused to make eye contact or slouched in their seats unlike those eager to present, but the professors had an uncanny ability to home in on those who hadn't read the materials. They also had no reservations about embarrassing them in front of their peers.

Entering law school, Cam committed to do everything necessary to keep up in all his classes. He struggled at first, but somehow found his rhythm, even while being pummeled by personal tragedy. His responsibilities only multiplied when his brother and sister came to live in his house. Now, not only did he have to deal with the constant demands of his classes, but he was committed to helping Ilana and Max manage the challenges of their lives.

Not long after his siblings moved into the house, he had a long conversation with Gabrielle about withdrawing from the mock trial competition. At that point, he couldn't imagine taking on more and thought he would implode if he added to what was already on his plate.

Gabrielle expressed support for any decision he might make and indicated she wouldn't be upset if he needed to drop out. Had it been a solo event, Cam would have withdrawn, but he wanted to support Gabrielle, so he never wavered from his commitment to her and the competition. He second-guessed that decision hundreds of times while putting in the hours to prepare.

Cam sat in the living room of the house alone. He had his Employment Law text opened but couldn't concentrate. An envelope torn open, with a white, official-looking letter on top rested next to his book.

Since the end of the mock trial competition, his other major life-altering stressors loomed on the horizon. On Monday, their second semester finals would begin and take up most of the week. The cyclical nightmare of long hours cramming, trying to sneak in a few hours of sleep, followed by a two-hour, ball-busting final would repeat itself for four straight days.

But even after enduring the torture of finals, Cam would still not be able to relax. He leaned forward and grabbed the letter to read it again. The banner at the top indicated it came from the Family Court Division, the body reminded him that the hearing determining his suitability to be guardian for Max and Ilana would take place the following Monday.

Yes, even after suffering through his tests, he would have no reprieve. Instead, he would head into a courtroom and watch while some judge decided if his family should stay together. He read the final lines of the notification: "The determination of the appropriate residential situs for the minors, Ilana Crewell and Max Crewell, will be adjudicated at the hearing. You are invited to participate."

Cam threw the letter onto the table.

You better believe I'll be there to participate.

CHAPTER FIFTY-THREE

CAM'S BODY ACHED. HIS head throbbed. He turned the handle on the front door and entered the house. Sophia, Gab, and D'Andre slouched on the couch, cocktails in hand. Gabrielle jumped off the couch at Cam's entrance. "You're the last one. You made it!" She tried to hug him. "Let' me get you a drink."

Cam waved her off. "Not right now."

She jammed a hand on her hip and stared at him. "You just finished your last final. You need it."

He walked over to the dining room table and plopped into a chair. "I'm fried. Five tests in five days. I can't believe it's over."

Gabrielle placed a glass clinking with ice swimming in clear alcohol in front of him.

"Enjoy. You earned it."

Cam pushed it a few inches away. "Not feeling it. Where are Ilana and Max?"

Sophia yelled from the couch. "They're with friends. We suggested they might want a night away from the house. Might be something happening they shouldn't be seeing."

Cam stretched and leaned back in his chair. "I can't slow my head down. I think I might just go upstairs and try to relax."

Gabrielle pushed his glass closer to him. "This will help. You need to catch up with us." She smiled at him.

Cam grimaced in response. "Hey, you guys are all done. Your worries are over. I still have this hearing on Monday. I'm not ready to let loose, yet."

Sophia offered, "Marco and I have to be your lawyers at the hearing. We're spending tomorrow getting ready. We still got two days." She pouted. "Play with us tonight."

Cam pushed back out of his chair and stood. "I can't get it all out of my mind. I'm not ready yet. I'm heading upstairs so I can figure out a way to slow my head down." He walked away from the table.

Everyone watched him trudge upstairs and then returned to their celebration.

CHAPTER FIFTY-FOUR

CAM STOMPED AROUND HIS room holding a Roberto Clemente figurine. Gabrielle sat on the bed; concern etched on her face. She twirled a lock of hair around her finger waiting for a chance to offer some support.

"It's not fair. Nothing about this is fair," Cam raged, as he continued marching in random patterns. "These people don't know anything. They're just making it worse. Civil servants, that's all they are." He held Clemente in one hand in front of him and spoke to him as if Gabrielle wasn't in the room.

She raised her hand and twiddled her fingers at him, but he paid her no attention and continued, "So what if we end up living in three different places and never see each other again? They don't care. Just want to fill out their reports and look like they're doing something, even if it destroys our family."

He placed Clemente gently back in his place on the upper shelf of his desk and turned towards Gabrielle. His eyes were red, and creases raced across his forehead. "What the hell is their problem?" He threw his hands out to his side while noticing her for the first time in minutes.

She stood and walked over to him with deliberative steps. He remained motionless and she wrapped her arms around him. He lowered his head onto her shoulder and exhaled a slow, deep breath.

"I hear everything you're saying," she said, "but what they want to do, isn't the important question." She rubbed the back of his head. "You've got to focus on what you're doing."

"But they want to split us up," he said into her shoulder.

"Yes, but you can't control what they want. What do you want?"

He took a step back and glared at her. "You know what I want."

"Of course, I do, but you need to say it."

"I want us to stay together."

"And...?"

"I want to show them that this is the best place for them."

"Do you think whining about what they might do will get you what you want?"

Cam tilted his head and squinted. "My head spins every night when I try to sleep because I have no control over what's about to happen. My gut hurts all the time worrying that the court won't listen to us and will just accept what the bureaucrats claim is best. Nobody's listened to us so far."

"Cam, stop being a wuss. You have a mouth, and you have important thoughts. Make them listen to you. Tomorrow's your chance. Your brother and sister have it good here. Now it's up to you to make sure everyone else understands."

Cam shook his head. "I just don't think they want to hear anything from me. I shouldn't be a parent."

"Probably not yet, but that's the position you've been put in." She put her hand on his arm. "My opinion, you've done a damn good job so far. Unorthodox at times, but pretty commendable if someone were to ask me. Don't think any less of yourself just because you're young. Your brother and sister might've ended up in a bad place if it weren't for you."

"If it weren't for all of us." He started pacing around the room again. "They haven't dealt with a situation like ours before, but that doesn't make it wrong, it just makes it different. I hear what you're saying, Gab. I'm just scared."

Gabrielle jumped in front of Cam to stop his wandering and placed her hands on his shoulders. "You're their best hope. We all have so much confidence in you." She shook him. "You're up to the task."

Cam shuddered, his entire body twitching for a moment. "Won't be easy falling asleep tonight." He looked up at her and smiled. "You want to sleep over?"

She returned his smile. "Not tonight. You need to be rested for tomorrow. Go say goodnight to your brother and sister. When you come back, I'll tuck you in." She turned him towards the door and smacked his butt. "Move."

Cam turned in the doorway to face her. He shook his head. "Thanks. I needed that."

———

THE SUN WAS BEGINNING to illuminate the city when Cam, Ilana, and Max snuck downstairs to grab food before leaving for the hearing. Dressed in dark suits, they appeared as ready to go to a funeral as to court. The somber mood and paucity of speaking suggested they were anticipating something more akin to a death than a positive result.

Turning into the kitchen, Ilana exclaimed, "Oh, that is so sweet." She pointed straight ahead at fresh cut bagels in a basket, cream cheese, and an assortment of cut fruit on a platter. "Who did this?"

Cam shook his head and bit his lower lip, while Max

rushed forward and smeared a glob of cream cheese on a cinnamon raisin bagel.

As they placed food on plates, their roommates quietly entered also dressed in suits. "We wanted to make sure you were ready for today," Marco said. "More importantly, remember we will be there in body and will be rooting for you like nobody ever has before."

Kate engulfed Ilana in a hug. She whispered, "That's my lucky suit you got on. You have nothing to worry about. I got my first job offer wearing it."

Ilana reached around further and squeezed harder. "Thanks. I'm not worried." Her trembling body gave away her true feelings.

Cam shoved the last bit of bagel into his mouth. "We better move. Got to meet our attorneys at the courthouse."

"Lucky, you got the best lawyers money can't buy," D'Andre said grabbing Cam's plate out of his hand. "Get out of here. We'll meet you downtown."

Cam led his siblings to the door. They paused and then turned to wave. Cam put his arms over his brother and sister's shoulders. "Let's go kick some ass," he said as he slammed the door closed.

CHAPTER FIFTY-FIVE

CAM SPIED HIS BROTHER and sister seated on the long, wooden rows of benches at the back of the courtroom. Dressed in their dark suits, hair in place, a touch of makeup on Ilana's face, they picked at their clothes and fiddled with strands of hair that had fallen in their faces, pondering how the death of their dad seven months earlier had left them in a state of near purgatory, forced to deal with the unimaginable pain of his loss.

Their dad's passing had left them with no place to live, no parents to offer emotional support, and no long-term financial solution to provide a safety net during this most traumatic stage of their lives. Despite all these obstacles, they had found a path forward. They may not have been thriving the same way their friends were, but neither had they fallen apart. All three Crewell children continued to face the turbulent winds which now constantly blew in their direction.

The courtroom was small and intimate, in contrast to the behemoth venues featured in movies with overhanging balconies and wood paneling covering the walls. A low-level judge would decide their futures in this utilitarian space, with five cramped rows of seating and an oversized seal of the Commonwealth of Pennsylvania plastered to the wall behind the raised desk which served as the judge's bench.

Cam had placed himself in the back row fifteen minutes earlier and tried to visualize how the proceedings would unfold. He gazed at the witness stand, just a wooden chair sitting on a small platform to the right of the judge and imagined himself with his hand in the air, swearing to tell the truth. He pictured the attorney for the other side getting in his face, grilling him on cross-examination.

Cam wanted to project confidence in his ability to advocate for his family, but his lack of experience in this arena ate away at him. His shoulders slumped as he imagined the judge banging her gavel as Ilana and Max were led away to live with another family. His brain couldn't wrap itself around the finality of this day, and, good or bad, how the result would alter the fabric of his life.

Ilana and Max now sat to his right, appearing pensive, while also inspecting the courtroom as their heads rotated side-to-side. Cam detected a slight quiver when Ilana placed her hand on the arm of his suit jacket. He turned to her and noticed her leg bouncing up and down in a staccato rhythm. She looked at him, biting her lip, her eyes welling up. He put his arm around her and pulled her closer. He whispered, "We've got nothing to worry about. We got this in the bag." He turned away, his upper teeth biting down hard onto his lower lip.

———

MINUTES LATER, the courtroom door slammed open and Marco, tugging a rolling briefcase, led a group of young adults in. Once he made it to counsel table, he unloaded his materials, creating three large piles of documents. Sophia stood next to him, placing two thick binders in front of them.

They sauntered over to Cam's family and sat down. "Everyone ready?" Sophia asked, smiling with her mouth, but not her eyes.

Cam nodded, but Ilana and Max didn't look up or utter a sound.

"C'mon guys, we're good," Sophia said. "We've been over your testimony how many times now?"

"Too many," Max muttered, staring at his feet.

She smacked his shoulder. "This is scary. We get it. I'm pretty scared myself. It's our first time being in court."

Ilana rolled her eyes. "Probably not real smart to keep reminding us."

"Point is, it's not easy being in court for anybody, but just remember the points we want you to emphasize."

Ilana nodded. "Got it."

Max looked up. "What if they ask me a question that we haven't gone over?"

"Don't worry. They will. We can't anticipate everything. First, you tell the truth. Even if you think it may hurt us, you tell the truth. But that shouldn't be a problem because I think the truth is only going to help our case."

Max leaned over. "Don't worry about her. She'll be fine. It's me that you should worry about."

"Why? We've been over all of this with you, too," Sophia said.

Max put his hand on his stomach. "I'm nauseous. I think it's nerves. I might get sick up there." He pointed toward the witness stand.

"C'mon, you'll be fine. This is old hat for you. You just testified in the mock trial competition. You rocked, Mr. Best Witness."

"That was a competition, not real. I didn't care if I screwed that up. I was playing a role. This is different."

Sophia nodded. "Of course. Remember how you made everyone pay attention to you and believe you at mock trial? Now that you'll be telling the real truth, this should be much easier." She patted him on his knee. "You're going to be great."

She turned to walk away and wiggled a finger at Cam, telling him to follow. They reached a secluded corner of the room. "Damn," she said, exhaling a big breath of air. "Your brother and sister might be falling apart. You should say something to them to focus them. We need to get this hearing started asap. The more time they sit here thinking, the more trouble I think we're in."

"Not sure what I can say to them. We've talked so many times about what to expect. If they aren't ready now, there's nothing more we can do about it. I'm a little sick also. I'm scared."

Sophia grabbed his hand. "Join the club. I've never said a word in court before and I'm about to give an opening statement in a case that has huge implications for a good friend. I'm dealing with as much pressure as you."

Before Cam responded, a seventy-ish-year-old man with a gut not well controlled by an ill-fitting suit, entered from the judge's chambers and yelled, "We are about to begin. Please take your seats. Judge Laskey will be out momentarily."

Sophia whispered to Cam, "Here we go." She pointed to the first row of seats where Cam would be sitting. "Good luck."

Cam nodded and took a deep breath hoping the unrelenting churn in his stomach would ease.

CHAPTER FIFTY-SIX

MARCO AND SOPHIA SHUFFLED papers while stationed at their counsel table. To their right, a newbie attorney made stacks in front of her. Marco turned to the crowd crammed into the few rows of spectator seating and found the supportive smile of Professor Hawkins. Assured, he took a deep breath and exhaled.

"All rise," the paunchy bailiff yelled as the judge entered the courtroom. "This court is now in session, The Honorable Judge Gretchen Laskey presiding." She wore the black, floor length robe expected of judges, but still projected an air of informality and affability. She waved as if swatting at a mosquito "Sit, please. People, sit."

Everyone in the courtroom took their seat. "We are here today for the final dispositive hearing in Commonwealth v. Crewell, et al. Are the parties prepared to proceed?"

The young attorney representing the Commonwealth stood. She wore a dark grey, pinstriped pants suit, starched white blouse, and a chiffon handkerchief with blue stripes tied around her neck. Her auburn hair framed her cherubic face. "Your Honor," she said. "The Commonwealth is ready to begin."

Marco stood and buttoned the top button on his navy blue suit. "We are also ready."

The judge nodded. "We are to determine whether the two minor Crewell youths should be removed from their current living situation and given over to Family Services for placement with a foster family. The Agency has the burden of proof so it will proceed first. Before the parties give their opening statements, are there any preliminary matters to discuss?"

Sophia stood. "Your Honor, we have provided you with a brief outlining the positions we are taking in this matter and the legal support for our arguments."

The judge grinned at Sophia. "The court has received your brief." She held up a bound set of papers. "I will utilize it to assist in making my ruling. I have not received any briefs from the Commonwealth. Am I correct?" She turned towards the Commonwealth's attorney.

She stood. "You are correct, Your Honor. We believe there are no unique issues of law, and the Court is aware of the governing standard."

The judge put aside the papers. "That reminds me. Mr. Crewell, you are utilizing law students as your attorneys. Is that correct?"

Cam, seated immediately behind Sophia and Marco, stood. "That is correct."

"Very well. Under the rules of this court, law students supervised by a licensed attorney may represent litigants in certain situations. I have previously certified their appearance to represent Mr. Crewell, so long as the lawyer supervising their activities is present. Professor Hawkins is in the back of the courtroom and has signed the appropriate forms indicating that she is supervising the law students and their conduct. I am comfortable these students are receiving proper supervision.

"One additional matter before we begin: I have received a signed stipulation that counsel representing Mr. Crewell are potential witnesses in this matter. Is that correct?"

Marco stood. "Your Honor, this is correct. Ms. Long and I both live in the residence at issue. We have agreed that we will not testify at any time in this matter. In exchange for that agreement, the Agency will not raise any potential conflict. We have provided the court with an executed stipulation with regard to this issue."

Judge Laskey held up a set of papers. "I have received it. Does you so stipulate, Ms. Boyle?" She pointed at the other attorney.

"We have agreed to this. We will not raise the potential conflict and counsel agrees that they cannot testify in this matter."

The judge shook her head. "I'm not sure I like this, but if both sides agree, I will accept the stipulation. Does either party have any other matters for the court to address before we begin?"

Both sides indicated they were ready to proceed.

"Good. We will start with opening statements. Ms. Boyle, as the moving party, your side will open first."

Boyle stood behind her table to address the court.

"Your Honor, through the filings in this matter you are aware of a living situation that is potentially harmful to the two minor children, Ilana Crewell and Max Crewell. Ilana is presently a senior in high school and Max is a freshman.

"Due to the untimely deaths of both of their parents, they are currently living in a house with six college students. Although their brother is one of the individuals living in that house, no one has established a clear indication as to who has primary custodial responsibility for Ilana and Max in their current situation.

"Their house lacks adequate privacy and has insufficient space for their individual lives. Further, no one exercises proper supervision to ensure attendance at school or to make sure they stay out of trouble.

"You will hear the testimony of Helen Cartwright, the case investigator assigned to this matter. Ms. Cartwright will tell you of the inspections she performed at the residence and how the conditions of the house fail to meet the applicable standards necessary to comply with governing regulations.

"In addition, a family member will offer testimony about Cameron Crewell and his lack of ability to raise these children."

Boyle turned in Cam's direction. "It will be clear from the testimony that due to Mr. Crewell's inability to provide a safe and nurturing environment, removing the children from the household and placing them in a foster home more capable of providing what these children need at this important time in their development, will be in their best interests." Boyle nodded at the judge and said while taking a seat, "Thank you, Your Honor."

Judge Laskey looked at Sophia over her horn-rimmed glasses and pointed her pencil in her direction.

Sophia stood and walked over to Cam and touched his shoulder. Ilana on his left and Max on his right side both inched in closer. "This family," she began, "has suffered enough already. They lost their mom four years ago and just last year had to live through the unexpected death of their dad. They don't have much extended family and were left with nowhere to go."

Sophia moved forward, away from Cam and his family. "Cameron Crewell--Cam to everyone who knows him, was just beginning his first year in law school. The first year is an incredibly stressful and trying year, but instead of dumping his brother and sister on the state, Cam and his roommates took in Ilana and Max, and gave them a place to live.

"And the evidence will prove, from the mouths of these three incredible people, how living in this house has brought them together and made the best out of a terrible situation.

"Cam's not going to tell you it's been perfect or that he is a perfect parent. I'm not aware of many perfect parents. But the picture you will receive once you hear from the three of them is that they live in a loving home, where they look out for each other and take care of each other. The only conclusion you will be able to reach after hearing their testimony is, this is the best living situation for Ilana and Max, and separating them at this point would only add to the terrible pain they have suffered since losing their parents. Thank you."

Sophia took her seat. There were no other sounds in the courtroom other than her chair sliding back into place. She put her hands in her lap to help them to stop shaking.

———

THE COURT DECLARED a five-minute break allowing Marco and Sophia to meet in the hallway outside the courtroom. Marco put his arm over her shoulder and whispered, "You were great. It was better than any other time you did it in class."

Sophia beamed, but then put back on a serious face. "We have to focus and be ready to cross their witnesses. You got the old bag, Cartwright, don't you?"

Marco nodded and then shook his head. "I hope those kids are ready. They were about to lose it before we got started."

"That's how I felt before I stood to open. I thought I was

going to puke on you, but once I got going and let it flow, I was fine. Hopefully, they will hold it together."

As they were about to head back into the courtroom, Cam approached. "What were they talking about in their opening? Who is the family member?"

Marco shrugged. "We'll have to deal with it if they call someone unexpected." He paused and looked at Cam. "You okay? Your face has no color."

Cam shook his head. "I'm fine. Don't worry about me. You got enough to think about." He tapped Sophia on the shoulder. "The opening was great. Keep it up."

She touched his arm and then grabbed Marco to return to the courtroom. "We've got some cross-examination to do," she said as she tugged him away.

CHAPTER FIFTY-SEVEN

THE PARTICIPANTS AND THE spectators were still returning to their seats when Judge Laskey commanded, "Call your first witness."

"The Commonwealth calls Helen Cartwright.

Rising without effort from her seat behind attorney Boyle, Cartwright carried a binder towards the witness stand. She swept imaginary dust off the seat and sat without making a sound. All eyes fixed on her as she waited for her first question.

"Please tell the court your name," Boyle stated while standing behind counsel table.

"I am Helen Cartwright. Senior caseworker for the Children's and Youth Services."

"How long have you worked in that capacity?"

"Twenty-two years and seven months."

"What are your job responsibilities?"

"I am responsible for investigating the living situations of minors who may be in need of alternative living arrangements. As part of CYS, we are charged to make sure that minors are living in appropriate conditions which would mean they are safe, secure, well fed, and someone has taken the responsibility for their education and general well-being."

She turned her body to direct her comments to the judge. "I evaluate the conditions children are living in and make recommendations for their future care. When we get involved, we have temporary authority to remove children from volatile or unproductive situations and place them in homes more conducive to their well-being, subject, of course, to court review."

"Ms. Cartwright, did you do a similar type of investigation into the living situation involving minor children, Max Crewell and Ilana Crewell?"

"I did."

"Why?"

"Our agency was notified that young Mr. Crewell, then age 15, had been taken to the hospital due to alcohol poisoning. That by itself might have been enough for us to investigate, but the hospital reported that Max did not have a legal guardian and was brought to the hospital by his older brother, Cameron, and a woman friend of his. A minor who is hospitalized for excessive drinking who is living in our jurisdiction without a legal guardian will get our attention."

"So, what did you do?"

"Our procedure is to open a file and then conduct an investigation. The first part of the investigation is to research the living situation. I found that Ilana and Max were living with their brother, Cameron, age 22, in a house with five other young adults. I learned that their mother had died approximately four years earlier and their father had recently passed away. He had remarried, but the wife left the area after his death."

"Given what you found in your research what did you do?"

"Clearly this was a problem. We had two underage children

living in a house with six other young adults, while the children had no identified legal guardian. Max had been hospitalized for excessive alcohol consumption. I absolutely had to do further investigation."

"What does that involve?"

"The next step is to perform an unannounced home inspection. The purpose is to examine the living situation and determine if an immediate need to remove the children exists."

"When did you do the first home inspection and what were the results?"

"May I look at my notes?"

Boyle nodded her head. Cartwright opened her file and continued, "I went to the home on October 12, last year. Cameron answered the door and I identified myself and the purpose for which I was investigating. He let me into the house, and I did my inspection."

"What were the results of your inspection?"

"I performed a rather cursory inspection--the initial one always is--but I found a number of troubling matters occurring in the home."

"Please give more detail of your initial inspection."

"When I entered the house, I found a number of young men and women intermixed in the living area. In the open, there was a clear indication of drug use as I located a bong and other paraphernalia consistent with the utilization of illegal, recreational drugs."

"Anything else?"

"Yes, no indication existed of a specific responsible adult who was in charge of taking care of the kids. Six young adults cohabited in the house. All were students with significant responsibilities to their schooling, but no identifiable person who would have primary responsibility for the children's welfare. I found this quite concerning."

"How long did this inspection take?"

"Oh, not long. A few minutes, but I can learn a lot in that amount of time."

"So, what is the next step?"

"After leaving, I wrote up my notes and did an initial evaluation. Here, the welfare of the children did not appear to be in imminent danger. They were being fed and were going to school. The house was reasonably safe. Based on those factors, I did not believe I needed to seek immediate separation. However, I was concerned about their long-term outlook, and I wanted to conduct a more involved investigation."

"How do you do that?"

"Essentially, I schedule a second, planned home visit. This provides me with a better sense of what is happening in the house and allows me to interview the children to determine how they are doing."

"When did that happen?"

"About a month later I returned. Cameron was expecting me and let me into the house. He and his siblings were the only people in the house that day. I spoke with Cameron about his guardian role of the children and how he managed to parent them and also keep up with his schoolwork. I examined the entire house to determine how appropriate the living arrangements were. Finally, I spoke with Ilana and Max to evaluate how they were responding to their particular situations."

"What did you find during that visit?"

"Truth be told, I was rather alarmed. After talking with Cameron, I was not satisfied he understood what it took to raise two high school students. He seemed cavalier. His attitude was 'don't worry, everything will work out.'"

"Anything else?"

"Of course. Cameron relied too heavily on the others living in his house to take on the guardian responsibilities. As he explained it to me, they shared in the tasks involving the children. One person might assume the responsibility for getting the children off to school and another might cook dinner that night. Cameron assumed some of these tasks but no more than anyone else. It appeared that if a crisis arose, the children would have no one who would advocate for them."

"Did you also interview the kids?"

"I did." Cartwright flipped the pages in front of her. "I first spoke with Ilana. She is a kind and smart twelfth grader, who did not appear to have a strong relationship with Cameron. When I talked with her about her activities, she indicated that one of the women in the house had assisted her with dance and that Cameron had taken little time to assist her. She also indicated Cameron was extremely busy with his studies and that she didn't spend significant time with him. Often, she went to bed before her brother returned from his studies."

"What did your interview with Max reveal?"

"Max is a ninth grader who is on the school's basketball team. Here, Cameron seems to have taken an interest and has gone to a few of his basketball games. On the other hand, like Ilana, Max seems to have bonded more with the others in the house than Cameron. For example, the housemate, D'Andre has been training Max for basketball and the other, Marco, has tutored him in several subjects. Again, however, I didn't find much of a bond between the two brothers."

"Ms. Cartwright, what conclusions did you draw from the home inspections you performed?"

She looked down at her notes. "The family has suffered significant tragedies by losing both parents at such a young age. I always base my decisions on the concept of what is in the best interests of the child. Here, I do not believe they are receiving appropriate supervision. Soon after the kids moved into their brother's house, Max went to a party, consumed a significant amount of alcohol, and nearly died in a hospital. I would think that a different family environment with more suitable supervision would be able to prevent this from happening again.

"Based on my visits to the house, clearly alcohol consumption and illicit drug use happens on, at least, a semi-regular basis. I question whether Cameron demonstrates the appropriate behavior so that Max doesn't believe alcohol and drug use is condoned."

Cartwright grabbed the plastic cup which the bailiff had filled with water and took a sip. "The situation with Ilana is a bit more nuanced. She plans on attending college next year, so she would not be spending as much time in a foster situation as her brother would. That said, I believe she would benefit from a more nurturing environment. Without a mother in the house, she is left to copy the behavior of a group of very young adults. I can only imagine what occurs in that house, but I suspect much of the behavior is not the type I would want high school kids to emulate.

"Accordingly, based on my investigation and understanding of the living conditions present at the home, my recommendation to the court is that Max and Ilana Crewell be removed from their present living situation and moved to foster living conditions which would provide a more stable and nurturing environment. In my opinion, it's in the best interests of the two children that they be removed from an environment that likely will be detrimental to their long-term development and into one more conducive to academic growth and emotional support."

"Thank you, Ms. Cartwright. I have no further questions."

Ilana turned and buried her head into Cam's shoulder sobbing. He gently rubbed her head.

CHAPTER FIFTY-EIGHT

EVEN BEFORE BOYLE HAD returned to her seat, the judge eyed Marco and asked, "Cross-examination?"

He stood and shook his arms at his sides to release the tension of his first ever cross-examination. He had a general concept of the rules: Ask leading questions. Don't ask questions where you don't know the answer. The reality of doing this for real, with actual stakes, struck him like a baseball bat to the face. He stepped forward to begin.

"Ms. Cartwright, it's your job to separate kids from their family, isn't it?"

She smirked. "Absolutely not. It's my job to evaluate living situations and make a recommendation as to whether a child would be better off in a different environment. Many times, it is my recommendation that the child stay with the family, perhaps with some modifications, but keeping the family intact. Here, however, I believe the minor children would be better served in a more stable environment."

Marco shook his head recognizing the witness was controlling him when he needed to exert control over her. "Let's get a few facts first. Your decision is based on the two home inspections you undertook?"

"Not just the home inspections, but the investigation and research I also performed."

"Let's focus on the home inspections first. The first one took about ten minutes, didn't it?"

"That's fair. Yes."

"And the second, it took a total of thirty minutes which included the interviews of Cam, Max, and Ilana."

"Probably a little longer, but that's close."

"So, your only interaction with the family totaled less than one hour."

"Correct."

"You never interviewed anyone else in the house, did you?"

"I did not."

"So, you cannot offer any opinion as to whether those individuals might be positive influences on Ilana and Max, can you?"

"Well, what I can say is that it is not optimal to have so many disparate people living under one roof when considering what's in the best interests of the children."

"I understand that the living situation is unusual, but isn't it possible the other members of the house are positive influences on the kids?"

"Perhaps."

"Yet you never considered that possibility."

"Again, given the living arrangements, I believe a dual parent situation without the extra young adults would be much more preferable."

"But it's the policy of the Department that living in a family unit with actual family members is preferable to living without family."

She shifted towards Marco. "True, but often I will recommend moving a child out of a house with family members into a different one without family."

Marco stared back at her. "Will you agree that nothing in their academic performance indicates there is a problem?"

"I suppose you are correct. Both children are doing fine in school."

"In fact, their attendance in school is exemplary, and their grades are actually better this year than they were last year."

"Yes, their grades are marginally better."

"There is no evidence they are being denied any of their basic needs, correct?"

"I'm not sure what you mean."

"Well," Marco looked at his yellow pad, "Both are adequately fed."

"True."

"You made no indication in either of your reports that there was a problem with their diet, in fact, in your report from your second visit you noted, 'regular meals are scheduled.'"

"I did write that, correct."

"So, it may be unclear who is preparing meals, but they are getting adequate nutrition?"

"Yes."

Marco again flipped a page on his pad. "Now, let's talk about Max's night where he ended up in the hospital."

"You mean when he drank too much alcohol?"

"Yes, ma'am." Marco nodded. "Soon after Cameron assumed responsibility for his brother and sister, this unfortunate event happened, didn't it?"

"Yes, it was less than three weeks after they moved into the house."

"Ms. Cartwright, sometimes bad things happen in a family and it's not necessarily the fault of the parents."

"Perhaps."

"Or to put it another way, many other kids have utilized drugs or alcohol and haven't been taken out of their home and placed in foster care."

"True. Drug and alcohol use among high school kids is at high levels."

"More importantly, in many of those instances, the drug use or alcohol use is repetitive, with the kids using either drugs or alcohol on a consistent basis."

"Certainly, many kids consistently consume drugs or alcohol."

"But here, Max made a mistake, and drank too much alcohol, but did it once. You have no indication Max ever drank alcohol again, or ever used drugs at any point."

"That is true, but as he demonstrated, even one time where alcohol is misused by a young person, significant deleterious consequences can arise."

"Ms. Cartwright, this may be true, but Cam did what a good parent should do after a significant mistake and educated Max on the potential dangers of alcohol and made sure there wasn't a second mistake."

"I guess that's true."

Marco nodded. "Good. Now regarding Ilana, you have no reports of any issues, do you? No reports have been made to the police about her, have they?"

"No."

"And no trips to the hospital."

"I am not aware of any."

"In fact, there haven't been any reports from the principal at her school and nothing but praise from her teachers, true?"

"Yes, you are correct."

"Ms. Cartwright, if Max and Ilana were living with their parents, you would never recommend putting them in foster care, would you?"

"Absolutely not."

"So, the reason you claim they should be taken out of their home is because they are currently living in a non-traditional setting."

Cartwright scooted forward "Let me reiterate. Living in a house with six young adults where none of them takes primary responsibility for their welfare and where the young adults are focused at running their own lives rather than supervising the lives of the two youths, I believe is detrimental to their development. In a home where two adults are charged with their care and who focus on their care, this is a better situation for their development than their current situation. Absolutely."

Marco mentally kicked himself for asking one too many questions. He said, "Thank you ma'am. I do not have any further questions."

Helen Cartwright walked off the witness stand offering a smile to the Crewell children. No one returned her smile.

CHAPTER FIFTY-NINE

THE ANNOUNCEMENT, CALLED OUT with what seemed like undue emphasis, disoriented Cam, sending a gut-wrenching wave of nausea through his body. It was so unexpected, causing its effects to hit that much harder.

"We call Miranda Crewell to testify."

As Cam searched for her, Ilana squeezed his knee so hard he almost squealed.

Marco flipped through his notes and examined the pretrial list of witnesses the County had filed. He shook his head and leaned over to Sophia, "They listed her as a potential witness. We just never thought they would actually call her. You'll have to figure out a way to cross her."

Her face contorted into a wince. "Awesome," she muttered. She slammed her binder. "No outline. We're screwed here."

Marco placed a hand on her back as Miranda walked in through the side door of the courtroom and took a direct path to the witness stand without allowing her eyes to waver from her destination. Her chiffon skirt, cut just above her knees, swayed with each step she took. The sheer emerald blouse, contoured to her body, was neither too tight nor overly loose. Her low, clunky box heeled shoes, which exposed the sides and tops of her feet, made a marked tapping sound as she walked.

Even though he was thirty feet away from her, Cam swore the same flowery scent he had detected at their last dinner when she told him they were on their own wafted over him.

She brushed the front of her skirt as she sat.

"Please state your name," Boyle requested after she was sworn in.

"Miranda Crewell." She took a sip of water.

"Where do you live?"

"Right now, I am living in a small house in San Diego, California.

Boyle stood in front of her and allowed her arm movements to mimic Miranda's. "Mrs. Crewell, what is your relationship with Cameron, Ilana, and Max Crewell?"

"I married their father a little more than three years ago. Although I was not their mother, she died a few years before I met Henry, I was their stepmother."

"As their stepmother, how was your relationship with the children?"

"I would say it was okay. I tried." She sighed. "I never wanted to replace their mom, but I always wanted to serve as a proper role model and exercise appropriate guidance for their development."

"Were you able to be a proper role model?"

A grimace crossed her face. "No, I was never given a chance. They're good kids, but they told me they didn't want another mother. I was not replacing their mother, but I was one of the adults in the house. They were out of control and wanted to impose their will on everyone. Henry, their father, was a good man, but he couldn't control them. My understanding is that their mom was the one who was in charge, but when she passed away, Henry lost all control."

"Please explain what happened in the house."

"It was hard. They didn't do anything overtly criminal, but they had no interest in listening. They basically told their dad what they would do and then did it. I tried to impose a little order in the house, but there were too many of them."

"Mrs. Crewell, would Cameron be able to run a house and offer a reasonable home for Max and Ilana?"

With added vigor, she scoffed. "Seriously? He was the one who was most out of control. He wasn't around much because he was supposed to be at college, but he seemed to be home more than at school. He never did anything but complain, that is, except when he was up in his room getting high."

"Please explain further."

"Well, he never did anything to help around the house. His room was a mess when he was there. Meals, he always expected them to be cooked for him, but never did anything to help make them or clean up from them. Being in charge of the other two, well, I didn't see him offer anything to those two while I was in the house. I can't imagine what he could offer them now."

"What about the other two?"

"Again, they are nice kids, but..." She paused and gazed up at the ceiling. "I don't know what to say, they need a lot of attention. Ilana is always asking questions. Needs lots of rides. I wouldn't say she has much independence. Max is sullen, lost in his thoughts. He needs so much guidance to do his homework, figure out his schedule. He has trouble just figuring out where he is supposed to be."

Boyle stepped closer to Miranda. "So, based on what you observed while you lived in their house, would Cameron be able to run a household and offer sufficient supervision to Ilana and Max?"

Her eyes narrowed as she glanced to the side and when her eyes returned forward her face had no expression, only a cold stare directed towards the back of the courtroom. "Could he run a household? I don't think so. He's so into himself, I'm not so sure he has any idea what's going on in their lives. His dad was so worried he wouldn't make it through college, so I guess it's a good thing he's getting his life together. Running their lives, I got to believe the court has a lot of options which would be much better for them."

Boyle stepped back. "Thank you and no further questions."

Judge Laskey leaned forward. "Cross examination."

Sophia stood, her brow etched with lines. "Your honor, may we have a few minutes to confer with our clients?"

The judge nodded. "We'll resume in ten minutes." She slammed her gavel.

———

IN THE HALLWAY, Sophia smacked her hand against the wall and muttered something inaudible. Marco approached, but kept silent, waiting for her to talk. He didn't have to wait long. "Shit." She smacked the wall again. "This is the first witness I have ever cross-examined, and I have nothing prepared." Rapid bursts of breath escaped her mouth.

Marco leaned over her. "You've just got to show that she doesn't know anything about the family, especially anything about how the family has been doing since she left."

She rolled her eyes. "Great. I'll just snap my fingers and she'll cower because I'm so freaking intimidating. This is going to be humiliating."

Others from the courtroom passed by, but Professor Hawkins stopped to join them. "This happens at trial. A witness surprises you with their testimony. How can we solve it?"

Sophia's eyes welled up. She shrugged her shoulders. "Why did she come to this hearing? What does she have to gain from this?"

As she finished her thought, Cam joined. His clenched jaw accentuated the redness of cheeks. "I may have some stuff that will help," he said.

"What do you have?"

"I have some e-mails and a few other documents. Give me a couple of minutes so I can highlight some of the relevant portions. It might help."

"I hope so, Cam. She's looking pretty credible right now, which means you're not."

Professor Hawkins patted Sophia on the back. "Good. You might have to do some quick thinking on your feet. You can do it."

Cam ran down the hallway holding up his phone and yelled, "I'll send you some good stuff. Use it."

Sophia shook her head. "It better be good dude, or your case is shot," she whispered in a voice so quiet she was the only one who heard it.

CHAPTER SIXTY

GOOD MORNING, MRS. CREWELL," Sophia said, hesitating because she still was not quite sure what to ask or where to start.

"Good morning," Miranda said with a pleasant, almost robotic smile, as if she had never met Sophia.

"Had you ever been married before your marriage to Mr. Crewell?"

"I was. For about four years."

"It ended in divorce, didn't it?"

"Yes, it did."

"You didn't have any kids, so you had no experience raising them."

"True, but I was really looking forward to getting to know them. I thought I had a lot to offer them, if they were willing to listen."

"Isn't it true, that you had no interest in being a parent to these kids?"

Miranda's head shot back. "Oh, no, that's not true. Henry and I were a team and I so wanted to help raise his kids. It's just that they wouldn't let me."

Sophia looked at her pad, but nothing jumped out to help her find a path forward. As she thumbed through the pages, a small ping rang out from Marco's phone laying on counsel table behind two books. He tapped it and his eyes widened as he read. He jumped out of his seat and handed the phone to Sophia. She studied it until a smile crept across her face.

She turned her attention back to Miranda. "Mrs. Crewell, you said you so wanted to raise the kids, but let me show you an email you wrote to Cam a week after his dad died."

"Objection," Boyle yelled. "We've never been provided this document. And using their phone to show a witness evidence is improper."

The judge leaned forward. "Given this is cross-examination I will give counsel some latitude. I will allow her to show Mrs. Crewell the email so long as hard copies are provided to the court by the end of this hearing."

Sophia nodded. "We will, Your Honor." She walked towards Miranda and handed her the phone. "This is an email you sent to Cam, isn't it?"

"Yes, ma'am. It is."

"And it says in the second paragraph, 'I know I haven't been much of a mom to you. That wasn't supposed to be my role. Your dad wanted to be the parent. I wanted to be his wife. I know you don't understand, but that's how we both planned it.' I read that correctly, didn't I?"

"Yes."

"So, one week after Cam's father died, you admitted that you never requested the role of mother to these kids and never really tried to be a parent."

"I guess you could say that."

Sophia stopped in her tracks. "I didn't say that, you did."

"I guess."

Marco's phone dinged again causing Sophia to lift it up and stare at it. She raised her head. "Mrs. Crewell, you testified that Cam never helped out and essentially just hung out in his room when he was home. Let me read from another email you sent Cam after his dad died. You wrote, didn't you, 'Cam, you are a wonderful young man. I know losing your dad hurts, but you are strong. I haven't been around the family for a long time, but I loved spending time with you and appreciate all your help in making my time with the family better.'"

She held the phone up to Miranda. "Yes, that's what I wrote, but that was right after his dad died. Of course, I'm going to say nice things to him." She shrugged.

"Mrs. Crewell," Sophia move a step closer, "do you have any emails or letters or any documentation to support your contention that Cameron did nothing in the house?"

Miranda turned her head towards the judge. "I didn't realize I was supposed to bring anything with me."

"So, the answer is 'no,' you don't have any."

She nodded, "I guess so."

Sophia glanced at her phone again and a near-smirk appeared on her face. "I have two more documents to go over with you. The first is an email you sent to Cam while he was at college a year before his dad died. Tell me if I've read this correctly. 'Just wanted to let you know how proud I am of you and what you have accomplished. You are doing so well at school and your dad couldn't be happier. You seem to have everything under control, and you do it all so effortlessly. The picture you sent of your dorm shows how organized you are. I see big things in your future.'"

Sophia moved back in front of Miranda. "Did I read that correctly?"

"You did."

Sophia stepped back to counsel table. "Last matter." She

again looked at the phone and then allowed herself to smile. "When your husband Henry died, he had a will, didn't he?"

"He did."

"And as part of the will, there was a trust, wasn't there?"

"Yes, I believe so."

"According to Paragraph nine of the trust, you receive four thousand dollars every month, don't you?"

"That sounds right."

"I'm going to read from that Paragraph of the trust and again, please let me know if I've read it accurately. 'The monthly allowance is paid to provide for the expenses associated with caring for and raising my three children.'"

"Yes, that's accurate."

"And it continues, 'If Miranda is to die prematurely, or for any other reason, and my son Cameron assumes responsibility for caring for the two minor children, then the monthly allowance shall be paid to Cameron for expenses associated with raising the other kids. If Cameron does not assume responsibility for raising the kids, Miranda shall receive the monthly allowance until she dies.' Did I read that accurately?"

"I think so." She waved her hand in the air. "I just don't understand those legal documents."

"Mrs. Crewell, by the terms of your husband's trust, you will lose four thousand dollars every month if Cameron becomes the legal guardian of Ilana and Max?"

Miranda's hand shot up to her mouth. "I have no idea about what that document says. I just came here today to tell the truth."

Sophia mumbled, "I'm sure," and then said for everyone to hear, "No further questions."

Boyle stood. "Your Honor, can we take a five-minute break so we can finalize our evidence?"

The judge nodded and announced a quick break.

BACK IN THE HALLWAY, Sophia beamed as she conferred with Cam. "Damn, you kept sending those documents to Marco's phone with the important parts highlighted. All I had to do was read them. It was like you were doing the cross-examining, not me."

Cam responded, "If I was questioning her, it would have gotten physical. You showed much more restraint than I ever could have." He shook his head. "The bitch tries to surprise us by showing up at this hearing. Never said 'hi' or 'bye.' Hope to never have to be in her presence again."

Sophia turned to Max and Ilana who approached. "You two ready? I think they might be done with witnesses. Max, you're up first. Can you handle it?"

Max's gaze remained on his shoes. "Sure," he mumbled.

Sophia bit her lip. "Don't worry," Ilana said, "we're both ready." Sophia forced a hopeful smile.

CHAPTER SIXTY-ONE

THE SUIT RODE A LITTLE high, exposing his black socks and suggesting a recent growth spurt. The spots of acne on his cheek revealed his adolescence. The inability to look anyone in the eye on his way to the witness stand belied his terror. Max stood six-foot-two, but slunk low when seated in a futile attempt to disappear.

Marco dove right in to lessen the opportunity for Max's nerves to take over completely.

"Please tell the judge your name."

"Max Crewell," he said, although nobody in the courtroom heard because his head pointed down at the floor and his voice was directed at his feet. The court reporter threw up her hands to signal the judge she was unable to transcribe his testimony.

The judge leaned over the witness box. "Mr. Crewell, you will need to keep your voice up so we all can hear you. Pull the microphone closer. That will help." She offered a smile. Max responded with an undetectable one of his own, his eyes still focused downward.

"Max," Marco began again, "everyone wants to hear what

you have to say, but you have to speak up for that to happen." Max's head lifted a bit, so Marco continued. "Tell everyone where you live."

Max gave the address of the house where he grew up and then corrected himself offering the address for the home where they lived now. Marco followed by asking about his schooling and how life in high school was for him. As he answered a few questions, his body lost a bit of the lingering rigidity and his head lifted allowing him to take in some of the supporting faces in the courtroom.

"I want to ask you about some difficult times right after your dad died."

"Go ahead."

"Well, tell us what it was like for you after he died."

"He died last year, right at the end of the summer. I was really sad. I love my dad. We had his funeral, and the house was kind of empty without him. Is this what you want?"

"Sure, keep going."

"I expected that things would kind of be like they were before—just without my dad."

"What happened?"

"Apparently, Miranda, you just heard her, she didn't want to stay anymore, and she didn't want to take care of us."

"So what happened?"

"Ilana and I had to figure out where to live. Well, that's not quite right. I had no idea what to do, so Cam figured things out and had us move in with him."

"Is that what you wanted?"

"I wanted everything to be like ordinary, but they weren't. I wanted to live in my normal house, but we couldn't do that. What else could we do?"

"How was moving into Cam's house?"

"Really weird. It didn't feel like our house at first, like we were visitors. I didn't know his roommates very well. So, I just hung in my room most of the time."

"Did it improve?"

"Absolutely. My room was pretty much like mine at my old house, only bigger. School started so I didn't spend as much time at home and had more things to do with my friends and at school. Soon, it started to become like home. Cam's roommates are really cool. They moved out from upstairs and let the three of us have the three bedrooms up there. They've all been great. Kind of like aunts and uncles. We respect them, but they don't always act like our parents."

"What do you mean by that?"

"It's just that they are all so good to us. Ilana spends a lot of time with the girls. And all the guys have been helpful to me. D'Andre, he worked with me day-after-day playing basketball and making me a better player. He made me get up early and we would go down to the park and he would work with me. He didn't have to, but he did. Then I made the basketball team at school, which I never would have been able to do without him."

"So, tell us Max, is it good having all of these young adults in the house?"

Max smiled for the first time. "When Miranda kicked us out of the house, it was the hardest time in my life. Worse than when my mom died because I felt like I had no one left. Cam was dealing with his feelings at first. So, yeah, I didn't want to move into the house, but right away everyone in the house started looking out for us and making sure we were okay. We needed that. Now, I'm not sure what I would call everyone, but they have been so great."

"Let's talk about Cam. How has he been since your dad died?"

"Like I said, right after my dad died, he had his own stuff to deal with. He was starting law school. We didn't have a place to live. He figured everything out and made a plan. He's our brother, not our dad, but he's the one in charge. He's made a plan for us and made sure we did well in school. He tried to keep us out of trouble, but at first I messed that up."

"What do you mean?"

"I screwed up. We had just moved into the new house. I was hanging out with some friends, and they got some alcohol. I drank some—a lot. I ended up in the hospital. Almost died." His voice got quiet.

"Why did it happen?"

He shook his head. "I don't know. It just did. It's all my fault."

"Why?"

"Because I did it. It wasn't because of Cam. It was just stupid. It would have happened no matter where I was living."

"Have you done any drinking since then?"

"None. Cam has made sure of that."

"How about next year?"

"I learned my lesson. No."

Marco walked over to the table and glanced at some notes and then walked back to where he was standing. "How are your grades this semester?"

Max's head bobbed side-to-side. "Not bad. High school's a lot harder than middle school, but I'm working at it, and my grades are better than last year."

"Good. Tell us about studying at the house."

"Sure. Cam makes us study every night. We're supposed to do our homework when we get home from school. I'm not great about doing that, but once Cam gets back from his classes, we make dinner. He usually doesn't make me clean up much so I can do my homework. I'm not allowed to do anything after we eat until my homework is done. He tries to check it each night, but if he can't someone else in the house will."

"Good. Let me ask you one last question, would you be better off in another house with other adults as guardians?"

Max looked back down at his feet, but then raised his eyes to meet Marco's. "There is no way that living anywhere else would be better for us. All six of the adults in that house worry about us and take care of us. We are better off with the way things are now."

Marco started to follow up, but instead said, "Thank you Max. I have no further questions."

Boyle stood and peered at her notes. She understood that she should take caution with cross-examining members of certain populations but couldn't decide whether Max fell into any. Her heels clicked against the floor as she walked towards the witness.

"You ended up in the hospital, didn't you, after you drank all of that alcohol with your friends?"

"Yes."

"You almost died, didn't you?"

"I guess."

"You were a ninth grader, fifteen years old and you were out drinking with your buddies."

"Yes."

"That night you left the house and your brother, who was in charge, had no idea where you were going, did he?"

"I guess not." Max's eyes were once again cast downward towards the floor.

"He wasn't acting like a father that night. He had studying to do."

"I don't remember what he was doing. I just wanted to go hang out with my friends."

"Max, wouldn't you agree that if you had a real parent that night, one who was focused on your needs and your safety that you wouldn't have ended up in the hospital?"

He shook his head. "What I did was stupid, I know that. It wasn't Cam's fault. It was totally mine. It probably would have happened no matter who was watching out for me. If my dad was still alive, it would have happened the same way."

Boyle paused and then asked, "Isn't it true that your brother is often busy with his studies? He has classes and has to study at night."

"Sure. He has lots of responsibilities."

"Well, doesn't that mean that he doesn't have enough time to make sure your needs are taken care of?"

Max looked at the ceiling. "No. I don't think so." He lowered his eyes and met Boyle's gaze. "Like I said, he has lots of responsibilities, but one of them is us. We always have food. Our laundry gets done—sometimes even by us. There's always someone to make sure we do our homework or if we need to be somewhere that we have a ride. I think Cam's done a pretty good job of making sure that we are okay."

Boyle opened her mouth to ask another question, but responded, "Thanks Max. That's all of the questions I have."

Marco stood quickly and said, "We have no further questions."

The judge wasted no time in announcing, "Please call your next witness."

CHAPTER SIXTY-TWO

SOPHIA ROSE. "WE CALL Ilana Crewell as our next witness." Ilana approached the witness stand in her suit, her hair pulled back from her face, to be sworn in. A smile born of overwrought nerves and a need to be heard took over her face. She told the court her name and gave her address.

Sophia lowered her head to ask, "Tell us what it's like living in the house where you moved after your dad died."

"Truthfully, I was really happy when we moved in. A little nervous maybe, but I was happy to be moving to a house where we were wanted."

Sophia took a step back to allow her to say more. "And..."

"And I was glad to be moving out of our old house. Both of my parents died when we lived there, and then Miranda said she had no interest in us. It kind of ruined all my memories of the house. I didn't want to stay anymore."

"I understand. So, what was it like moving into the new house?"

"A little crazy at first. We had to pack and move in like two days. All of Cam's friends got the house ready for us. We have the three bedrooms on the top floor. They made us feel welcomed."

Sophia smiled. "How?"

"It was the little things. Somebody put a stuffed bear on my bed with a note telling me how excited they were we would be living in the house. It made me feel like I wasn't an intruder. The bear still sleeps in my bed with me."

"Anything else?"

Ilana squirmed. Memories of the days after her dad died and the feelings of loneliness and rejection flooded back to her. "It's just that they've never acted like we shouldn't be living in the house. Never said anything nasty about us. Once we moved in, they acted like it was our house too."

"How has it been since then?"

Ilana offered a smile and Sophia couldn't help but smile back. "It's been pretty great. Not perfect. When test time came around, it was pretty stressful. Max and I had midterms at the same time they had their first big tests. The tension was kind of thick for a few days."

"Tell me about your relationships with Cam's friends."

Ilana slid forward in her seat and turned to face the judge. "What can I say? They've been awesome. I'm probably closer to the women, like Max's closer to the boys." She found Kate in her seat and caught her eye. "All of them have been great to me, sort of like having three aunts always around to help me. One, in particular..." her words stuck in her throat. She grabbed the plastic cup and took a sip. "One of the women, I just connected with her. She helped me with school and with my friends, but mostly she understood what I was going through. I hadn't had that since my mom died."

She didn't let her gaze waver from Kate, who pulled a tissue out of her bag and dabbed at her eyes.

"Ilana, are Cam's friends in charge of you?"

She rolled her eyes to the ceiling. "That's not an easy question to answer. They aren't my parents, but the way things are, if they ask me to do something, I'll do it. I respect them enough that I listen to them. I guess what I'm saying is that in many ways it's better than them being my parents. I know they are looking out for me, but I can talk to them in a way I never could with my parents." She shrugged. "Is that a good answer?"

"You're doing fine." Sophia glanced down at her notes. "Let's talk about your brother. What's his role in the house and in your life?"

"He's my brother," she said without irony, like it was the most obvious answer. "He'll always be my brother, but since my dad died, it's different. He's in charge of us and that's changed the way he is and how he acts around us. It used to be when he lived at home that he would just leave whenever he wanted. He never told anyone where he would be and we never knew when he would be coming back. Now, we know when he'll be home. He tells us what his schedule is at school so we can all plan around it. If he's not going to be home, he'll figure out who can help us if we need it. It's a lot for him to do."

"And how well is he doing it?"

Ilana shrugged, her lips closing tight. "I've never had to worry about being a parent or being responsible for anyone other than me. Now he has to worry about his grades, but also mine and Max's. I think he must be doing a pretty good job. It just seems natural, like this is the way it's supposed to be. Living at the house isn't perfect, but for me, it's now my home."

Sophia sat back at counsel and said, "Ilana, I don't have any more questions for you."

Boyle brushed the hair out of her face when she stood while also trying to adjust her glasses which only made it appear like she was smacking her own face. She walked three

269

steps towards Ilana and then retreated back to where she had been.

"Can I call you Ilana?"

Ilana nodded.

"Ilana, will you agree that your brother is too young to be raising kids?"

Ilana let out a small huff of air. Her eyes lifted and her face emitted an unintended glow. "That's not an easy question to answer with a yes or no. Of course, under normal circumstances Cam wouldn't be raising kids right now. You've pointed out he has a lot going on. I think being a first-year law student is really difficult and it would be better if he could focus entirely on just that. Our parents always stressed our education and told us to wait until finishing our studies before starting a family. Pretty good advice, I think. But that was in a perfect situation, which of course we are not in."

Boyle let Ilana finish her answer while looking down at her feet and when she was done talking lifted her head to ask her next question. "Wouldn't being in a house with two parents able to focus their attention on you be better for you?"

"In some ways maybe, but overall no. Sure, it would be nice to have people focused on me, but I don't think it's real. It would be great if both of my parents were alive, but that's not happening. Cam is doing his best for us and himself. He's doing a lot of the same things that our parents did and is, I think, trying to make decisions like they would."

"Ilana, your parents wouldn't have let Max drink himself into the hospital, would they?"

Ilana clenched her jaw while her face turned crimson. "That's so unfair. Yes, it's horrible what happened. Who knows what would have happened if my parents were alive." She pointed a finger at Boyle. "You don't. It was bad, but I can tell you that we all learned from it. And again, I think this is what my parents would have wanted. They always told us that we would make mistakes, but they wanted us to learn from them. It's clear that both Max and Cam learned from what happened to him. So, I think my parents would have been okay with how Cam responded." Ilana folded her arms across her chest.

Boyle thumbed through her pad, but recognized Ilana wouldn't budge in her assessment of her family situation. "I have no more questions," Boyle said before turning to take her seat.

With a serious scowl plastered on her face, Ilana left the witness stand. As she passed by counsel table, Sophia lifted her head and gave her a quick wink. Ilana offered a subdued smile and then took her seat.

CHAPTER SIXTY-THREE

BACK IN HIGH SCHOOL, when his emotions controlled most of his actions, Cam would sit in the rear of a classroom wanting to pay attention, but always thinking about anything other than the day's lesson. His inability to focus combined with his desire to escape destroyed his GPA and inhibited his ability to get a sniff from a decent college. Walking to the witness stand he felt the familiar urge to withdraw, to avoid conflict and run. He managed to do what he couldn't do when he was younger and pushed the feelings to the back part of his consciousness.

He settled in the witness chair and forced a smile.

"What's your name?" Sophia asked, standing back near her counsel table to offer Cam the spotlight.

"Cameron Crewell. Ilana and Max are my sister and brother." He turned his head a bit towards the judge, who continued to take notes.

"Mr. Crewell, are you the guardian of Ilana and Max?"

Cam shrugged. "I'm not sure what that means legally. I've never been appointed guardian, but since my dad died, I do everything in my power to make sure they are okay. They are my responsibility."

"Tell us about your home life and how you take care of your responsibilities towards them."

"You've heard a lot of it already. At the beginning of law school, I lived in a house with five other first years. My dad died and his wife Miranda left town. That left no one responsible for my brother and sister. We thought about finding a different place to live, just the three of us, but there really wasn't any way I could afford a new house. My housemates were cool and wanted to help out, so they kind of redid the house and the three of us now live on the third floor and the rest of them live of the second floor."

"What did you do to make sure Max and Ilana were okay?"

Cam squirmed and swiped at his hair. "It was really hard at first. We were all hurting after my dad died. Never expected it, but we had to deal with it, because Miranda wouldn't." His eyes scanned the courtroom. but couldn't find her. He mumbled, "She's gone again. Just leaving her destruction."

Sophia stepped forward to redirect him. "Tell us more about what you did to make the transition easier."

"First, we all made sure they were comfortable in the house. We got all their stuff and set up their rooms. Pretty much like they were in the old house. We wanted the third floor to be our private area. Which, for the most part, it has been. Everybody in the house has been really respectful."

"What else did you do right at the beginning?"

"I had to make sure they were good at school. They didn't have to transfer, but I made sure the school knew how to contact me with any issues. I talked to every one of their teachers, so they had my contact information if they needed to talk. I made sure they were up to date on doctors' appointments and going to the dentist. Things like that."

"And then how did things progress after that?"

"It's hard to describe. I just had to make sure we were on top of everything. I set up a schedule for when they were supposed to do their homework. I made sure someone was always home to help them with their assignments or to get them to where they needed to be. I had to be more mindful of food in the house, so we set up a schedule for cooking. Everybody had a day of the week where they were responsible for making sure there were meals for everyone. Ilana and Max have to cook every Sunday for the whole house. It actually helped all of us knowing we would be eating dinner together most of the time."

"You make it sound easy. Was it?"

A scoff escaped from Cam's mouth. "Of course not. It was really hard. I didn't have much of a clue of what I was doing. I hadn't been a parent before and never even thought about being one. I made a lot of mistakes and I still make a lot of mistakes. Every time I think of Max in the hospital, I feel horrific. I was responsible for him." His voice trailed off. "But," he began again, "I've learned from everything that's happened."

"Cam, how would it be if you brother and sister were moved to a new home?"

Cam paused to gather his thoughts before turning his body to face the judge. "It would be the absolute worst outcome for them. And for me. I understand this is not the perfect situation and I'm not the perfect parent. But this is so much better than splitting us up. I don't care if you have the greatest parents in the world ready to step in, it would be much worse for them."

He pointed to Ilana and Max. "They are thriving in our house. I'm not sure why and I wouldn't have planned it this way, but our house—our home—is the best place for them."

He took a deep breath and crossed his arms.

"I don't have any further questions," Sophia said.

BOYLE'S SHOULDER slumped when she stood to face Cam. She brushed her skirt away as she picked up her notes. "You agree you've made some mistakes, don't you?"

Cam nodded. "Yes, I just said that."

She glanced at her notes. "You were making mistakes in high school, long before either of your parents passed away."

Cam's eyes narrowed and his lips tightened. "Yes. I've made lots of mistakes, haven't you?"

Boyle ignored the question. "Let's go through a partial list of your problems in high school. Suspended ninth grade for getting into a fight. Suspended in tenth grade for yelling at a teacher. On academic probation in eleventh grade. Nearly flunked out."

"Yes," he spit out before taking a deep breath. "Those are all true, but it ignores that I managed to get my act together by twelfth grade. Made academic honors and got myself into a decent college."

Boyle gritted her teeth. "True, but then you managed to find yourself back on academic probation in college and had to take a year off."

"You want to go through all of this? Fine, but let's paint an accurate picture. I had trouble in college at first keeping up academically. Probably because I didn't prepare myself properly in high school. I dropped out after a year. I worked fifty hours a week and after that year was better prepared to deal with college. I went back. Worked hard and got myself into one of the top law schools in the country."

He glared at Boyle and said before she had time to ask another question, "You know what? My problems in high school have helped me with Ilana and Max. I want them to learn from my mistakes. I'm pretty open about them and we talk about how they can avoid repeating what I did wrong."

"How about your drug use?"

"What about it?" Cam shot back.

"You've had problems with drug use before, haven't you?"

"I wouldn't put it that way, but again, I will try to be as transparent as possible." He shifted forward in his seat. "In high school I smoked weed. In my first year at college, I smoked a lot of weed. My smoking was a significant contributing factor in my failing grades my first year. When I got home, I got my act together and essentially stopped smoking."

"Essentially?"

"I smoked a few times once I returned to college. Nothing since I started law school." He stared straight at Boyle unblinking.

"Will you agree that drug use continues to occur in your house, even since your brother and sister moved in?"

Cam scoffed again. "What I can tell you is I haven't done anything since I started law school. Also, neither my sister nor my brother have done anything since I've been watching out for them."

"Mrs. Cartwright found evidence of drug use during her house inspections."

"She saw a bong. She has no idea if anyone ever used it."

"Let me be direct, have any of your housemates used any form of recreational drug while your brother and sister have been living in the house?"

Cam continued to stare. "And let me be equally as direct, there has been nothing that anyone has done in the house that is illegal or improper while Ilana or Max have been around."

"There's beer in the house, isn't there?"

"Yes, and we are all over twenty-one."

"It's available for Ilana and Max, right?"

"No. They know not to touch it."

"Yet, when you were in charge, you let Max drink so much alcohol he ended up in the hospital."

Cam forced himself to speak with deliberation. "He didn't get any beer from the house. He drank with his friends. It was stupid—and scary. The good thing about it is that he's learned his lesson. He hasn't touched alcohol since. Yes, I take responsibility for what happened, and I've made sure it won't happen again."

"Mr. Crewell," Boyle said with equal deliberation, "how can you be so sure? You're in law school and busy so much of the time. You have a job offer in another city for the summer. High school kids are unpredictable. You have to be there for your brother, so I ask you again, how can you be so sure?"

Without hesitation, but without rushing, Cam said, "Because my mom, my dad, and I have raised him right. He's not perfect, but he's learning all the time. And since my dad died, I have noticed a maturity in him that wasn't there before. So yeah, I know it's not going to happen again."

Cam looked out and caught Max's gaze and locked on it. Boyle stepped back and said, "I have no further questions."

The judge looked at Sophia. "We rest," she said before taking her seat. She reached and touched Cam's arm.

The courtroom was quiet with the recognition of near finality. Judge took off her glasses and announced. "We will take a fifteen-minute break. Generally, I do not need closing arguments from counsel. I have listened to all the evidence, and I have reviewed both parties' pretrial submissions. I am aware of the issues and the positions of both sides. When I return, I will inform you of my decision."

CHAPTER SIXTY-FOUR

SOPHIA BOLTED INTO THE HALLWAY, her head jerking side-to-side trying to find Cam. The verdict was impending, and she wanted to check on Cam's state of mind. He desperately wanted to win, yet he hadn't been forthcoming with his feelings prior to the hearing. Her lack of experience clouded her ability to predict how the judge would rule and her emotions roiled inside of her, causing a wave of despair to rise from her gut. Without a clue as to how Cam would react to a good or bad result, she quick-walked past the elevators wanting to tell Cam how well he had testified, yet brace him for any conceivable result.

She moved past empty offices and into an area more deserted than the area near the courtroom. In a far corner, she overheard hushed voices. As she got closer, she saw three silhouetted figures lumped together. Even without much lighting, she recognized the Crewells, clung together, barely making any sound. The noises coming from them nearly broke her heart.

Ilana made some primitive sounding moans as she cried on

Cam's shoulder. Max wheezed as he hyperventilated while holding Ilana's hand. Realizing there was nothing she could say to ease their fear, Sophia turned to return to the courtroom.

———

THE LATE AFTERNOON sun caused long shadows to drift down the walls of the courtroom. A low hum from the many whispered conversations hung in the air until the door at the front opened and the judge re-entered carrying a sheath of papers. She trotted up the steps and took her seat. She grabbed a pair of glasses resting next to her and put them on while organizing her papers.

Everyone took their seats. "I have listened to all of the evidence," she began, "and have reached a decision." She spoke without raising her voice, almost apologetically, eyes alternating between the three lawyers. "I will give you my ruling from the bench and follow up with a written opinion. But my decision today will remain final."

Cam, Ilana, and Max leaned into each other, waiting for finality. Sophia half-turned and put a hand on Cam's knee. They all tightened their lips.

"I have been a judge for fifteen years," the judge continued, "and this case has proven to be perhaps the most elusive I've handled. The standard I must follow is 'what is in the best interests of the children,' and that is the standard that guides me in reaching my decision.

"So, what is in the best interests of Ilana and Max? Clearly, having two engaged parents who have the time, energy, and resources to give to the kids is the best option. Cam Crewell did not set out to be a parent and his life is not structured for being a parent. He is a law student and I understand what it takes to be a law student. It takes a commitment of time and energy of

279

huge proportions just to manage the commitments of attending school. To do law school right, a student must maintain a certain selfishness and dedication to study to get through.

"Yes, Cam's roommates have agreed to act in pseudo-parental roles to try to fill in the gaps when Cam is not available. It's admirable, but no one would argue that it's optimal. They have no legal obligation to protect the minors and the court has no real enforcement mechanisms to make sure the roommates fulfill whatever promises they have made to look after and protect Ilana and Max.

"And of course, having minors live in a house with six young adults is fraught with danger. In her visits to the house, Ms. Cartwright found evidence of drug use. Now the court is not prudish, and it recognizes what happens in real life, even if it can't condone it, but this sort of conduct is much more likely to occur in this type of environment than in a more traditional setting.

"The problems inherent in this type of living situation played out immediately. The court must note that Max had to be taken to the hospital after excessive consumption of alcohol and the court finds that this resulted from the lack of structure which existed in the house at the time this occurred.

"In sum, this court has major reservations about the nature of the living environment in general and about many of the specifics existing in the home presently. I would well be within my powers and could easily justify removing the two minors from the house, based solely on these issues."

She stopped and looked up to find a silent courtroom. The three Crewell kids huddled waiting for the court to impose its judgment. "Before I can remove any of the children from the house, I must consider all the facts. As I stated, this is an unusual situation, but simply because it's different, does not automatically guide my decision. "

She leaned forward and looked at Cam. "I must take notice of the following: Despite the demands of law school, the evidence suggests you are an active presence in the lives of your brother and sister. They have testified that you are a positive influence and I agree with their assessment. Up to now you have had no legal obligation to assume the care of them, yet you have accepted that responsibility.

"You are young, and in ordinary circumstances I would shy away from putting kids under your care. But there is also no doubt that they have responded to you as the head of your household and accept your authority. This is no small feat. Moreover, there is clearly love between all of you which I cannot ignore. In fact, one of our guiding principles is not to upset the status quo when the status quo is working."

The judge took her glasses off and spoke directly to the family without reading. "I have accepted that this is an unusual situation, but I also recognize that I cannot be a slave to potentially outdated concepts. I find that despite all its peculiarities, this situation is presently the best one for Ilana and Max. I am ruling that they are to stay in their current living situation and that Cameron Crewell will be appointed legal guardian until the minor children reach the age of majority."

Cam stared wide-eyed at his sister, who threw her hands over her mouth. Within moments she had engulfed him with a huge, body-encasing hug. Max buried his head in his hands and let his head fall onto Cam's shoulder. Everyone in the courtroom watched as they enjoyed their moment.

Without an overwhelming desire to tamp down the outbreak of enthusiasm, the judge tapped her gavel allowing people to shift their focus back to her. "I understand the outburst, but I still have more to say." She allowed a small smile to crack the edges of her mouth. "Mr. Crewell, the court has confidence in your ability to provide guidance and supervision

281

in the house. That said, the court's confidence is bounded by the realities it has witnessed where seemingly stable environments implode and families, once rock solid, begin to split apart. With that in mind, the court will continue to exercise its supervisory responsibilities over you. I'm ordering Ms. Cartwright to conduct four inspections per year to ensure that you continue to abide by the court's rules. She will report back to me and if necessary, I will order further hearings."

She looked over the top of her glasses at Cam. "Generally, I look to maintain the status quo, but trust me, I will move your brother and sister if you do not meet my standards." She glared at Cam, who nodded.

"I will also want to address the issue of money. Your father's will appears to have provided money to the person who has legal responsibility for the children. I am ruling you are that person. Although this is not the subject of this hearing, and I am not making any rulings regarding the applicability of any provision of the will, I am ruling that you are the legal guardian of the two minor Crewell children. Should there be any issue with you receiving the money owed to the guardian of the children, please do not hesitate to contact my chambers."

"This is my ruling. A written opinion and an order memorializing my findings will be issued. Do the parties have anything further the court needs to address?"

Boyle was already packing her bag, so the judge slammed her gavel, picked up her file, and headed out of the courtroom. Once sure the judge was gone, Sophia turned to Cam and let out a guttural scream. He leaped and engulfed her with a hug. Ilana and Max followed and thanked Sophia and Marco. They hung together until the crowd in the courtroom thinned.

Cam spied Professor Hawkins in the back of the courtroom. She had been present all day but allowed the students to handle the hearing. Her lawyer team performed well enough that she was able to remain unnoticed in the back of courtroom. He waved at her and mouthed, "Thank you."

She clasped her hands in front of her chest and smiled. "You are so welcome," she mouthed back. Ilana and Max waved at her as they threw on their coats.

Cam put his arm around Ilana to guide her to the door. "Now that I am officially in charge, there's a whole new list of chores that will be awaiting you when we get home."

Ilana rolled her eyes, but remained attached to Cam as they left the courtroom.

CHAPTER SIXTY-FIVE

PLENTIFUL LAUGHS FILLED THE dining room. Everyone, except the high schoolers, toted a glass of champagne. The eight members of the house gathered to celebrate the judge's ruling. Finals were over and the lingering stress of potentially losing Max and Ilana had evaporated leaving only a slight residue. Kate stood next to Ilana, her arm draped around her waist as they ate while gabbing about anything, laughing at everything, and feeling almost giddy.

Max snuck over to the cooler holding a load of beers, but any intention of nabbing one was stopped in its tracks when Cam shot him a stare. Cam nodded his head in appreciation while acknowledging to himself how quickly he had learned "the look" which his dad had deployed throughout their childhood. Without a word he had quelled any misbehavior and reminded Max of his authority. For a moment, he felt smug, like he had this under control and Ilana and Max would always follow his lead and stay away from imminent harm.

His mind flashed back to a funeral his parents had forced him to attend when he was about nine. He bristled when they him to made dress up and then complained the entire drive to the church. His parents explained that his third cousin, a young adult who had just moved out west, was killed in some random act of violence. He tried to care, but was annoyed because had never met this guy and he wasn't at home playing video games.

The service was horrific. Everyone bawled without any attempt to hold back. The parents of the kid looked comatose, not able to comprehend what fate had dealt them. Cam took in the pain this death had caused everyone in the community and began to feel their pain. He didn't know his cousin, but the trauma of the event started to attack him from the inside. He began to sob in uncontrollable, breathless heaves, and ran out of the church.

His dad caught up to him outside where the bright sun contrasted with the dark mood inside. "Why did you make me come?" he wailed. "This is horrible."

His dad bent down in front of him and stared him in the eyes while grasping his shoulders. "Cam, we knew this would be hard on you, but we wanted you to understand that sometimes bad things happen to good people."

"But, this shouldn't ever happen."

"I know." His dad looked up to the sky. "But it does sometimes. We just want you to know that we love you very much and hope you never, ever, have to experience anything like this again."

Cam grabbed his dad and buried his head in his chest. They waited outside sitting on a low brick wall for his mom to come out after the service was over.

The thoughts of the funeral years before evaporated as he stepped over to Max. He motioned to Ilana to join them and then guided them to a corner, out of hearing range of everyone else.

"I wanted us to have a moment together so I could say

285

something," he said as he bit down on his lower lip. "I tried not to let you know, but I don't think I've ever been so scared in my life. That hearing took a lot out of me because I thought I was going to lose you." He glanced at Ilana and then locked eyes with Max. "I can't imagine us not being in this together and I can't imagine how I would have handled things if the judge ruled differently."

Ilana grabbed his hand. "You don't have to say anything. We were feeling the same."

Cam stepped back. "No, I do have to say it. We spent too long not saying anything growing up. I knew mom and dad loved us, but how often did they say it. They were great parents, but we need to say what we feel. I love both of you."

Ilana grabbed him and yelled, "I love you too."

Max flushed, but forced out, "Love you."

Cam yanked him in closer and rubbed his head. "It'll be easier with a little more practice."

They broke apart and Ilana turned to head back to the others. "One second," Cam said, holding up his hand. "I got one more thing to say."

Ilana rolled her eyes and stomped back. "What else?"

Cam shifted his feet. "I made a decision. I'm not taking the internship in New York."

Ilana's mouth hung open. "What? Why?" Her eyes didn't blink.

"It's just not the right time. Not now."

Ilana pressed forward. "But it's what you've wanted, like forever."

A rueful smile came to Cam's face. "I think it's what I used to want. Now, I'm not so sure. I think it's important that we stay together this summer." He looked at Ilana. "Before you go to college, I want us to be together as long as possible."

"But I'm staying in town for college. We'll see each other all the time."

"Maybe. But when you're in college you're going to want to spend time with your friends, and that's the way it should be. We'll be here for you, but only for backup."

"But what are you going to do about a job? New York paid a lot of money."

"It did, but there's good paying jobs here. I have a couple of interviews this week. I'll find something."

"You better," Max said, "I have big plans for the summer."

"Don't worry. I'll make sure the freezer is stuffed with Hot Pockets."

Max turned to Ilana as they walked back to the others. "You know, with everyone out of the house this summer, there's going to be a lot of empty space. Maybe we'll have a couple of parties when Cam's not paying attention."

Ilana laughed. "Good thinking. Maybe we can invite Mrs. Cartwright. I'm sure she'd love to come." She smacked him on the shoulder before running over to Sophia and Gabrielle who opened their arms offering a big hug.

CHAPTER SIXTY-SIX

THUNDER RUMBLED IN THE DISTANCE, predicting change from clear skies to possible rain. Even with its looming threat, the noise had no effect on the activity in the street. Three car trunks slammed almost in unison signaling that they were packed and ready to go. The eight housemates stared at each other, not ready to commit to leaving.

Sophia stood next to the green, dented sedan with her hand against the door. She turned and stared at Ilana before running to her side. "You going to be okay?" she asked, as she brushed some hair from Ilana's eyes.

Ilana smiled. "You don't need to worry about me."

Sophia hugged her and moved to allow Kate space to say her goodbyes. "I'm going to miss you," Kate said, wrapping her arms around Ilana. "I left most of my clothes here. I got another stash at home. Wear whatever you want. Make the boys drool a little."

"Whatever," Ilana replied. "It won't be the same without you here."

"We'll be back in a couple of months. You better be coming

over for dinner every Friday. The food here will be better than in the dorms."

"Doubtful." She smiled. "I'll be too busy."

They hugged again before Sophia and Kate sauntered over to Cam and Max. They gave their final goodbyes and hopped into their car. Before anyone could react, they were heading down the street, gone for the summer.

Marco and D'Andre waited for their turn at the side of the road and once the path cleared, they jogged over to Max. "Little man," D'Andre said to the boy who stood two inches taller than he did. "You need to work on your crossover and quickness. An hour a day will be spent on ball drills and another hour on fitness and agility." He raised an eyebrow.

Max nodded.

"Picture yourself starting the first game of the season every time you're practicing," D'Andre said. He smacked Max on the back. "Also, read a book." He grabbed Max in a bear hug and lifted him up. "I can't wait till we're all back in the house again."

"Just have a great summer," Marco said. He turned to Ilana. "You enjoy getting ready for college. Can't believe you won't be living in the house come the fall. I'll miss you."

They hugged for a long moment.

Marco and D'Andre pulled Cam away. Each offered a bro hug and a smack on the back.

"Crazy year, wasn't it?" D'Andre asked. "Don't think second year can top this. Let me know when you get your grades, so we can compare."

Cam laughed. "You just want to know that you beat me again. But I'll text you." Cam locked eyes with Marco and then D'Andre. "Guys, thanks for everything. This isn't what you signed on for when we started in the fall. I couldn't have done any of this without you."

They fell into silence before D'Andre squawked, "This was an awesome year. Can't wait for the next one."

They turned and headed towards the other car waving again before getting in. They headed out with squealing tires leaving Cam and his siblings alone in the street.

They looked around like they were expecting other people to be nearby, but no one else was there. The street remained quiet.

Cam shoved his hands in his pockets and headed up the front steps towards the house. The door creaked a bit when he opened it. Ilana and Max each placed a hand on one of his shoulders as they walked into the house together.

Dear Readers,

Thank you so much for taking the time and energy to read *Guarding Innocence*. To me, knowing that people out there are reading my books makes the long hours of writing and editing even more worthwhile.

While I mainly write for personal reasons, I get so much personal satisfaction when readers let me know they enjoyed what they have read.

One way you can help me is to review the books you have read. Reviews help prospective readers determine if a book they are considering is one they want to try. With Amazon's algorithms, reviews also help a book get more attention.

Please consider leaving a review on Amazon.
Reviews on Goodreads and Bookbub are also helpful.

ABOUT THE AUTHOR

James Rosenberg has been a practicing attorney for nearly thirty-five years. He spends much of his time in a courtroom and has cross-examined every type of witness imaginable.

Every trial is a story and the people involved believe that their case is the most important in the world. When you listen to these people, they have great stories to tell.

When not trying cases, James spends much time with his wife and three kids. They are getting older now, but also have great stories to tell.

Sometimes, when everyone is out of the house, James gets to talk to Allie the wonder dog. She is a great listener.

ALSO BY JAMES ROSENBERG

The Jersey: A Story of Loss and Redemption

Verdicts and Vindication Series

Legal Reserves

Unclean Hands

Guarding Innocence

Each book in the Verdicts and Vindication series provides an enhanced look into what a lawyer goes through in taking a case to trial. From the beginning of the case, to the jury's verdict, you will experience the sacrifice, intelligence, and often, the courage it takes to push a case to the end. Every case takes a toll on the litigants and the lawyers, and the ramifications of even the simplest trials extend far beyond the courtroom and into the lives of the people who participate in a trial.

Made in the USA
Middletown, DE
19 January 2025

69810232R00166